DIG TWO GRAVES

John Colgan

BIOGRAPHY

John Colgan was born and lived in Greater Manchester for a number of years. He is married with three grown up children. He lived in North Cheshire before moving to Wiltshire where he lives with his wife. This is his first attempt at writing.

This book is published by John Colgan and printed by Createspace.

It would soon be dusk and the water had been slowly rising up Tom Shannon's body. He was going to die he was sure of that. The water was now up to his chest and he was so cold that he believed that he would die from hypothermia before the water suffocated him. His concern was heightened by the fact that Sean Keane, a good friend and a man who had saved his life in the past, was in the same predicament. They had both been tied securely to wooden supports holding up an old, battered jetty at the mouth of a river and the tide was coming in. He wasn't exactly sure where they were. All he was certain of was that they were on the coast somewhere in Donegal, Ireland.

The two men who had done this to them were sitting in their cars in a clearing near the embankment. They could hear music coming from a car radio and occasionally some raucous laughter. No doubt they were waiting until the job was done and perhaps hoping to hear some screams of panic. Shannon was determined not to give them that satisfaction. Shannon was angry and sad. Angry because it was his fault that they were going to die. Sad because Keane had a wife and two small children and he wasn't going to see them again.

Shannon had reacted irrationally to a tragic incident that occurred a few years ago. This set him on a path seeking revenge, which he was warned would bring him pain and lead to disaster. This warning came from someone whom he loved very much. He was thinking about her now and remembering how distressed she was when she learned what he was planning to do. She told him that seeking revenge was a recipe for disaster, not just for those on the receiving end of his actions but also for himself.

is heart ached when he thought of the unhappiness he had caused her. Why hadn't he listened to her? She was his grandmother and his only living relative. She had years of life experience and she knew what she was talking about. She had said "when seeking revenge, dig two graves – one for yourself." Now it looked as if that grave was going to be a watery one. Once again he struggled with his bonds although he knew it was pointless. Keane looked over at him and shook his head. They both knew that there was no escape. All those who would have rescued them didn't know where they were. Shannon knew that that was his fault too. He had made his move too soon and didn't let his contacts know where he was and what he was doing. In spite of all his training and experience he had fouled up. Now he was going to die and so was one of his best friends.

1

THREE YEARS EARLIER

The blind man shuffled down River Street in Belfast, feeling his way with his white stick. It was about nine-thirty in the evening. Although the sun had retired it was still fairly warm. The light from the full moon cast a silvery sheen, picking up various objects and creating an eerie atmosphere. Except for the blind man the street was empty, the silence broken only by the tapping of his stick. He moved cautiously along and the sound of the tapping ricocheted around the silent street. Most of the inhabitants in their terraced houses had settled down for the evening.

Suddenly at the other end of the street two army vehicles screeched to a halt and several soldiers jumped out. The sound of their boots echoed as they charged to the other side of the empty road and began to bang on the doors. If the doors weren't opened immediately they were kicked in. There was screaming and shouting as the soldiers began to search various houses. The blind man hesitated, he appeared to be listening but after a moment he continued down the street. When he arrived at the place where the army vehicles were parked he stopped, then bent down as if to fasten a shoe lace or perhaps to remove a pebble from his shoe. In the light from the street lamps it was difficult to tell.

After a few moments he stood up and continued his journey ignoring the chaos taking place only a few yards away from him. He stopped once again near a lamppost then continued on his way. The tap, tap of his white stick was drowned by the uproar coming from across the street. The soldiers concentrated their search on half a dozen houses with uncompromising zeal. The doors and windows of the remaining houses remained closed. It was unlikely that they were unaware of the pandemonium taking place and yet no one ventured out to see. Only the flutter of curtains could be seen as the curious peered out into the semi-darkness of the street. Suddenly there were two small explosions and the two army vehicles were ablaze.

The early morning television news reported that the army had raided a number of streets in the Province. Weapons had been found in some of the houses searched and a number of arrests had been made. In one street two army trucks had been set alight by incendiary devices but no soldiers or civilians had been hurt. A calling card was found taped to a lamppost near the burning trucks. In a later news bulletin the Assistant Chief Constable of Northern Ireland, Gordon Murray, was interviewed and he expressed his concern about this terrorist who left calling cards. He had done untold damage to police and army vehicles and his activities had caused chaos in the city.

Colonel McDonald, an anti-terrorist army officer from England, had been posted to Belfast in order to capture this man. He went on to say that this terrorist was having calling cards printed with a red rose on one side of the card. All the known printers in the city had been checked but there was no evidence that they were involved. It was possible that some private individual may have a printing press. He emphasised that it was everybody's duty to report to the authorities any suspicious activity in their neighbourhood and to let them know if they knew of anyone who had a printing press.

2

Martha Adams had returned to Belfast a few months ago after spending about five years in England. Her husband, Bill, was an engineer and he had been transferred to Manchester when he was promoted. Their son, Paul, wasn't happy with the move because he had a lot of friends in Belfast with whom he shared a passion for playing football and tennis. He was too young to leave behind so Martha and Bill decided to keep their Belfast home to make it easier to keep in touch with relatives and friends. They made regular weekend visits and when Bill was working abroad, Martha and Paul sometimes spent a little longer there. Martha's sister, Sarah, and brother-in-law, Martin Norton, lived in Belfast and so they were able to see them more often than they had originally anticipated. Paul had a very close relationship with his Aunt and Uncle and things seemed to work out fine.

Bill was promoted again but with promotion came a heavier work load. Paul was offered a place at Manchester University, reading mathematics and information technology, which pleased Martha and Bill. It was a few weeks after Paul had graduated that Bill had a heart attack when he was attending a meeting in France. He was flown home and hospitalised but only survived a few days. Paul had become good friends with Michael Jones, who was also a student at the University and coincidently also came from Belfast. When they graduated, they told Martha that they had both been approached by a government representative, who had offered them a job. Paul and Michael had been reluctant to give Martha any details about the work. All they were prepared to say, was that initially they would be joining the army and after training, would be posted somewhere on special duties. It would mean that they would have to go away on a training course for a few months and the job offer would depend upon them successfully completing the course. Martha had to admit that she wasn't too happy about Paul joining the army and she asked Paul what Michael's parents thought about it. Paul said that Michael always avoided talking about his parents and so Paul decided that for some reason the subject was taboo. He and Michael had become good friends and he believed that if Michael had a problem talking about his family, then he must have a good reason. He was prepared to respect his friend's right to privacy. When Paul and Michael had left to attend the training course, Martha decided to return home to Belfast.

On her return to Belfast, Martha was informed that Bill's company had gone into liquidation and some of the directors had been arrested for embezzlement. The pension fund had been spirited away and so Martha would now have to depend upon her savings and whatever state pension she may be entitled to. Just when Martha thought life had reached an all time low, things had become even worse. After a few weeks, and with her sister Sarah's help, she got a part-time job with a local accountancy firm. Shortly afterwards she was delighted when both Paul and Michael, who had successfully completed their training course, were posted to Holywood army base. Holywood was only about twenty minutes drive away. Martha was now able to see Paul frequently and Michael also kept in touch. She began to believe that her life was taking a turn for the better until the doorbell rang one evening. Martha opened the door to find her very distraught sister standing there.

'Sarah, whatever is the matter?' exclaimed Martha.' She could see that Sarah had been crying and was still fighting back tears.

'Come in and sit down and I'll make you a cup of tea,' invited Martha. A cup of tea was Martha's answer to all problems.

'I must tell you right away,' began Sarah. 'Martin has been arrested.'

'Why, what has he done?'

'They've accused him of killing a policeman but it's not true. He was in the pub with his pals when the shooting took place.'

'Well, I'm sure that the police will be able to check that and then they will have to release him.'

'The problem is, that some of the men who were with him are said to have connections with the Provisional IRA, although Martin didn't know that.'

'There may have been other people in the pub who could verify that he was there and I'm sure that the police will find them eventually. Why did the police suspect Martin?'

'Charlie Perkins was the policeman who was killed. You'll remember Charlie. He had a crush on me when we were younger and he was always pestering me for a date. He walked me home from the Rugby Club annual ball one year. It was the year before Martin and I got together. It was dark and I thought I would be safe if a guy was with me, even though home was only five minutes' walk away from the club. I was wrong. Charlie had other ideas and I had to fight him off.'

'You never told me that.'

'Charlie was quite nasty. He said that if I ever told anybody, he would say that I was the one who made the first move. He was a police officer so I thought he would be believed so I kept quiet. I didn't want any trouble.'

'Oh, I'm so sorry; it must have been awful for you.'

'A couple of weeks ago Charlie met Martin in the pub. They had both had too much to drink. Charlie told Martin how he had walked me home from the Rugby Club one night and claimed that I had given him a "good time." Martin lost his temper. There was a struggle but some of the fellas in the pub separated them so it was a bloodless fight. I suppose that the police believe that Martin has a motive.'

'Let's hope that someone reliable comes forward and can remember that Martin was in the pub at the time of the killing,' said Martha hopefully.

'He has been held at the police station for five hours and they won't let me see him,' sobbed Sarah, 'I'm so glad that Brian is away on a school trip this week.'

9

'Why don't you stay here tonight and......?' Martha began but was interrupted by the door bell.

When Martha opened the door, she was surprised but delighted, to see Martin. When Sarah heard Martin's voice she ran into the hall and they embraced.

'Martin, what happened?' asked Sarah.

'The pub landlord came to the police station and confirmed that I was in the pub at the time of the shooting.' explained Martin.

'Why did it take him so long to come forward?' asked Sarah.

'He had taken the afternoon off to go on a golfing trip with some of his friends. On the way back they stopped off for a meal and they only got back about an hour ago. As soon as he heard about the arrest, he went to the police station and made a statement.'

The next evening Paul arrived home saying that he had been given some leave and would be staying for a few days. He and Martha were having their evening meal when the door bell rang. Martha answered it and was met by a neighbour who was extremely distressed.

'Martha, I'm so sorry. I've got some very bad news. I don't know how to tell you,' she said.

'Please come in,' said Martha who was now looking quite upset. Paul, hearing the conversation, joined them in the hall.

'What's the matter Jennifer?' asked Paul.

'Oh, I'm so glad to see you are home Paul. I'm afraid something terrible has happened. Someone has thrown a bomb into the window of Sarah and Martin's house.'

'Oh no,' cried Martha now appearing to collapse. Paul held her, took her into the living room, and helped her into an armchair.

'Are they still alive?' asked Paul.

'I don't know. They've been taken away in an ambulance. It didn't look good. I'm afraid I can't tell you anything more.'

'Jennifer, would you stay here with Mum so that I can go to the hospital?'

An hour later Paul returned home, his face was ashen.

'I'm sorry Mum; they were both dead on arrival.'

Brian, the son of Sarah and Martin, moved in with Martha. He was sixteen years old and Martha decided it would be better for him to return to school as soon as possible after the funeral. He was an exceptionally bright boy. Like his cousin Paul he excelled in mathematics and computer studies. Paul told Martha that he was working at the Holywood army base updating the communications system. The army base was only a short drive from Martha's house so Paul was able to spend a lot of his spare time with Brian. Brian was amazed at Paul's computer skills and he became very fond of his cousin. Martha did everything she could to soften the cruel blow that Brian had suffered and she noticed that he was beginning to recover from the death of his parents. She felt sure that this was mainly due to the attention he was receiving from Paul and she was happy with that. She was, however, concerned about Paul. The murder of his Aunt and Uncle had devastated him and after an episode of fits of rage, he often had periods of melancholy. He blamed the police for the death of his Aunt and Uncle. He argued that the wrongful arrest of his Uncle had thrown suspicion upon him. He always managed to hide his behaviour from Brian and she often heard them laughing when they were messing about on the computer. She came to the conclusion that they were good for each other. Perhaps in time Paul would come out of what she felt was his grieving period.

Brian had always been interested in drama and it was something he was good at. He spent two evenings each week at school rehearsing for the annual school play. He was usually home by eight o'clock but this particular evening he hadn't returned by eight-thirty. Paul rang the school and caught one of the teachers as she was locking up. She told him that rehearsals had finished at seven-thirty and Brian had left with the other students soon after that. As Paul put the phone down it rang.

'Hello, yes this is Brian Norton's home,' answered Paul. He listened for a several minutes and then said, 'I'll come right away.' He put the phone down.

'Has something happened to Brian?'

'He's in hospital,' replied Paul and seeing the alarm in Martha's face he quickly said, 'It's not life threatening. Somebody has mugged him.'

When Martha and Paul arrived at the hospital they were met by a nurse.

'How is Brian Norton? Can we see him?' asked Martha anxiously.

'He's not in any danger,' replied the nurse, 'the police are interviewing him at the moment so I will have to ask you to wait for a few minutes.'

'How bad are his injuries?' asked Martha.

'The doctor will let you know shortly,' replied the nurse. As the nurse left the doctor appeared.

'I'm Doctor Smithson and I understand that you are Mrs Adams, Brian's Aunt.'

'Yes, how is Brian?'

'He has suffered two broken ribs and some cuts and bruises.'

'Can we see him doctor?' asked Martha.

'Yes, I believe that the police have finished interviewing him,'

They were shown into the ward. Martha walked quickly to Brian's bedside. His head was bandaged and he had a dressing on his nose. She could see several bruises on his face and arms. Tears filled her eyes as she fought off the need to cry out.

'Brian, my love, who did this to you?

'It was Constable Perkins. He said my dad killed his brother and so he was going to punish me. He said he was going to keep beating me up until I told everybody that my dad was a murderer,' replied Brian, who had become quite distressed.

'Brian, I'm sure that the police will deal with him,' said Martha.

'I don't think they believe me. I told them he was not wearing his uniform and he smelled as if he had been drinking. They asked me several times was I sure it was him and was there anyone else who would have reason to do this to me.'

Paul was sitting on the opposite side of the bed to Martha and throughout the conversation he hadn't spoken. Martha could see that he was very angry but was trying to control himself.

'If the police don't do something about it,' threatened Paul, speaking for the first time, 'I will.'

Martha was going to speak but was interrupted by the arrival of the doctor.

'Mrs Adams, I want to keep Brian in hospital overnight for observation,' said the doctor, 'if there are no complications, then I will discharge him tomorrow.'

3

Constable Len Perkins had just finished a pizza and was enjoying a lager when the door bell rang. He was quite irritated because it was ten o'clock at night and he was watching a film on television. By the time he reached the door he was very angry. He opened the door and was met with an old man with white hair and a white bushy beard. He was shabbily dressed and so Perkins immediately assumed that he was a beggar who was going to hassle him for money. His anger turned into a rage and he grabbed the old man by his lapels and began to push him away from the door. He pushed him so hard that the old man fell over. Perkins kicked him in the ribs and was about to kick him again, when the old man grabbed his foot, twisted it, and Perkins found himself on the ground. The old man waited until Perkins got up. Perkins took a right swing but the old man swerved and he was taken by surprise, when the old man delivered a mind exploding right hook, which floored Perkins. Once again, the old man waited until Perkins got to his feet. Perkins was now more cautious, he circled around the old man and then tried a left hook but the old man swerved again and Perkins took a number of severe blows to his ribs and head and he was unconscious before he hit the ground.

Perkins woke up in hospital feeling very sore. He also woke up feeling very terrified. When the ambulance collected him, they found a calling card tucked into the top of his shirt. On one side of the card was a message, "TIME TO CONFESS" and Perkins knew, only too well, what this message meant. He had guessed who had attacked him and the calling card confirmed it. The assailant was, indeed, a man to be frightened of. Perkins fear was such that an armed policeman had been stationed outside his hospital room. What he couldn't get his head around was that apparently the assailant had called the ambulance. Perkins knew why he had been attacked and he wished that he could turn back the clock so that he could have the opportunity to behave differently. What he had done a couple nights ago had now put him firmly on this dangerous man's black list. He also believed that there would be no escaping him until he had done what this man wanted him to do. All the security forces had been trying to catch this very elusive man for over two years but all in vain. Colonel McDonald, an experienced and successful anti-terrorist soldier, had been seconded to the Province in order to put an end to this terrorist's activities. Although McDonald had broken up a number of Loyalist and PIRA cells he had not been able to capture this mystery man. Perkins was convinced that this would not be the end of it. He was sure that he would hear from this terrorist again.

The rider on his Harley-Davidson was moving with speed along a dark country lane. It was a little after midnight on a cold but dry night and the lane was empty of traffic. Occasionally a rabbit would make a hasty retreat into the hedgerows as the biker approached. Eventually the rider arrived at Connery cottage. It was a single storey building with white walls and a thatched roof standing in about half an acre of land. The moon suddenly escaped from behind the clouds and flooded the front of the cottage. The rider parked his bike in the garage and entered the cottage. He drew the curtains before switching on the light. It had been an exciting but dangerous night and as the adrenaline subsided he began to feel tired and weary and his ribs were sore, very sore. He hadn't expected Perkins to attack him. He also felt emotionally drained. The path he had set himself on had not achieved what he had expected, the removal of this agonising pain in his heart. Perhaps he would never recover from this horrendous grief. He felt certain that his present activities were not easing the pain. He had a shower then made a mug of tea and took it into the bedroom. He lay on the bed but sleep escaped him and his thoughts turned to Laura.

He became sad and angry as the memory of that fateful day flooded his mind. He began to recall the day he first met her. It was at the Manchester University Graduation Ball. She was standing with Peter Blake and Peter's parents. He and Peter had just graduated with good law degrees. At first he had assumed that she was Peter's girl-friend but was delighted to learn later that she was Peter's sister. She was a very beautiful girl with shoulder length, blond hair and the biggest blue eyes he had ever seen. He knew that this was the girl he was going to marry. Now she was dead.

He jumped up off the bed, grabbed the empty tea mug and flung it against the wall. He was in a rage. His heart was full of sadness and grief but his mind was full of anger. He felt as if he was going to burst with hatred and the need for revenge. Revenge, his grandmother's words came back to him as if they were being whispered in his ear:

"When seeking revenge, dig two graves – one for yourself"

Half way through PC Perkins's second day in hospital the doctor told him that the x-rays showed that he had two broken ribs and a broken nose. After the doctor had gone he lay back on the pillow and reflected on the past few days. He recalled the evening he left his local having had too much to drink. He was feeling angry and sad because his brother had been shot dead. He was convinced that the killer was a guy called Martin Norton, rumoured to have associated with members of the PIRA. After a police investigation Norton was found to be innocent. The day before the police made this announcement Norton and his wife were both killed by a bomb thrown into their living room window. Perkins didn't believe that Norton was innocent. On his way home from the pub, in a drunken stupor, he met Norton's son Brian, a sixteen year old boy, who was returning home from school after rehearsals for a school play. He grabbed him and pushed him up against a wall. He tried to make him say that his father was a murderer. The boy refused so he started to punch him so hard that the boy began to slide down the wall. Perkins lifted him up and gave him a further beating and the boy lost consciousness. Perkins staggered home leaving the boy on the ground. Sometime later a couple walking home found the boy and called an ambulance. The police made a thorough investigation but were unable to find any concrete evidence to charge Perkins. Brian Norton gave a convincing description of Perkins, saying that he was not in uniform and smelled of drink. Perkins denied being in the area at the time of the assault and the police were unable to prove otherwise. As Perkins lay in bed thinking about the incident he realised that he had two choices. He could confess to the assault which would result in him losing his job and probably a term in prison. The other choice was to keep tight lipped and hope that the matter would go away. He really didn't believe that it would go away. The "calling card" terrorist, as he was often described, never left a job unfinished. He was also aware that his colleagues in the police force suspected that he was guilty and their attitude towards him had changed, positively cool. Perkins felt that his only hope was for the security forces to catch him but that looked unlikely. He was still mulling over these choices when a doctor came in.

'How are you feeling today, Mr Perkins?' asked the doctor.

'I'm feeling very sore.'

'Let me make a few checks.'

After checking Perkins' temperature, pulse and a quick look at the bandages the doctor started to make a few notes. When he had finished he handed a sealed envelope to Perkins.

'It will take a few days before you start to feel better. When the nurse comes in give her the envelope she will know what to do. Your health will be assured if you follow the instructions.' The doctor left without further comment.

When the nurse arrived Perkins handed her the envelope.

'This is for you, Mr Perkins,' said the nurse after she had opened the envelope. She handed him a calling card.

'Oh my god,' exclaimed Perkins, as he read the message on the calling card, "PERKINS - CONFESS OR SUFFER THE CONSEQUENCES -

THIS YOUR LAST CHANCE." The armed policeman sitting outside the door ran into the room when he heard Perkins scream.

A few days after Brian Norton was released from hospital, it was reported in the press, that Constable Len Perkins had been badly beaten at his home. The police claimed that it was the work of the mysterious terrorist because a red rose calling card was found tucked into the constable's shirt. Martha, remembering Paul's threat, wondered if he had been involved. The police had failed to charge Perkins because there was no witness and Paul had become extremely embittered at what he described as a cover up. Paul arrived home that evening a little after six o'clock. Brian was upstairs doing his homework. Martha decided that she would have to raise the matter with Paul.

'Paul,' began Martha as she began to prepare the table for the evening meal, 'do you remember saying that if the police didn't deal with Constable Perkins; you would?'

'Yes,' replied Paul, 'I was angry.'

'Were you involved in the beating of Constable Perkins?'

'What kind of a question is that?'

'Paul, I know you have been trained by the SAS so you will have the kind of skills to deliver that kind of punishment and you have a motive.'

'Mum, you should have been a detective.'

'Paul, are you this man who leaves calling cards or are you involved with him somehow?'

'Mum, I'm in the army. I don't remember being trained to beat up civilians or policemen.'

'Why do I feel that you are avoiding answering my questions?'

'I'm not sure what.......' began Paul but he was interrupted by Brian bouncing into the room with his usual greeting of "gimme five" and Martha was thwarted.

Next morning when breakfast was over, Paul asked, 'have you seen the morning papers?'

'No, I haven't,' replied Martha.

'Well, you will both be pleased to know,' smiled Paul, 'that Constable Len Perkins has been charged with assault.'

Paul laughed as they both cheered.

'Is he likely to be convicted?' asked Brian.

'Yes,' said Paul, 'because he has confessed.'

'Why did he confess?' asked Brian, 'there were no witnesses. It was his word against mine and the police obviously believed him.'

'Receiving a red rose calling card and one or two slaps made him see the error of his ways,' laughed Paul as he threw his fist into the air, 'he was made to do what the police should have made him do.'

Martha, with concern in her eyes, looked at Paul.

4

'Our man with the calling cards seems to have caused a great deal of havoc since he joined us,' said Sean Keane as he took a seat next to Declan Brady.

'Maybe but I don't like his maverick style. He hardly ever reports to us and we're never sure where he is. We don't even know where he lives. He doesn't live with his grandmother because I've checked,' complained Brady as he took a sip of his Guinness.

'That was the deal, Declan, we agreed to give him a month's trial and if he proved himself he would be allowed to do his own thing. You have to admit he has been brilliant and he has created havoc without taking life.

The two men were in The Trooper, a popular pub with Republicans, off the Falls Road. They were part of a Provisional IRA cell. Keane was a tall, lean man with light brown hair and brown eyes. He had the presence of a man in control. Brady, in contrast, was a short, thick set man with black hair and cold, pale blue eyes which never seemed to smile. He was a hard man with a foul temper. They were both in their early thirties.

'What's so brilliant about not taking life? Killing some of the bastards will make them sit up and take notice. And that's my point, he should be controlled by us and be part of the overall plan. He should be doing what we tell him to do and not doing his own thing.'

'Don't you see? That's his strength, apart from the two of us nobody knows who he is or what he looks like. That reduces the chance of him being caught or betrayed. He's effectively invisible and the calling cards are having a scary effect. There are a number of us who believe that taking life does not further our cause but engenders hatred for us.' argued Keane.

'Leaving calling cards is a bit over the top. I think he's seen too many bloody films or he's been reading too many comics. And what's the point of the red rose? I still don't trust him,' continued Brady, now getting quite irritated and completely ignoring Keane's argument.

'We checked him out. He was born in Derry and lived there until he was ten years old when his parents took him to England. That's why he has an English accent. His grandmother still lives in Belfast. As you know he keeps in touch with me to make sure his activities don't interfere with our plans. Come on, Declan, admit it. He's more than proved himself during the two years he has been here. I don't know why he has a red rose printed on the cards.'

Before Brady could answer, two other men who had been getting drinks at the bar joined them.

'These red rose calling cards are certainly making the headlines,' said Frank Doyle as he took the only vacant seat next to Keane. Brady glowered at him but didn't say anything. The other man, Peter Byrne, took a chair from another table and sat down.

'This week he wrote off two army vehicles, caused panic in Marks and Spencer's and dealt with that child-beating bastard of a cop,' said Peter Byrne unable to contain his glee, 'and interestingly it is the first time that he has used violence. He put PC Perkins in hospital.'

'And it's only Wednesday,' smiled Doyle.

Byrne and Doyle were cousins but looked so much alike that they were often mistaken for twin brothers. They were over six feet tall with blond hair and brown eyes. They both had the same infectious sense of humour but they also had a dark side.

'Sean, I think you and Declan did the right thing keeping the identity of this guy a secret. He's become something of a hero and he's bloody good for morale,' said Byrne.

'This cop, Perkins,' said Doyle, 'is in hospital and still hasn't admitted beating up this kid. Everybody is waiting to see what our mystery man does next. I don't know where you got him from, Sean, and I don't want to. I'm bloody glad he's on our side.'

'Perkins is in the City Hospital,' said Brady, 'and I don't think that there is any chance that he will be able to get to him because he's being given round the clock police protection.'

'That's where you're wrong Declan,' said a man who was approaching their table.

'What do you mean Dave?' asked Brady.

'You obviously haven't read the morning papers perhaps because it wasn't on the front page,' said Dave Connors, 'Perkins has confessed to beating up this young teenager.'

'Why would he do that?' asked Brady, 'it was the teenager's word against the police officer's. Surely they would believe the police officer.'

'Well, it would seem that our man, disguised as a doctor, got into Perkins private room at the hospital,' answered Connors, ' after pretending to examine him he made some notes which he left in a sealed envelope for the attention of the nurse. When the nurse turned up she opened the envelope which contained a message for Perkins written on a red rose calling card. It was a final warning for Perkins. I suppose Perkins realised that he wasn't safe anywhere and so confessed.'

Keane's mobile phone rang. He took the call, listened for a few moments then left the pub.

5

When Paul Adams's leave ended he returned to Holywood army base. On the way back to the base he smiled when he remembered his mother's suspicions. He almost laughed out loud when he recalled that he had referred to her as a detective and she certainly didn't miss anything. He wondered if her suspicions would make her more worried about him. He decided that when he arrived at the base he would give her a call and attempt to allay her fears. At the base he went into the communication room where he found Michael Jones. He and Jones had become good friends at Manchester University and their friendship was still strong. Jones was very secretive about his parents and always clammed up if Adams accidentally mentioned them so he tried hard to remember to keep off the subject. He wondered if there had been some tragedy in the family and Jones was still trying to come to terms with it. He had made up his mind not to push Michael on the matter. He was sure that when Michael was ready to talk about it he would let him know.

'Hi, Michael,' Jones looked up from the piece of equipment he was working on.

'Good to see you back, Paul. Did you have a good leave?' Paul told him about the beating that Brian had received at the hands of Perkins and the subsequent beating that Perkins suffered.

'I did read something about it in the paper. It would appear that Perkins got his just desserts. Anyone who spoils somebody's life should not be allowed to get away with it. They should be punished severely.'

'He won't do it again. I think he will be punished appropriately. In addition to the beating he may have to go to prison and will most certainly lose his job.'

'That's good because, believe me, if they have any influence, they do get away with it. They have the means to cover everything up.' Jones was obviously very angry.

'It sounds as if you've experienced some sort of injustice.'
Jones immediately clammed up and was silent for a few moments which, to Adams, felt like hours and then Jones broke the silence but his voice sounded very strained, 'Is your mother well?'

'She's fine, now that Brian is home and recovering from the beating.'

'Good, very good,' said Jones but his mind seemed to be somewhere else.

'How's the new equipment?' asked Adams hoping the question would bring Jones back from wherever he was.

'It's good. Of course, there is state of the art equipment on the market but Captain Cosgrove says it costs more that the budget allows.'

'Well, if he said that I'm sure it's true. He's been pretty good to us since we were posted here. He's given us a lot of freedom with the work we do but he has to work within the constraints of the budget.'

'I know but when I have the money I'm going to buy some of that equipment and then I'll show them what can be done.'

'Rule the world, perhaps? Don't forget Cosgrove has recommended us for that new anti-terrorist unit which is being set up in Manchester. We may get promoted and then you'll have more money.'

'Yea, if only. I don't think army pay will buy the kind of equipment I would like to get my hands on.'

'If we are accepted by the anti-terrorist unit you may have access to some better equipment.'
Paul was getting worried about Michael. All this surveillance technology seemed to have taken him over. He hardly ever took any leave and spent a lot of money on books and magazines on the subject. Paul believed that with the amount of time he spent studying the technology he would probably become a world authority on it.

'Well,' said Jones, 'you may be right. Colonel McDonald, who is setting up this unit, has an outstanding reputation. He has had experience all over the world and he is highly decorated. I'm sure he will have lots of influence. These guys at the top always do.'

'Wow, you seem to know a lot about this colonel. Do you know him?'

'Of course not,' replied Jones with much more than a touch of irritation in his voice.

Adams was surprised that his question had caused such annoyance particularly after the silence his previous question had generated. He had certainly hit a nerve. Something was seriously upsetting Jones but what? It was so unlike Jones who, although very sensitive about questions with regard to his family, wasn't easily upset and was usually quite placid. He decided to let it go. Nevertheless, he thought, it was a strange reaction.

6

After Sean Keane listened to the call on his mobile phone, he left The Trooper and made his way to the local park, some three hundred yards from the pub. He entered the park and sat on a bench not too far from the entrance. After a few minutes a tramp entered the park and sat on the bench at the opposite end. Keane remained silent although he gave the tramp a couple of side long glances. After a few moments the tramp spoke, 'Can you spare a pound for a cup of tea, Mr Keane?'

'I think so, Mr Shannon. I suspected it was you, Tom, but I wasn't sure. Your disguises always manage to fool me. So why do you want to see me?'

'Sean, I'm getting out.'

'What's brought this on?'

'After I beat up that bent cop I wasn't too happy with myself. I had only intended to give him a warning but when he attacked me I lost it. I'm afraid of becoming violent and I'm concerned that I may start to like it. More importantly they seem to be making some progress with the Peace Process. I think we should make a contribution by pulling out.'

'Tom, I think you are absolutely right. If we expect peace then we have to play our part. We are not achieving anything and in my opinion we are making the situation worse. There are quite a number of us who feel that way. Somebody has to make the first move. Mandela was referred to as a terrorist and he managed to unite his country and become a great man. Wouldn't it be fantastic if we could achieve something like he did? I think I am probably in dreamland because I'm afraid that there'll be a few hard cases who won't give up.'

'When I joined you I told you that I had my own personal agenda and you never asked me what it was.'

'That's your business, Tom. I was only interested in what you could offer the Republican Cause. You proved to be a very valuable asset to us and if you'll forgive the cliché you became a legend in your own lifetime. Your methods were very risky and I must admit that I was amazed that you never got caught. You will remember that I tried to persuade you not to join us. Your grandparents were very good to my parents when they needed help and I know that your grandmother was upset by what you had decided to do. It's important not to underestimate Colonel McDonald. He is a very competent soldier and he has broken up a number of cells on both sides of the divide. I think it's good that you have decided to go. I don't think your luck will hold out indefinitely.'

'I'm relieved that you feel the same way. Perhaps one day I'll tell you what motivated me. I know that Brady wasn't happy with me and probably gave you a bit of grief.'

Keane chuckled at this. 'You're right; Brady had a bee in his bonnet about you. I think he was jealous because you were admired by everyone and he wanted to control you. He even tried to find out where you lived.

'I was living in my late grandfather's cottage. His name was Tom Connery and ever since I was a child the locals called me young Tom Connery and the name stuck. It has been good cover over the past few years.'

'Well, I'm never going to tell Brady,' laughed Keane, 'it'll be a lifetime puzzle for him.'

'I suppose this is goodbye then,' said Shannon'

'I suppose it is. Good luck, Tom. I hope we meet again in better times. Apart from Brady and me nobody knows who you are or what you look like so you should have no trouble getting away.'

'I have to see my grandmother before I leave the country. She'll be relieved to know that I am going back to England. She was very unhappy with what I've been doing. There are also some of my maternal grandfather's affairs that need sorting out.'

The light was failing as the two men shook hands and then Shannon disappeared into the gloom.

7

Three or four weeks later, Tom Shannon was on the W3502 flight
from Belfast to Manchester, leaving behind a part of his life he wished
to forget. His grandmother had warned him that he would regret his
decision. She pointed out to him that his actions would not ease the
pain nor make him any happier. She was right. He wasn't any happier
and the pain was still there. He certainly felt as if he had been buried
in guilt and regret. Shannon's thoughts were interrupted by the
captain's announcement that the plane was preparing to land at
Manchester Airport. On arrival, he made his way through the terminal
and within a few minutes he was in a taxi making his way to Bowdon,
a leafy area south of Manchester, which was fifteen or twenty
minutes away from the airport. The taxi dropped him off outside a
detached, two storey Victorian house and Shannon walked up the
drive to the front door. He hadn't visited the house for a little over
two years and he felt sad as he turned the key in the lock and opened
the door. He put his luggage down on the hall floor and went into the
living room. The furniture was as he had left it, covered with dust
sheets. He took out a bottle of Jameson's whiskey from his holdall and
went into the kitchen. His mother was a great cook and she loved this
kitchen and she had had it designed to her own strict specifications.
He and his parents had been happy living in this house. The family had
left Belfast because Shannon's father had taken up a post as a lecturer
at Manchester University when Shannon was ten years old. Shannon
had been successful at school and eventually graduated from
Manchester University with a good law degree. It was at the University
that he met Peter Blake, also reading law, and they became good
friends. When he met Blake's sister, Laura, he believed his life was
complete. He had met the girl of his dreams. He sat down at the

kitchen table and poured himself a generous glass of whiskey and then his thoughts turned to Laura.

Tears filled his eyes as the memory of that fateful day flooded his mind again. He began to recall the day he first met her. They both knew that they were meant for each other. They had made such plans. All that seemed a lifetime away.....

Shannon snapped out of his reverie. He had to focus on getting his life back to something that resembled normality. He had to find Peter and hope that he would understand why he hadn't been in touch for more than two years. That could be difficult, very difficult. How much could he tell him? Perhaps it would be wise not to tell him anything at all. Peter's parents, Harry and Rachel Blake, lived nearby and he had to make an effort to see them too. They may not understand his long absence and wonder why he had not been in touch with them. They too had suffered deeply. Should he phone them or turn up at their home unannounced? He decided he would have to face them. If he had hurt them then he owed them a visit to apologise personally because he had some explaining to do. A phone call seemed a coward's way. It only took him about ten minutes to walk to the Blake's family home. When he arrived at the door, he reached for the door bell and then hesitated; his hand shook. The guilt and shame of how he had neglected them began to overwhelm him. How could he have treated them so badly? He wasn't sure he could face them. How would he be received? Would he be able to do this? He had to do it. He rang the door bell.

8

Colonel Jim McDonald was sitting in his Belfast office. McDonald was in his early fifties with steel grey hair. He had a strong face with piercing, blue eyes. He had earned a reputation for successfully fighting terrorists in many parts of the world. He was staring at a calling card on his desk. On one side of the card a red rose was printed. On the other side of the card in handwriting it read *"Goodbye Colonel"* McDonald smiled. It was strange that he should smile because this was the card of a clever terrorist. McDonald had spent nearly two years trying to capture this man and he had been a pain in the proverbial but he also secretly admired him. He admired the skill with which this man could suddenly appear and just as quickly disappear. He chuckled when he thought of the audacity of the man to leave a calling card. This was a man he knew he could use. He was clever and resourceful and seemed to have the ability to make himself invisible. This was a terrorist who had created havoc without taking life. McDonald knew this because all his acts of terrorism were accompanied with his calling card. Nevertheless, it was important to stop him because he had become iconic. The youth of the Province worshiped him and the danger was that they may try to emulate him. He had become part of the games children played in the streets. All the boys wanted to play the part of the mystery man who left red rose calling cards.

McDonald wondered what was meant by *"Goodbye Colonel."* Did it mean that this man was giving up his terrorism or did he know that McDonald had been recalled to England? It was true that there had been none of his activities reported for four weeks or more so perhaps he had returned to England. The reason McDonald thought he may have gone to England was because the only clue to his identity was that he had an English accent. McDonald had been successful in breaking up some terrorist cells of the PIRA and the Loyalists. Under interrogation, the terrorists who claimed to have seen this mystery man gave various descriptions from tall and slim, through to small and thick set and various colours of hair, from blond to black. From all the information McDonald gleaned there was only one common factor, this terrorist had an English accent. That was the only information McDonald was able to find out in spite of threats of long term imprisonment or promises of amnesty. He came to the conclusion that no one really knew who he was and he probably worked alone although he had a feeling that someone in the PIRA must know who he is. Although McDonald was disappointed not to have caught this infamous terrorist, he was looking forward to returning to England to see his family and to organise a new anti-terrorist unit in Manchester.

9

Shannon needn't have been nervous. Rachel Blake opened the door when he rang the bell.

'Tom,' she cried, 'what a lovely surprise,' she gave him a big hug, 'come in, Harry will be so pleased to see you.' She took his arm and took him into the living room.

'Hello, Tom,' said Harry Blake, 'where have you been hiding yourself?' They would obviously be very curious about his absence which was to be expected. Shannon told them that his grandfather, Tom Connery, had died and left him a cottage in Northern Ireland along with a Harley-Davidson motorcycle. This, of course, was perfectly true. He said that he decided to live in the cottage for a while and look up some old friends. That was only part of the truth but it would have to do. He became very emotional when he explained that he had felt that he had nothing left to live for. All his dreams had been shattered and his heart had been full of hate and revenge. He had this great need to get away.

'We understand, Tom,' said Rachel as she put her arm around him in an attempt to comfort him, 'losing our beautiful daughter was a great shock to all of us and you also lost your parents in a car crash only a short time before. It was a dreadful time for you.'

'I blame myself for taking Laura to Belfast,' said Shannon.

'No, Tom, it wasn't your fault. It was an accident,' said Rachel, 'please don't blame yourself for what happened. We know how much she meant to you. She wouldn't want you suffering this way.' There was a silence for a short time as Rachel continued to hold Shannon.

'What are your plans now?' asked Harry. Rachel knew that Harry was trying to change the subject because this was his way of dealing with emotion. It had been a bad couple of years since Laura had died.

'Harry, give the boy time to get his breath,' scolded Rachel.

'Sorry, Tom,' apologised Harry, 'sit down my boy.'

'I've just made a pot of tea, Tom,' announced Rachel, 'would you care for a cup?'

'Thank you,' answered Shannon, 'that would be great.'

After Rachel had poured the tea, Harry said, 'So what have you been doing with yourself?' which invited a frown from Rachel.

'As I said,' answered Shannon, 'I went back to Northern Ireland. I spent some time with my grandmother and then I thought it would be good for me to look up some old friends.' Shannon wasn't feeling too happy not telling the whole truth but how could he tell them what he had really been up to? Rachel and Harry were decent people and he was sure they would be shocked.

'We did get in touch with your grandmother,' said Rachel, 'she told us that you were with her for a couple of weeks. She said you became restless and told her that you needed to get away somewhere,'

'That's true,' said Shannon, 'I felt that I had to do something. I didn't know what. I was too devastated and I was angry with the world.' Shannon was grateful that his grandmother hadn't disclosed what he was really doing. She wouldn't have wanted to worry them. He felt ashamed of himself at the worry he must have caused his grandmother.

'You poor boy,' sighed Rachel, 'I hope you managed to find your friends.'

'I did find some of them,' replied Shannon, 'some of them had moved on chasing their careers. I eventually decided to stay in my grandfather's cottage. Grandad had left me a Harley-Davidson motorbike so I used it to get around the countryside.' It wasn't a total lie but not exactly the truth either. He was hoping that they wouldn't press him for any more information because he wasn't prepared to tell them what he had been doing in Northern Ireland. He also wanted to avoid telling them any serious lies. He had to try to change the subject.

34

'I would like to get in touch with Peter,' said Shannon, hoping to divert the conversation in another direction, 'did he join a law firm or set up his own company?'

'No, he's a cloak and dagger man,' said Harry, 'he's a spy.'

'Take no notice of him, Tom, Peter got a job with the MOD so all his work is confidential. His working hours are so erratic that he thought it would be more sensible to have a flat in the city. He will be delighted to see you. I'll give you his phone number and his address.'

When Shannon got back to his parent's home he sat and looked at Peter's telephone number which Rachel had given him. He was relieved that he had managed to steer Rachel and Harry away from asking him for more detailed information about his activities in Northern Ireland. He didn't think Peter would be such an easy pushover and he was beginning to realise that meeting him would be fraught with difficulties. If he didn't get in touch with Peter then Rachel and Harry would know and wonder why. More importantly they would be hurt and he had to try to avoid that. How much should he tell Peter? Would he be prepared to tell him a plethora of lies? He had no choice. He had to ring him. On the third ring Blake answered.

'Peter, it's me, Tom.'

'Tom, where the hell have you been? Nobody, but nobody, knew where you were. I began to believe you were dead. I'm assuming you're in England. I want to know everything you've been up to. We'll have to.....'

'Whoa! Slow down. I understand that you have a busy schedule and your work is confidential.'

'You must have been speaking to my parents. They were worried about me. I'll explain when we meet. Why don't we meet this evening at my flat? Should we say eight o'clock?'

'That's fine, I have your address.'

Shannon took a taxi to Peter Blake's flat in the city and arrived a little before eight o'clock. The door was opened by Blake and they gave each other a hug and a lot of back slapping.

'You're looking very fit,' said Blake, 'with the short haircut you look like an SAS trooper.'

'I don't think I'm that fit.'

'What's your poison?' asked Blake as he stood in front of the drinks cabinet.

'Jameson's would be fine, if you have some.'

'I've always kept a bottle in stock in case you turned up one day.'

'What a sweet, considerate young man you are.'

'Less of the Blarney, you old sod and tell me what you've been doing for the past however many years.'

This was a question Shannon was afraid of. He didn't feel ready to talk about it. How much of the truth could he tell Peter? He was beginning to regret making contact with him. Perhaps it would have been better if he had remained in Northern Ireland. He didn't relish telling Peter a pack of lies. He would have to stall.

'You first, your Dad says you're a spy.'

'Yea, that's what he calls me. I told Mum and Dad that I was doing some confidential work for the MOD. I didn't want to worry them. My hours of work can be quite difficult, sometimes late nights and early mornings. Mum and Dad were getting a bit concerned so I found this flat in the city. I told them this would cut out the time commuting and so be less stressful. I didn't tell them that I'm helping to set up an anti-terrorist unit here in Manchester, code name Ironclad. I think that would have alarmed them. My job is mainly to do with communications and administration. We're still recruiting but we have acquired a big old house called The Priory on the south side of the city. That will be our headquarters.'

'Peter, this sounds like classified information. Should you be telling me?' Shannon was feeling very uncomfortable. This was worse than anything he could have imagined. How could he tell Peter what he had been doing for the last two years or so when Peter was working for an ant-terrorist organisation?

'Tom, I trust you. In any case we haven't got off the ground yet. We're still recruiting.'

'You'll have to be careful, Peter. I could be a terrorist.'

'Funny you should say that. Colonel McDonald was saying the other day that he needs men like this terrorist in Northern Ireland who has the cheek to leave calling cards. You didn't come across him in your travels did you?'

'I'm sure he was joking,' replied Shannon, ignoring Blake's question.

'No, he was serious. He spent nearly two years trying to catch him but all he got were his calling cards with a red rose on one side. Jim never found out the significance of the red rose. He said if he could turn him, he would offer him a place on his team.'

Shannon was only too familiar with the name Colonel McDonald but could he tell Peter that? His mind was racing looking for a way out. He wanted to jump on the next plane back to Northern Ireland. But how would he explain that to Peter? Blake spoke interrupting his thoughts, 'Why don't you join us, Tom. I'm sure that Colonel McDonald would find a place for you.'

'I don't think that I'm qualified for that kind of work.'

'That's nonsense. I remember you were always at the gym and indulging in those outward bound courses. You're education is the same as mine. You are young and fit and you will be offered training. You could help with the administration and setting up all the communication systems. We would be working together even though it is not as we had originally planned.'

'I'm fairly confident that I'm the last person the Colonel will consider recruiting.'

'Let him be the judge of that when he meets you.'

Meeting Colonel McDonald was not on Shannon's agenda. He hoped that Peter hadn't made any arrangements for that to happen. In the unlikely event of a job being offered he wouldn't be able to accept. He would have to reveal who he was and that would have serious consequences. It would be dangerous not to admit to his past activities because these things have a habit of coming to the surface. He had to think of something to discourage Peter from arranging a meeting. He decided that it would be safer for Peter if he didn't know anything about his pursuits in Northern Ireland. He was trying to think of some excuse to leave.

'Peter, I don't think it would be a good idea for me to meet Colonel McDonald.'

'It's all arranged. He'll be here any moment.'

The door bell rang. Shannon met Colonel Jim McDonald, in person, for the first time.

Shannon looked at this man who had been his adversary in Northern Ireland. He was tall, about fiftyish, certainly fit. He had white hair and the bluest, piercing eyes Shannon had ever seen. He felt as if they were looking straight into his very soul.

After introductions the men sat down and Blake poured drinks. There was silence for a while and then Blake, looking at the Colonel, spoke.

'Tom has spent the last two years or so in Northern Ireland.' Shannon cringed.

'Is that so, Tom? Were you working there?

'No, Colonel. I was visiting my grandmother and friends and sorting out my late maternal grandfather's affairs. I was born in Northern Ireland but lived in England from about the age of ten.'

'Ah,' said the Colonel, 'that accounts for your English accent.'

Shannon was getting more uneasy. If McDonald started to ask more probing questions then he could find himself in big trouble. McDonald was no fool. He had the reputation of being able to get at the truth very quickly. If Shannon made one slip then McDonald would seize the moment. He had to come clean for Peter's sake. There was no mileage in beating around the bush; he decided to come straight to the point

'Colonel,' said Shannon, 'I have to confess that I didn't want to meet you. I tried to tell Peter but I found it too difficult. Now I've put myself in a more difficult position.'

'Tom, what's this all about?' asked Blake.

'Let him speak, Peter,' interrupted McDonald.

'I have probably reached a point of no return and I now need to protect Peter.'

'Protect me from what?'

'Peter, I'm sorry, I shouldn't have made contact with you. You don't realise it but you are now compromised. What I have to tell you will shock both of you. I have to come clean because truth always seems to come out eventually and at a time when it can do most damage. This is going to be difficult.

'Tom, what can be so bad that I need protection?' asked Blake.

'Peter, I think it would be a good idea if you poured some more drinks,' said McDonald, 'large ones I think. It may help Tom.'

Peter handed out the drinks and after Shannon had downed a good measure he relaxed.

'I'm not going to beat about the bush.' Shannon put a red rose calling card on the table. The silence was deafening. After a few minutes the Colonel spoke.

'That must have taken a lot of courage,' said McDonald, 'what you have just disclosed has put you in a very vulnerable position, to put it mildly. I'm assuming that you are telling us that you are the man we often called the "calling card" terrorist. You caused devastation but I don't think you ever killed anyone, well, not according to my records.'

'I am happy to accept the authority of your records. I certainly tried to avoid taking life. So what happens now?'

'What I have to say may surprise you,' said McDonald, 'it may even shock you. I want you to join Ironclad. It's a new anti-terrorist unit. Shannon was silent. Blake became quite excited and made his way to the drinks cabinet returning with more drinks.

'This is an occasion for celebration,' grinned Blake.

'Hold on, Peter, I don't think Tom shares your enthusiasm.' McDonald had been watching Shannon's face and had detected some concern.

'I have just had about two years dodging bullets, hiding from the police and the army. Never sure if I was going to get caught or killed;

having to change my appearance on a regular basis. When I first started on this mad life I was full of hate and seeking revenge. I believe that it is out of my system now and I want to lead a more peaceful, lawful life. Some of the terrorists were fighting for a cause that they believed in and no doubt some of them had suffered injustices. I had a different motive. My motive was revenge; revenge for the shooting of Laura. I now accept that it was an unfortunate accident but at the time I was consumed with grief and anger and I wanted to hit out at somebody.'

Shannon could see that Peter had become upset. He had been very close to his sister and her death had been a shock to him and his parents too. Not only was Laura very beautiful but she also had an attractive personality and she was loved by everyone who knew her. Peter was obviously reliving the grief that he had suffered at the time of his sister's death. Shannon, more than ever now, wished that he had stayed in Northern Ireland. He could see that he was causing more hurt. His thoughts were interrupted by McDonald speaking. Blake remained silent.

'You said earlier that Peter was compromised by you revealing who you were. Peter, of course, didn't know who you were and so is not to blame. You are correct, however, sometimes the best of kept secrets will out and he may have been affected by association. I know that you will be aware that there will be consequences.'

'Yes, I agree. I was going to ask for amnesty. I must make it clear that....' McDonald interrupted.

'Before you make a decision hear me out first,' McDonald paused for a moment to take a sip of his drink, then continued, 'the way I see it is that you have two choices. One, you may be offered amnesty. The reason I say, may be, is because of your notoriety. I can't guarantee that you won't serve a prison sentence. The police and the army in Northern Ireland have been after your head for a long time and so will resist you being allowed to get off scot free. You particularly embarrassed the police. Even if you didn't serve a prison sentence, your real name will be known to the public and there may be some hotheads who will want to have a go at you or someone close to you.' McDonald paused to check on Shannon's reaction. Shannon's face did not betray how he was feeling.

'And the second choice?' asked Shannon

'The second choice is that you join us. Your real identity will never be known to the public, or perhaps I should say, that no one will ever know the real identity of the terrorist with the red rose calling cards. He will disappear from the face of the earth and it will be assumed that he was killed in some skirmish or other, we can easily set off that rumour.'

'I must admit, I never thought about the possibility of someone having a go at my grandmother or me, when my identity was in the public domain.'

'I think the chances of that happening are very high,' said McDonald, 'there's always some idiot who wants to be the fastest gun in town. Everybody knew about the red rose calling cards. You were a legend and certainly a hero to many people in Northern Ireland. However, to many people you were a terrorist and they may come seeking revenge.'

'I must admit I hadn't thought it through. I just wanted to get away from all that stupid madness. It would seem that I have no choice but to accept your offer of a place on your team. Perhaps it will give me the opportunity to make some reparation.'

'Why the red rose?' asked McDonald.

'I think I can answer that question,' said Blake, who hadn't spoken for some time but was now smiling at Shannon, much to Shannon's relief, 'and I now understand why he became a terrorist. That was my sister Laura's favourite rose.'

Shannon was on the train travelling to the SAS training establishment in Herefordshire. He smiled when he recalled his meeting with Colonel McDonald, in Peter's flat, over six months ago. He suppressed a laugh when he remembered Peter's face as he listened to the conversation Shannon had had with McDonald. It had been risky, risky for Shannon but necessary for Blake's future with the anti-terrorist unit. McDonald surprised them both; even Blake, who wasn't totally sure that McDonald would offer Shannon a place on his team, after Shannon had disclosed who he was. When Shannon had given the situation more thought he quickly realised that there was no alternative. McDonald was right, amnesty was not an option. He certainly found it difficult to believe that McDonald had arranged a shortened version of the SAS training programme for him and offered him a place on his Manchester team. It wasn't the career he had planned but when McDonald had spelled out the alternatives, he realised that he had no choice. If he had turned down McDonald's offer, then the life of the person who meant most to him could be in jeopardy. He wondered what his grandmother would think about his decision, exchanging one dangerous activity for another. He wasn't sure he would be able to tell her. He decided to assign that decision to a lower priority file for the time being. There was no point in upsetting her until he could see how things panned out. He was also relieved that Peter's position in the team was secure and that his character would not be tarnished by his association with Shannon. McDonald was very much aware of Shannon by reputation and yet seemed very keen to take him on board. Shannon now felt sure that it would be an opportunity to make some reparation. He had high expectations and was looking forward to the training.

10

The Peace Process in Northern Ireland was under way. The Provisional IRA agreed to lay down their arms although there were those members of the public who were very sceptical. The Loyalist paramilitary organisations had still to commit themselves. Some PIRA and Loyalist terrorists had joined forces and turned to criminal activities. Many of them had indulged in drug dealing and prostitution previously. Declan Brady was ex-PIRA. He was sitting in his favourite pub, The Red Lion, in Tomb Street in Belfast with a couple of his ex-PIRA mates. The PIRA cell he had belonged to had been disbanded and now crime had become his full time occupation. He was a short, thick set man with black hair and cold, blue eyes which never seemed to smile. He was a hard man with an unpredictable, foul temper.

'Listen, you fellas, we're going to rob a bank,' declared Brady.

'You've got to be bloody joking,' said Martin Nolan.

'Declan, I don't think you've thought this through,' suggested Michael Donovan, 'with all this new technology the banks are high risk.'

'*I'm* not going to break into a bank, you daft eejits. I'm going to get someone else to do it for me.'

'Well, you can count me out,' said Donovan.

'And me too,' joined in Nolan.

'Not you two, you stupid morons,' snapped Brady, 'but I want you both to help me to set it up.'

'If you're getting somebody else to break into the bank isn't that a big risk. Can you trust this fella?   Who is he?' asked Donovan.

'He's the assistant bank manager. He's going to open the bank for us,' whispered Brady as he looked furtively around the pub.

'Declan, I don't know what you've been drinking but I think it's gone to your head,' said Nolan.

'Will you shut your mouth and listen,' barked Brady, 'you stupid bugger.'

'Okay, okay, keep your hair on,' said Nolan.

'Do you remember me telling you that I bumped into an old school pal of mine a few days ago? He was brilliant at school and went on to university. Well, he's an assistant bank manager now but he's very unhappy. After a few pints he told me that he feels he's wasted his life in the banking business. He's been passed over for promotion a number of times. He's looking for revenge so I explained how he could achieve that. I made a deal with him. Later this evening we're going to pay him a visit to make sure the deal is honoured.'

'How much are we talking about here?' Donovan asked.

'At least ten million pounds, probably more,' said Brady.

'What about the risk?' said Nolan.

'Hardly any risk at all,' replied Brady, 'in fact you two won't go anywhere near the bank.'

'That's fine by me,' said Donovan.

'I can live with that,' said Nolan.

At about eight-thirty that evening Brady, Donovan and Nolan, wearing masks, were standing outside a detached house in the suburbs of Belfast. The sky was heavy with cloud and it seemed to have become dark earlier than usual. A slight drizzle had begun to fall and was made more unpleasant by a cold breeze. Brady rang the door bell. The door was opened by a man. He was of medium build with dark brown hair which was quite grey at the temples.

'Why have you come this evening?' the man whispered, looking worried.

Brady had removed his mask when the man had opened the door.

'Surprise always gives us an advantage, Eddie,' said Brady as he replaced the mask, 'let's go inside shall we? It's cold out here.'

As they walked down the hall a woman's voice called out, 'Eddie, who's at the door?'

Before Eddie could answer they had entered the living room.

'What's going on? Who are these men Eddie?' screamed the woman.

'We're Eddie's friends, Mrs Carson,' said Brady.

'Eddie, what's going on? Why are these men wearing masks?'

'It's all right, Sylvia, they're not going to harm us,' said Carson, trying to calm her down.

At that moment a young girl appeared at the living room door. She was about thirteen or fourteen years old with long blond hair and big blue eyes. She was a smaller version of her mother. The similarity was remarkable.

'Mummy, what's the matter?' she asked looking very distressed.

'Nothing darling,' said Carson, 'go back upstairs and .....' Before he could finish Brady interrupted.

'She stays down here.'

Sylvia began to get agitated. 'For God's sake, Eddie, who are these men?'

'Gag her and tie her to the chair,' said Brady, looking at Donovan.

'Declan, please, there's no need for that,' pleaded Carson as Donovan forced Sylvia into a chair and began to tie her wrists.

'Mummy, Mummy,' screeched the young girl.

'Gag and tie up the girl too,' ordered Brady.

'Declan, that's unnecessary,' said Carson, 'you'll be quiet won't you Sandra?'

'Okay, no gags but they have to be tied to the chairs until the job is done.'

'Eddie, what does he mean? What job?'

'So you haven't told your sweet, darling wife what you're up to, Eddie. Have you?' mocked Brady.

'Sylvia, you know I've been very unhappy with the way the bank have treated me over the past few years. The last straw was when they promoted that incompetent Blackwell instead of me. This is my way of getting back at them; a bit of revenge.'

'Eddie, what in God's name are you going to do?'

'There won't be any risk for me. I'm going to open the bank in the morning before any of the staff arrive. Declan will be with me. When we've finished we will come back here and that will be the end of it. We'll have financial security for the rest of our lives.'

'I don't believe this,' said Sylvia, 'and what makes you think you will get away with it?'

'It's easy, Mrs Carson,' interrupted Brady, 'you and Sandra will be here with my men as hostages. Eddie will tell the police that the robbers threatened to kill you if he didn't do what he was told. You won't be able to tell the police who we are because we have masks on. The only name you know is Declan and that may not be my real name.'

'It seems that Eddie knows who you are.'

'I don't think Eddie will be telling anybody anything, especially when he gets his cut of the takings. Do you, Mrs Carson?'

'Eddie these men are criminals. When they get their hands on the money they won't need us. How can you be sure we will be safe?'

'I've known Declan a long time. We were in the same class at school. He's not a stranger.'

A faint flicker of alarm registered in Brady's eyes. Sylvia now knew too much and he also saw her as something of a loose cannon. It was also obvious that Eddie was also careless and may prove to be a problem in the future. He would have to give this some thought. Perhaps there would be too many loose ends.

'Mummy, I need to use the bathroom,' said Sandra, cutting into Brady's thoughts.

'I'll take her,' said Brady, 'and she'll have to leave the bathroom door open. I don't want her escaping out of the bathroom window.'

'Eddie, this man is going too far. Stop him, please.'

'Declan, you promised my family would not be hurt in any way. Sandra's thirteen years old and she is entitled to her privacy,' said Carson, 'let me take her. I have a vested interest in this job going smoothly.'

'Okay, you can take her but remember I have your beautiful, darling wife here tied to this chair and you don't want to leave her too long with me do you?' said Brady as he stroked Sylvia's cheek.

When Carson and Sandra returned, Donovan tied Sandra to the chair again.

'Declan, is it necessary to tie them to the chairs?' asked Carson, now beginning to feel a little nervous about the situation.

'Well, it's obvious that you haven't told them what you're up to,' said Brady, 'and I'd say that they are in shock right now. When people are in shock they do stupid things, such as trying to escape. You should have warned them, Eddie, and then all this trouble could have been avoided.'

'You weren't supposed to arrive until early tomorrow morning,' said Carson, 'Declan, I told you there was a time lock on the safe so we can't open it until seven-thirty. I was going to explain everything to Sylvia tomorrow. I didn't want her to be awake all night, worrying.'

'Like I said earlier, Eddie, surprise always gives us an advantage. I didn't want any last minute cold feet. Anyway, this will be more authentic. Can't you see the headlines? "ASSISTANT BANK MANAGER'S FAMILY TERRORISED AT GUN POINT OVERNIGHT IN THEIR HOME" When the police start asking questions, your wife and daughter will be able to genuinely describe the terror they experienced, as they were threatened by gunmen. They will be able to show the police the marks on their wrists. They will be able to honestly say that this was because those big, bad robbers tied them to the chairs.' Brady looked over to Donovan and Nolan and winked.

The news of the bank robbery was too late for the early editions of the newspapers. The television news reported that a bank in Belfast had been robbed of fifteen million pounds. The police believed that Mr Carson, the assistant bank manager, had been forced to open the safe whilst his family were being held hostage in their home. The bodies of Mr Carson and his family were found in their home later in the day. All three had been shot in the head. The bodies of Mr Carson's wife and their daughter had been found tied to chairs. The police were asking neighbours to report anything suspicious they may have seen near the home of the Carson's.

47

11

Shannon arrived at the SAS training centre and was shown to his quarters which were made up of a single bedroom and a bathroom, small but adequate. He had been told that the course was in three phases, first, Endurance, followed by, Escape, Evasion and Tactical Questioning, and finally, the Killing House. He was unpacking his holdall when the door opened and in walked a sergeant. He was tall, broad and had obviously kept himself at the peak of fitness. He had a weather-beaten face, thick, black eye brows almost obscuring his dark, brown eyes and wearing the famous SAS beige beret.

'I'm Sergeant Campbell and I am your training instructor. You will be doing a shortened version of the training programme. Don't expect any preferential treatment because you are one of Colonel McDonald's boys. Do you understand?'

'Yes, Sergeant.'

'This is a tough course and I'm not going to make it easy for you. If you step out of line or fall below standard I'll jump all over you. You are free for the rest of the day but I want you in the gym tomorrow morning at seven hundred hours. Be in the mess at eighteen hundred hours for your evening meal. Do you have any questions?'

'No, Sergeant.' Shannon thought it wise to continue addressing him by his title because he guessed that this was what Campbell would demand. He didn't want to antagonise him because this man was not a happy bunny, but why?

'Your first job is to go to the Quartermaster's store and draw your kit. Go on; get your ass out of here.'
Shannon left and Campbell followed.

Shannon expected the course to be tough and he appreciated that the SAS would demand a very high standard from all candidates. It looked as though he was going to have a problem with Campbell. Was it because the course had been watered down for him? Was this the reason Campbell was so unhappy? Shannon wondered if perhaps Campbell had had a disagreement with McDonald in the past. He thought that was very unlikely because McDonald had had an outstanding career in the SAS. He was one of the highest decorated officers and was very popular with all the troopers. He told himself not to become paranoid, perhaps all recruits were treated this way as part of the breaking down and building up process. Time would tell.

Shannon had some time left before he would have to go to the mess so he decided to have a look at the gym. He had always kept himself fit, jogging most days and attending the gym as often as he could. Sergeant Garry Ellison was the gym instructor and Shannon thought he was a breath of fresh air after his experience with Campbell. Ellison put him through several health tests and then set up a training programme suitable for him. Ellison was surprised to hear that the only training arranged for Shannon was working out in the gym. He explained that the Endurance Phase was scheduled to take place the day after tomorrow and he would have to carry a bergen weighing fifty pounds along rough country. Ellison explained that a bergen was a rucksack used by the SAS. He believed that Shannon would be doing about twenty miles which was roughly half of the usual distance expected of SAS candidates. Sergeant Ellison pointed out that it was absolutely essential that Shannon should have some experience carrying weights.

'Shannon, this is strictly between the two of us,' said Ellison 'some supervision should have been arranged to help you with your training. The usual procedure is for the weights to be increased gradually over a period of time. I suggest that you begin carrying weights on your back as soon as possible. Campbell is in charge of your training so strictly speaking I shouldn't interfere but I'm concerned about your lack of training. Be careful Campbell isn't a guy you want to cross.'

Shannon took Ellison's advice and filled a bergen with weights and set off around the compound. He continued the training until nine o'clock with breaks for a meal and short rests. He repeated the same procedure the following day. Although he had always kept himself fit, he had not had much experience of carrying heavy weights on his back. At the end of the second day he was having pain in muscles he didn't know he had. Hot showers gave some relief but not completely. He hoped that he had done enough to complete the course tomorrow and so avoid the wrath of Campbell. It was dark when he finished his training and he was on his way to his room when he met Sergeant Ellison.

'Hi, Tom, I've been watching you from time to time doing your training and I'm impressed. You have kept up a good pace and on the second day your pace improved.'

'Thanks, I need all the encouragement I can get. Right now I'm aching everywhere.'

'I'm a qualified physiotherapist, if you come to the gym after you've had your shower I'll give you a massage with some of my magic liniment.'

'That's an offer I can't refuse,' smiled Shannon feeling better already. After the massage, Shannon felt very relaxed and some of the aches and pains seemed to have melted away. He began to believe that he would be able to cope the following day.

The day for the Endurance Phase had arrived. Shannon, along with other candidates, was taken to the Brecon Beacons area in South Wales. Shannon was given a map and a compass and informed that there would be check points along the way manned by SAS Directing staff. No help or advice would be given. Each candidate would be left to his own devices because it was necessary for them to be self-motivated.

'Shannon,' roared Sergeant Campbell, before Shannon could get started, 'I'll be watching you. These other guys have to complete the full hike. You only have to do half that distance so I expect you to be well on time or you will be in big trouble.'

Shannon walked off in silence hoping that he could make good time. The massage had worked wonders and he was in good spirits in spite of Campbell's threatening behaviour. The first few miles passed without a hitch. It was good to be out in the fresh air and the surrounding countryside was very dramatic. The area had a reputation for being wet but it was a sunny, dry morning with a cool breeze, ideal for walking. It would have been perfect, thought Shannon, if he hadn't got this dead donkey on his back and a sergeant barking at his heels.

Shannon's aim was to complete the course by seven in the evening. It was a little after twelve noon and he had made good progress having passed the half way mark. He was feeling particularly pleased with himself when out of nowhere Campbell appeared.

'Come on Shannon, you're too bloody slow, get your fat ass moving a bit faster or you'll never finish and then you'll be bloody sorry.' Campbell was red in the face, looking as though he was ready to blow a gasket. Shannon suddenly tripped over something and crashed down heavily on his left shoulder, striking his face against a protruding rock. He was shaken but managed to recover. He was absolutely certain that it was Campbell's foot but he wouldn't be able to prove it. His first thought was to punch Campbell in the nose but, as he scrambled to his feet, he thought better of it. He moved off and, as he did so, Campbell shouted after him.

'You stupid, clumsy Irish bastard, you can't stay on your feet.' That almost stopped Shannon in his tracks but he gritted his teeth and moved on. So that is the problem, it is because he is Irish. He didn't have an Irish accent so Campbell must have had access to his records. Perhaps the SAS needed to have information of each candidate's background so documents would have been sent automatically. He felt sure that Colonel McDonald would have ensured that a certain period in his career would have been omitted but his date and place of birth would probably be shown.

A few hours later he reached his final rendezvous point and was told that he had finished the course twenty minutes under the stipulated time. One of the Directing Staff noticed the wound on his head. A field bandage was applied and he was told to report to the Medical Room when he returned to Herefordshire. Back at the SAS Headquarters' Medical Room Shannon's wounds were examined, cleaned and dressed. No stitches were required. He was given some pain killers for the head wound and the bruising on his shoulder. He left the Medical Room and stepped out into the cool air of the evening. He was elated that he had completed the hike with twenty minutes to spare. He was also angry when he thought of Campbell's attempt to stop him. What was wrong with that man? Surely it was nothing to do with him being Irish. He couldn't imagine that that reason alone could generate such anger. There had to be some other reason; but what? As far as he could remember he had never met the man before. One thing he was sure of, Campbell was going to make this course as difficult as possible for him.

The next day all the candidates, except Shannon, were kitted out for jungle training in Belize. A group of troopers who had completed their jungle training joined Shannon for the Escape and Evasion and Tactical Questioning Phase. Instruction on escape and evasion was given in the classroom and some SAS officers and POWs spoke of their experiences under interrogation. Shannon found the rest of the afternoon both interesting and informative. As he was leaving the classroom he met Sergeant Ellison.

'Hi, Tom, I believe you had an accident yesterday. Was it an accident?'

'I don't think so but no witnesses I'm afraid.'

'I told you to be careful, Campbell is a dangerous man. It's not the first time he had a grudge against someone. Have you met him before?'

'No, but he seems to have a problem with the Irish.'

'That's interesting. The last time he gave a recruit a bad time, he was Irish. But you're not Irish.'

'I was born in Northern Ireland but brought up and educated in England.'

'Captain Thornton was surprised that you hadn't had any training before doing the hike. He's looking into the matter and is certain to want to speak to you and Campbell. Be careful because Campbell will have a good story to cover his back.'

Ellison was correct. Captain Barry Thornton had spoken to Campbell and now wanted Shannon to report to his office.

'Sit down, Shannon,' said Thornton pointing to a chair in front of his desk, 'I think you probably know what I want to discuss with you but I would like to do it informally.'

'I can guess sir.'

'I was surprised to see that you hadn't had any training before you went on the hike. Sergeant Campbell tells me that you were told about the training but failed to turn up. Do you have anything to say?' This completely wrong footed Shannon and he wasn't sure how to handle it. He decided it would be wise not to refute Campbell's lie initially and then see what Thornton had to say. He hesitated before answering and he was sure that Thornton had noticed.

'I must have misunderstood his instruction, sir,' said Shannon, perhaps a little too hurriedly.

'I see, well in view of the fact that you are a civilian and you must have suffered on the hike, I'm going to be lenient with you. This incident will not appear on our records and not on our report to Colonel McDonald. You may go.'

'Thank you, sir,' said Shannon with relief. As he was leaving the room Thornton spoke again.

'Shannon, I've been in the SAS a long time and I keep my ear to the ground and I know most of what goes on here. The problem usually is proving it because troopers won't inform on each other. From what

I've seen and heard about you I'm sure you would make a first class trooper.'

As Shannon was leaving Thornton's office he smiled and thought Thornton is no stone jug.

Shannon decided to put the Campbell problem to the back of his mind and concentrate on getting through the Escape and Evasion and Tactical Questioning Phase. He would be experiencing a modified version of the course. This meant that he only had to survive not much more than one day and one night. He was given a map, a compass, a torch and a bottle of water. His task was to reach allocated rendezvous points at certain times without being captured by the "hunters." The "hunters" would be in uniform and probably be the local Territorial Army. He had had lots of experience with evasion but not capture and interrogation so he was looking forward to the challenge. The exercise would take place somewhere in Gloucestershire. Shannon had no idea exactly where this would be, or the kind of terrain he would be up against but had been assured that there would be ample cover.

He was dropped off at the starting point at the edge of a forest at twelve noon. The sky was overcast and threatening rain. He realised that the most difficult part would be travelling during daylight. His strategy was to arrive at a point during the day which would make the final rendezvous point achievable during darkness. This meant that he would have to find a hiding place where he could sleep during daylight. He made good progress and arrived at the first rendezvous point without incident. He now had to be on the lookout for a suitable hiding place. After a few more hours he found some thick shrubbery and he managed to make his way into the middle. On his journey through the forest he had found a large plastic sheet, probably left behind by some picnickers. He folded the sheet down the middle and covered it with leaves. He then slid into it as if it were a sleeping bag.

He was very tired, probably due to the previous day's exercise and he was soon asleep.

When he awoke it was dark. He took a chance and used his torch to check his watch. It was ten-thirty; he had slept about five hours. He would have to get moving. Visibility was poor because the moon was obscured by the density of the trees. He ploughed on through rough terrain for what seemed an eternity. He was relieved that Campbell hadn't appeared and he was hoping he wasn't involved in this exercise. He had decided, however, that he had to assume that he may turn up because he had made it abundantly clear that he was out to make him fail the course.

Dawn was breaking and the sky was heavy with cloud. He heard some movement ahead. He dropped slowly to the ground and began crawling through the tall grass and found cover under some bushes. He could see about four uniformed men walking in a line obviously searching the ground. They kept on moving in formation and so missed him. The light was improving bringing with it a greater danger of being captured. This could also be an opportunity for Campbell to make his move. Shannon had checked his map and compass regularly and he felt fairly confident that he was progressing at a reasonable pace and in the right direction. He calculated that he could only be about two hours from the final rendezvous.

After about an hour the rain carried out its threat. It was torrential. Shannon thought this could be to his advantage if the rain caused the hunters' enthusiasm to dwindle. He heard some movement and what he thought were voices but the rain made it difficult to see. He lay very still and then slowly rolled under some undergrowth. Five hunters walked passed, very close to where he was hiding. He was certain that they couldn't see him because the rain was falling heavily. They seemed to be preoccupied with keeping themselves dry as they struggled to hold their rainproof hoods in place. They walked passed him and soon disappeared behind a curtain of rain. Shannon hoped they were the last patrol. An hour later and with no sign of Campbell he arrived at the final rendezvous.

On the way back to the SAS Headquarters, Shannon was relishing the thought of a really hot shower followed by a big breakfast with lashings of tea. It was eight-thirty when they pulled up in front of a single storey building. Too late for breakfast he thought unless they arrange sandwiches on these occasions. He decided he would be grateful if he could get out of his cold, wet clothes and have a shower. As he got out of the vehicle a corporal approached him and took him into the building. The corporal opened a door labelled "Briefing Room A" and Shannon entered. There were two troopers already in the room looking miserable. Shannon took a seat near them.

'I assume it didn't go according to plan,' said Shannon.

'They caught me,' one of them began, 'because.....'

Before the trooper could finish speaking the door opened and the corporal came in and beckoned to Shannon. He followed the corporal as he walked to the end of a long corridor. He stopped in front of a door which appeared to be made of metal. The corporal opened the door and without speaking pushed Shannon into the room. The door was shut and Shannon heard the key being turned in the lock. I should have realised thought Shannon, it's the interrogation. He looked around the room, it was about four yards square and there were no windows. There was a single light pendant hanging from the centre of the ceiling which gave off a very poor light. A wooden table and chair were the only furniture he could see and these had been placed in the centre of the room. He could see some metal rings had been fixed on one wall but he could only guess what these were for.

Shannon was feeling cold, tired and hungry. He sat down and waited. After half an hour the door opened and in walked a sergeant and the corporal he had seen earlier. They both carried canes.

'Who said you could sit down? Stand up,' yelled the sergeant as he slapped the table with his cane.

Shannon stood up. The corporal pushed him away from the table and the sergeant began prodding him with his cane.

'You're not a trooper so what are you doing here?' screamed the sergeant.

Shannon gave his name rank and serial number which had been given to him during the instruction classes.

'Answer the sergeant,' roared the corporal and he pushed Shannon with such force that he fell against the wall.

'Get up,' they both shouted.

'I'll ask you again,' said the sergeant, 'what are you doing here?' Shannon gave the same answer. The corporal pushed his face close up to Shannon's face and began to scream obscenities.

'I'll give you another chance,' said the sergeant, 'What are you doing here and who are you working for?'

Shannon repeated the same answer. The interrogation continued for what Shannon felt was a lifetime. Each NCO taking turns to scream obscenities at him and prodding him with their canes. He was feeling very tired and cold. He wanted to go to sleep and was finding it difficult to keep his eyes open. Suddenly a bucket of ice cold water was thrown over him. He gritted his teeth as his body went into a spasm of shivering.

'Take your shoes and socks off and strip to the waist,' ordered the sergeant.

Shannon fingers were extremely cold and he had some difficulty undoing his buttons.

'You're too slow,' said the corporal and he tore the shirt of Shannon's back.

Shannon was feeling the effects of not having eaten for twenty-four hours. He was wet and he was cold and his limbs were aching.

'You only have to tell Sergeant Booth you've had enough,' said the corporal, 'and the interrogation will end. It only gets worse from now on.'

Shannon kept silent. He knew that if he accepted the offer he would fail the exercise.

'Are you ready to tell me what you are doing here?' asked the sergeant.

Shannon remained silent.

'All right you've had your chance. I'm going to hand you over to the tough guys.' And the sergeant left.

A few minutes later the door opened and in walked Sergeant Campbell. Shannon felt sure that this was going to be a very painful experience. Campbell had tried to get him disqualified when he was experiencing the Endurance Phase by tripping him up. The fall could have been more serious and have made it impossible for Shannon to carry on. Now he felt that Campbell had a great opportunity to really hurt him.

'I see we have a terrorist on our hands. Did you know that, Corporal Banks?' Campbell was holding a cane with which he continually slapped his hand.

'No, Sergeant.'

'Aye, he's Irish. All Irishmen are terrorists. This bastard is a real terrorist. Isn't that right Shannon?'

Shannon didn't reply. He wasn't quite sure where Campbell was coming from. Was this part of the act? Perhaps Campbell had managed to get hold of some confidential information about him. He thought that was unlikely.

'Has he been cooperating Corporal?' Campbell slapped down hard on the table with his cane.

'No, Sergeant.'

'That's very bad.' Campbell began to prod Shannon with his cane forcing him back to the wall. He then threw two sets of handcuffs on the table.

'Corporal, cuff him to the rings on the wall.'

The corporal did as he was told and Shannon was spread-eagled against the wall.

'You've been asked before and I'll ask you again. What are you doing here?'

Shannon gave his usual answer. Campbell punched him several times in the ribs and as Shannon's head fell forward, Campbell delivered two blows to his head. Shannon was dazed. He shook his head and through the mist in his eyes he could see that the corporal looked concerned.

'Now will you talk, you Irish bastard or do you want some more of the same?'

Shannon was determined not to give in so he didn't answer. This prompted Campbell to have another go. He threw several punches to Shannon's body and finally a left and right to his jaw.

Shannon passed out.

He was lying in a gutter outside a Belfast pub. He tried to get up but he couldn't. His head hurt and his tongue felt as though it had spent the night at the bottom of a bird's cage. He couldn't remember how he got there. Had he been thrown out of the pub? He couldn't be sure. He remembered that he had been doing a lot of drinking over the past few months but always managed to get home. Home, where was home? He remembered. He had been staying in the cottage his grandfather had left him in his will. Where had he left his Harley-Davidson? This wasn't good enough. He had to try to sort himself out. Someone was bending over him, 'Tom, Tom, Tom Shannon.....'

Shannon opened his eyes. A nurse was speaking, 'Tom, Tom Shannon, how are you feeling?'

'Sore, what happened?' asked Shannon and then added, 'Oh yes, I remember.'

After the nurse had taken his temperature and checked his pulse he was taken to the x-ray department for a brain scan and an x-ray. Later in the afternoon the MO came to see him.

'You've certainly taken a beating. You have two broken ribs and a lot of bruising. I thought it advisable that you had a brain scan because of the extent of the damage to your head and face. There's no damage to your brain and surprisingly no fractures to your jaw. You must have a very tough jaw.'

'Is there any chance of my being discharged this evening?'

'No, I'm keeping you in overnight for observation then we'll see. You should take it easy for the rest of the day.'

Late the following morning Captain Thornton paid Shannon a visit.

'The MO was keen for you to have a good rest. That's the reason I've left my visit so late. How do you feel this morning?'

'I'm recovering, sir.'

'I've been trying to find out what happened to you. Candidates don't usually get so badly hurt. I've interviewed Sergeant Campbell and Corporal Banks and they both say you fell off the chair and hit your face against the table.'

'I can't really remember much about it so I guess that's what must have happened.'

'I'm not very happy with this explanation because your injuries are not consistent with falling off a chair and hitting your face against a table. According to the MO you have suffered a lot of bruising to your body and two broken ribs.'

'If you remember, sir, I did fall during the Endurance exercise so perhaps that accounts for the extra bruising.' Shannon was hoping that he sounded convincing.

'All right Shannon, if that's what you say,' said Thornton, obviously not convinced, 'but if you change your mind you know where to find me. I'm going to inform Colonel McDonald that you've had an accident and so will be spending a few days in hospital which may mean postponing some of your training. Do have a problem with that?

'No, sir.'

'Do you have any questions?'

'I would like to experience the Killing House. Would that be possible?'

'We'll have to wait and see how well you recover.'

After Captain Thornton left, Shannon closed his eyes and began to think about his experience in the interrogation room. Thornton appeared to be concerned that Campbell had meted out more punishment than was necessary. He certainly wasn't convinced by Shannon's explanation of his injuries. Thornton's visit had convinced Shannon that what had happened to him was extremely unusual. He began to wonder if he and Campbell had crossed paths sometime in the past. He knew that Campbell had a home in Belfast where he spent most of his leave time. He couldn't recall ever meeting him. If he had been subjected to some kind of personal vendetta then what was the reason? Had someone informed Campbell about his activities in Northern Ireland? If so who could that be? It was unlikely to be Colonel McDonald or anyone on his team. The only other people who knew who he was were Sean Keane and Declan Brady. He trusted Keane implicitly but Brady was another matter. Was there a connection between Brady and Campbell? Shannon found that hard to believe. Brady was a terrorist and probably still is but Campbell is a sergeant in the SAS; chalk and cheese? Only time would tell but Shannon decided that he would have to be on his guard until he could find out if Campbell had some connection with his past.

After two days resting Shannon began to feel much better and was discharged from hospital. He walked over to the gym to see if Sergeant Ellison would arrange a suitable workout for him.

'Hi, Tom, how are you feeling?'

'I'm okay now.'

'Tom, I've been doing some digging and I found out that Campbell's nineteen year old brother had been killed in Northern Ireland some six or seven months ago. He was serving with the security forces in Belfast when he was killed by a sniper's bullet. The Real IRA claimed responsibility. That must be the reason he hates the Irish.'

'It could explain his behaviour.'

'Perhaps it's his way of seeking revenge.'

'*Seeking revenge*, that sounds familiar.'

'What do you mean?'

'Oh, it was something my grandmother said to me a lifetime ago.'

'After you were taken to hospital Campbell was taken off the course. Captain Thornton is investigating the matter.'

After a health check, Ellison arranged a new workout programme for Shannon. Ellison told him that a celebration had been arranged in the mess for the following evening for all the course members. Shannon protested that he didn't really qualify because he had only done a shortened version of the training programme. Ellison said that Captain Thornton expected him to be there. He still had to do the Killing House and, as it was a team exercise, it would be useful to meet the other troopers who would be doing the exercise with him.

The following evening when Shannon arrived at the mess, the celebration was well under way. A group of troopers who were standing around the piano spotted him as he walked through the door. They raised their glasses in his direction and broke into a chorus of "For he's a jolly good fellow." Shannon was staggered. He was saved by Ellison who guided him to the bar. The singing changed to another tune and Shannon was grateful.

'Will you have a drink?' asked Ellison.

'A Jameson's would be fine.'

'I suppose that took you by surprise.'

'I've got to be honest, I'm gobsmacked.'

'You know how it is with small communities. Well, here it's like one big family. Everybody soon found out you were brutally beaten when you were cuffed to the wall. You didn't break even though you were tortured beyond what is normally allowed.'

'I think I need another drink,' said Shannon.

Captain Thornton joined them at the bar.

'It looks as if you've created a great fan base. All the guys think you would make a good trooper and I think you should sign on straight away,' said Thornton with a grin.

'It's not for me, sir, you guys are just too tough and anyway I can't sing.'

'I've arranged for you to be included in the Killing House exercise the day after tomorrow. The MO tells me that you are medically fit. Before you return to Manchester I would like you to call in my office for a chat. Enjoy the rest of the evening.'

'Thank you, sir.'

The celebration went with a swing and stretched on into the early hours of the morning. Shannon was made welcome by all the troopers who treated him as if he were some sort of hero. Everyone appeared to be there, officers, all the instructors and administration staff but no sign of Campbell. Shannon began to wonder if some of these troopers would be fit enough for the Killing House exercise even if it was the day after tomorrow. Some of them had been going hard at it all evening. As it got later Shannon noticed that a number of the guys had a dazed look in their eyes and the singing had died down to a drunken murmur. Shannon and Ellison decided to turn in. As they were leaving there was a loud, drunken chorus of what sounded a little like "Auld Lang Syne" and lots of waving and cheering. Shannon wondered if any of them would remember the celebration tomorrow.

Shannon learned a great deal from the exercise in the Killing House. Inside the house there were various corridors and a number of rooms leading off these corridors. The candidates were sent into the Killing House in teams. They were given a task. In order to achieve that task successfully, it was necessary for them to make quick and accurate decisions and to be able to distinguish between innocent bystanders and gunmen. They were trained to focus on the main objective and carry out correct procedures with regard to "injured" and "killed" team members. Shannon had had lots of practise with making quick decisions under pressure when he was working in parallel with the PIRA. He had also familiarised himself with various weapons although he had never used one in anger. This training had fine tuned him. He was satisfied that he had given a good account of himself. He had nothing but admiration for these SAS guys. They had to train hard and were often sent on very dangerous, difficult missions.

Before he left for Manchester, he called to see Captain Barry Thornton as requested.

'Ah, Shannon, I wanted to have a chat with you before you left,' he pointed to a chair, 'sit down, I won't keep you long. I wasn't satisfied with Banks' and Campbell's version of how you received your injuries. I asked two of my officers to look into it. After questioning, Banks admitted that his original story was untrue and that Campbell had beaten you into unconsciousness when you were cuffed to the wall. Banks said that he had a feeling that Campbell was wreaking some sort of personal vengeance against you, as if you had done him some sort of injury in the past. I don't know if that makes any sense to you. Have you met him before?'

'No, sir, I can't think why Banks should think it was vengeance.' Shannon couldn't remember meeting Campbell before. He was beginning to wonder, however, if Campbell had in his possession some details of his past that McDonald had buried. He didn't think this was likely but he wouldn't be able to suggest this as a possible reason. It was too risky. Someone other than himself would be at risk. The information had to remain buried.

'Campbell hasn't offered any reason for the way he treated you so it will probably remain a mystery. As you know Campbell was affected by the death of his young brother who was killed by a Real IRA sniper. That may be the reason for his behaviour. I have to accept some of the responsibility because I should have seen the warning signs.'

'What will happen to him, sir?'

'Both he and Banks will be disciplined. The MO is going to have a word with Campbell to see if he will agree to receive some counselling and psychiatric treatment. Then we'll have to wait and see.'

Thornton stood and shook Shannon's hand, 'well, goodbye, Tom. Don't forget what I said. If you change your mind and decide to join us give me a call.'

'If I were you, Captain, I wouldn't hold my breath,' smiled Shannon.

12

Shannon arrived back in his flat in Manchester around noon and he decided to give Peter Blake and Tony Clarke a call to see if they could meet him for lunch. Blake couldn't make it but Clarke agreed to meet him at the usual place. Clarke joined McDonald's team on the same day as Shannon. He was ex-SAS and excelled in all aspects of counter-terrorism. When Shannon first joined the Manchester team McDonald arranged for him to work with Clarke on some assignments. They gelled immediately and proved to be a very efficient twosome. Their investigations led them to believe that the Parker brothers, owners of the Half Moon club in Manchester, had some connections with a terrorist organisation. The police were also interested in the Parker brothers because they suspected they were drug dealers. Shannon and Clarke were still working on the case when Shannon's date for SAS training came up.

Over lunch, Shannon gave Clarke all the details of his experience at the SAS training establishment.

'It sounds as if this Campbell guy is a bit of a nutter.'

'Well, he certainly gave me a bad time.'

'Do think that he knew about your previous activities?'

'I think that's unlikely. If you recall my real name was never known to anyone and I used various disguises. Corporal Banks seemed to think that Campbell was carrying out some personal vendetta but as far as I know Campbell never admitted to that.'

'I remember Jim McDonald telling us about what he called "your previous life" after he swore us all to secrecy. I can't remember anyone mentioning someone called Campbell.'

'I remember the surprised look on every face,' smiled Shannon, 'as if they were thinking, has Jim gone mad, bringing an ex-terrorist into our midst? What were you thinking at the time, Tony?'

'I thought that I would rather have you inside the tent than outside. I didn't know you then, of course, but I'm still glad that you are inside the tent.'

'I'll take that as a compliment.'

'It was. What are you going to do this evening?'

'I'm going to catch up on some paper work and then off to the gym for an hour or so this evening.'

After leaving the restaurant Shannon went back to his flat in St John's Mews and spent some time sorting out the accumulated mail. Although he had kept his parents' house in Bowden, it had been more convenient having a flat in the city. He then realised that it was quite late and he had promised himself a workout at the gym. He had used his gym kit on the SAS course and had washed it before he left. He decided to change into his track suit before going to the gym. He opened his holdall and took out his gym kit. Something dropped out onto the floor. It was a calling card with a red rose printed on one side. Shannon froze. He turned the card over but there was no message on it. He had packed the holdall himself before he left and it wasn't there then. Who could have put it there? The first name that came to his mind was Campbell. If Campbell was responsible then he must know who he is or who he was. That couldn't be possible. He had never met Campbell before. He couldn't imagine who else it could be because whoever put it there was someone who was at the SAS Training Centre. Campbell was the only one who had given him some grief. Everybody else had been very helpful and supportive. Somehow someone had found out about his past and he didn't think it was a friend. He would have to watch his back.

It was twenty minutes to nine when Shannon returned to his flat. His answer phone message light was flashing. He pressed the play button,

"Meet me at Parsonage Walk at nine o'clock – urgent." It was Clarke's voice. Shannon looked at his watch, he would have to move. He had intended to shower and change but he wouldn't have time for that. He arrived at Parsonage Walk a couple minutes before nine o'clock. It had been a warm, sunny day and although the sun had gone down some time ago, it was still warm. About an hour earlier there had been a heavy shower and the light from the street lamps was reflected on the wet pavements. The silence was broken only by the murmur of the river flowing nearby. As the minutes ticked by Shannon began to believe that something had happened to Clarke. Working for Colonel McDonald was a very risky occupation. They had to deal with some dangerous, ruthless thugs. He looked at his watch. It was ten minutes after nine. It wasn't like Clarke to be late, especially when the phone message had said it was urgent. What could be so urgent in Parsonage Walk? His thoughts were interrupted by a sharp blow to the back of his head and he plunged into a pit of darkness.

Shannon was slowly waking up or was he? He could smell what he thought was antiseptic or was it alcohol? He wasn't sure. What he was sure about was that he was hurting all over. His brain was addled. Was he in that damned Belfast gutter again? Was this a dream or a memory revisited? If it was a dream why does it keep occurring? Perhaps it was guilt. He remembered that Sean Keane was in this dream or whatever it was. Sean tried to help him up and some woman was screaming, "leave the old drunk in the gutter where he belongs." Sean was shaking him, "Tom wake up, Tom, Tom Shannon..."

'Tom Shannon, wake up,' Shannon opened his eyes and the nurse smiled at him, 'welcome back, wherever you've been. How do you feel?'

'I'm not sure where I've been and if I said I feel rough it would be an understatement.'

'Well, I can tell you where you are now. You are in The Manchester Royal. Now that you're awake we're going to take you for some x-rays.'

After the x-rays Shannon was taken back to his room. As the nurse was leaving Colonel Jim McDonald came in. He was looking worried or was he angry? Shannon wasn't sure. Shannon was always amazed by the Colonel's blue, piercing eyes which, Shannon believed, seemed to look into your very soul. Right now, he thought, that was exactly what they were doing and it wasn't an experience he would recommend to anyone. Was this a prelude to an admonishment?

'How are you feeling because you look a mess?' asked McDonald as he sat down.

'I feel as if I've been trampled by a stampeding herd of cattle.'

'What the hell were you doing in that part of the city at that time of night?'

'I received a message on my answer phone to meet Tony at Parsonage Walk at nine o'clock that night.'

'Did you get back to him to confirm?'

Shannon felt sure that he was going to experience a reprimand. He was feeling uncomfortable now and not only physically. He realised that he had screwed up. The rule was that all messages left on answer phones should be checked.

'I didn't and on reflection his voice did sound a bit strange as if he had a sore throat. I should have suspected something.'

'Never mind that now, the important thing is that you're alive.'

'They didn't rob me so what was it all about?'

'I think they intended to kill you.'

'What makes you think that?'

McDonald explained that the attackers had soaked him with whisky and may have forced some down his throat. They then probably intended to throw him into the river so it would look like he had been on a binge and fallen in accidentally. Two police officers, who were patrolling the area, spotted them dragging him along the ground. They fled when they saw the police whose immediate concern was to get medical help.

McDonald stood up. 'We probably won't catch them now so it's important that you watch your back.' With that he turned and left the room. Shannon decided that he was probably angry with a touch of concern but at least he hadn't handed out a reprimand.

Ten minutes later Clarke arrived.

'How are you doing, Tom? Has somebody been trying to improve your face? My God, they've managed it.' Clarke stood at the foot of the bed with a big, silly grin on his face.

'Don't try to make me laugh, Tony, it hurts,' complained Shannon.

'So who did this to you, some jealous husband?'

'I wish I knew then I could do something about it. This is the second beating this month and I'm beginning to think somebody doesn't like me.'

'Now who's being funny?'

'What have you been up to?'

'I've been having a look at the area where you were beaten up and I found part of a cufflink. I'm having it checked out. It may not mean anything.'

'It sounds interesting. I'm hoping to be discharged tomorrow. I'm told that there is nothing broken, just some bad bruising.'

'Okay, if you are still here tomorrow I will pop in to see if your face has returned to its usual ugliness.'

Next morning Doctor Mark Stephens paid Shannon a visit. A special facility had been set up in The Manchester Royal for the exclusive use of McDonald's team and supervised by Doctor Stephens.

'As I suspected, Tom, the x-rays show that there are no internal injuries or broken bones although it looks as if you were careless with a couple of ribs not too long ago.'

'Ah, yes, that was a little SAS game.'

'I see. I'm going to keep you in for observation until this evening. If you seem all right then I'll discharge you.'

70

As Doctor Stephens was leaving he turned and said, 'I almost forgot, Tony Clarke left a change of clothing for you at reception. I'll have it sent up. Your track suit is quite dirty; it's in a plastic bag in the cupboard at the side of the bed.'

Shannon was discharged from hospital at five o'clock. When he arrived home at his flat in St. John's Mews he gave Peter Blake and Tony Clarke a call to let them know where he was. Clarke said he would call to see him immediately after dinner. Blake was still busy setting up some system but would catch up with him later.

Shannon was staring through the window of his flat at the street below, thinking about the beating he had received in Parsonage Walk. Clarke had jokingly suggested that Campbell had followed him to Manchester in order to continue his vendetta, if it was a vendetta. He didn't think it was anything to do with Sergeant Campbell but he couldn't be sure. Campbell, however, did have a home in Belfast. It wouldn't be stretching credulity too far to imagine that Campbell knew someone who had information about him. Perhaps his activities had affected Campbell or someone close to him. The question is, if Campbell knows who he is, who told him? He realised that he was very fortunate that the two policemen turned up when they did. His thoughts were interrupted by the sound of the door bell. It was Clarke. Shannon let him in and poured him a whiskey.

'How are you feeling?' asked Clarke as he made himself comfortable on the sofa. Clarke, like Shannon, was tall but with brown hair and brown eyes which was in contrast with Shannon's blond hair and blue eyes.

'Not too bad.'

'I checked Parsonage Walk where you were beaten up and, as I told you, I found a cuff-link, well part of one, lodged between two paving stones. It's twenty-two carat gold and has the letter "V" engraved on it. I traced it through the jewellers on Market Street to Max Parker. It was a special order with a request for his wife's name, Val, to be engraved on the back. Because of the damage it's not easy to read but the "V" is clear enough.'

'I think it would be difficult to prove that Max Parker was in Parsonage Walk that night.'

'You may be right. Let's pay him a visit tomorrow night and return the cuff-link. His reaction could be interesting.'

'Max is a wily bird and he'll probably have some plausible excuse up his sleeve.'

After Clarke had left, Shannon picked up his gym kit which he had left in the plastic, hospital bag. He was wearing it when he was beaten up. It would need to be washed. He took it out of the bag and found a calling card in one of the pockets of his track suit trousers. This one could probably be explained. The guys who beat him up must have put it there, whoever they were. The one which must have been planted in the SAS Training Centre was something of a mystery. Perhaps Tony's joke about Sergeant Campbell waging a vendetta against him was close to the truth. He couldn't understand the reason for this recent calling card, particularly as it would seem they were going to kill him.

13

Max Parker and his brother Raz owned a night club called The Half
Moon on Whitworth Street.

It had been suspected that they were dealing in drugs but the police
had been unable to get any real evidence against them. McDonald's
team were interested in them because they believed they were in
touch with terrorist groups. Their mother came from a wealthy family
in Iraq. Unfortunately her parents were killed during a British forces
attack and she never really recovered. The shock of it affected her
health. She became depressed and sometimes suicidal and had to be
watched continually. Eventually she took her own life. The Parker
brothers idolised their mother and were devastated by her death.
They didn't hide the fact that they were angry about the action of the
British forces.

Shannon and Clarke arrived at The Half Moon about nine o'clock the
following evening. Max Parker was standing at the bar with his back to
them, talking to a very good looking, blond woman. He seemed to be
having a serious conversation with her and his arm was around her
waist. Parker was a short, thick set man and most of his hair had
disappeared. His face was fleshy and sported a large, hawk-like nose.
The blond woman saw Shannon and Clarke approaching and said
something to Parker who turned to face them.

   'Well, well, look what's the cat's dragged in. And it looks as if it's
been having a go at one of them.'
Parker was smiling but his dark, almost black eyes told another story.
He turned to the blond woman, 'I'll speak to you later sweetheart.'
She got the message and moved away.

'Just look what the cat's left behind,' said Clarke, holding up the damaged cuff-link. He tossed it over to Parker who caught it and began to examine it.

'We believe it's yours,' said Shannon, not taking his eyes off Parker.

'I'm sure you've checked it out with the jeweller. It was mine but I gave the pair away to some guy who came collecting for charity.'

'Are you expecting us to believe that you gave away a pair of twenty-two carat gold cuff-links with your wife's name engraved on them?' asked Clarke, now getting a little impatient.

'I gave this guy a couple suits I got tired of. He said he was collecting for some charity. I remembered afterwards that I'd left the cuff-links in the pocket of one of the suits. Don't ask me the name of the guy or the charity because I don't know. If I knew I would have been on to him to get them back.'

Shannon and Clarke realised that they weren't getting anywhere and decided to leave. When they were a few steps away from Parker, he called after them.

'Hey, you two, let me know if you find the guy who nicked my cuff-links. He would've returned them if he'd been honest. The city's full of criminals, you should be chasing after them not honest citizens like me.' He then roared with laughter.

'It's quite strange,' said Clarke, as they were leaving, 'that he never asked where we'd found the cuff-link.'

'The thought had crossed my mind but then I suppose he doesn't care if he believes his story is watertight.'

'I think we'll have to scrub around this one for a while, Tom. I can't see how we're going to prove a connection with the attack on you.' Shannon nodded. He hadn't mentioned the calling cards to Clarke. He was beginning to believe that his past was catching up with him. Were these calling cards a warning? The first one must have been put in his holdall at the SAS Training Centre and that was a real mystery. The only suspect being Campbell. The second card was left in the pocket of his track suit on Parsonage Walk where he was beaten up and that could have been anybody. On this second occasion the police believed that they had intended to kill him. If they had succeeded then what was the purpose of the calling card? It could only have been a message for McDonald. Obviously someone wanted to advertise the fact that they knew who he was and where he was. Only two men from his past would associate him with the calling cards but Shannon felt that it was unlikely that they knew that he worked for Ironclad. Members of Ironclad knew who he was. Was there a mole in the camp? If so then they were all in danger. Perhaps it would be wise to raise the matter with Colonel McDonald.

14

The next morning Shannon arrived at The Priory around eight-thirty. The Priory was a large Victorian house on the south of the city. It was the headquarters of McDonald's unit, code name Ironclad, and it was also a safe house. State of the art surveillance equipment had been installed and armed military police were on duty around the clock. Clarke and Blake had already arrived and were sitting at the conference table drinking coffee. Shannon helped himself to a cup and joined them.

'I forgot to tell you, Tom,' said Clarke, 'a new recruit joined us when you were away on your course. She will be joining us this morning.'

'Did you say *she*? Having a woman on the team will be interesting but is she.....' Before Shannon could finish the door opened and in walked the new recruit. All three of them stood up and Clarke went to greet her.

'Tom Shannon, I want you to meet our newest recruit. This is Flight Lieutenant Stella Bellamy.' Shannon took her held out hand as she said, 'please call me Stella.' Shannon's jaw was resting on his chest and he held her hand just a little too long.

'You can close your mouth now, Tom, or you'll be catching flies,' whispered Clarke.

Shannon muttered something unintelligible and released her hand but somehow couldn't stop gazing into her eyes. They were deep pools of green and he felt he was going to drown in them. Her hair was a golden colour which was swept back into a ponytail. She held his gaze for a few more seconds. The moment was so intimate, as if they were alone in the room. Stella suddenly seemed flustered and quickly said, 'I must report to the Colonel.' It had been a long time since Shannon had felt like that and he sensed that she felt the same or was it just wishful thinking? Clarke was operating in mischievous mode. 'Well, I never thought I would see the day when an Irishman would be lost for words. Could it be his English education?'

'I don't know what you mean,' said Shannon but his mind seemed to be somewhere else.

'You went weak at the knees and you couldn't take your eyes of her.' Clarke could see that his tease had missed the mark.

They had just finished telling Blake about their visit to The Half Moon club when the door opened and McDonald came in with Stella Bellamy. They all sat around the conference table having recharged their coffee cups. McDonald said that he wanted them to spend the afternoon catching up with their paperwork. He wanted all reports on his desk by six o'clock that evening. He smiled when he saw the long faces and then added that he wanted to see them all at the Midland for dinner at eight o'clock. He went on to say that Paul Adams and Mike Jones, who were two more new recruits, would be joining them from Holywood army base in Northern Ireland.

It was eight o'clock and everyone had turned up at the Midland. McDonald had ordered the drinks and the starters had been chosen. McDonald said that because some new members had joined the team he thought it would be useful if everyone met socially as a means of getting to know each other better. He brought smiles to their faces when he described it as a sort of team building exercise without the exercises. After a couple of hours the party was going extremely well. Everyone had relaxed, no doubt helped by the alcohol. Shannon was sitting next to Stella and was amazed at how comfortable he felt with her. He got the feeling that she too was enjoying his company. He found himself telling her all about the effects Laura's death had had on him. Something he had never discussed outside the Blake family. He didn't mention his Northern Ireland activities because he assumed that McDonald would have given her information on a need to know basis. They were so interested in each other that they hadn't noticed that McDonald and Clarke had gone to the bar and Blake, Adams and Jones were deep in conversation.

'I believe that you were beaten up the other night,' said Stella, 'did you find out who did it?

'No, Tony suggested that Campbell, the sergeant I was telling you about, had followed me and given me a beating. That's Tony, of course, always the joker.'

'Yes, I've become very much aware of that. He's been teasing me about you, trying to get a romance started.'

'That's Tony, always ready to play cupid. I hope you're not upset.'

'No, I think it's rather sweet. I can see that he is a good friend of yours.'

'Yes, Tony's a good guy. I hope we will be good friends too.'

'I'm sure we will.' Shannon thought he detected a little blush on Stella's cheeks.

McDonald and Clarke had returned from the bar followed by the waiter carrying a tray with another round of drinks. As McDonald was handing out the drinks, Paul Adams joined Stella and Shannon.

'Have you enjoyed yourself, Paul?' asked Shannon.

'Yes, it's been great,' said Adams, 'as you know Mike Jones and I are stationed at Holywood at the moment so it's good to meet the rest of the team.'

'Jim does this sort of thing now and then to take the tension out of the job. He's got us all together to do a bit of bonding. I think that's what it's called. I can see that Peter and Mike have got their heads together,' said Shannon.

'Yea, they're probably designing a new computer system,' said Adams, 'they're a couple of geniuses.'

'I hear you are something of a genius too, Paul,' said Stella.

'I'm slowly catching up with Mike. Well. I'm going to push off now. It's late. Nice to have met you.'

'And you,' said Stella.

'See you at the meeting tomorrow, Paul,' said Shannon.

As Adams was leaving Clarke and McDonald joined them. McDonald said it was past his bedtime and he was leaving. He reminded everybody about the meeting next morning. Clarke sat down next to Stella.

'Have you two got to know each other better?' asked Clarke, with a cheeky grin.

'Yes, we have,' said Stella, 'and I've found out that you are something of a joker.'

'Who me?' smiled Clarke, 'never.'

'I believe you've been playing cupid,' said Shannon.

'If I ever saw two people who should be together, it's you two.' Stella looked a little embarrassed.

'What about your love life, Tony?' said Shannon, trying to change the subject, in an attempt to spare Stella's blushes, 'anything serious going on?'

'No, alas, no fair maiden has cast her eyes in my direction. They don't know what they're missing.'

'That's true,' said Shannon, 'a lifetime of teasing.'

'Now you have cut me to the quick and my heart is broken and it will never heal.'

'See what I mean, Stella,' said Shannon, 'he never stops.'

'You are both very lucky,' said Stella, 'to have the sort of friendship you have. I've enjoyed the evening but I'm afraid it's late and I must go.'

'Tom will walk you home,' said Clarke with a twinkle in his eye, 'it's on his way home.'

'It's okay, I'll get a taxi.'

'Tony's right. It is on my way home and I would be delighted to escort you, my fair lady.'

'Don't you start too,' laughed Stella.

Stella gave Tony a kiss on his cheek and she and Shannon left.

When they arrived at Stella's flat they both stood at the door for a moment.

'Will you come in for a coffee?' asked Stella suddenly.

'Er, I think so. I mean yes, that would be great.'

Stella unlocked the door and they went in. The flat was tastefully furnished and tidy with everything in its place and yet it had that lived in, warm, welcoming atmosphere. The woman's touch was very much in evidence. Stella had definitely put her stamp on this place thought Shannon. Stella had gone into the kitchen to make coffee and Shannon began to look at Stella's collection of CD's.

'I see you are a fan of Kenny G,' said Shannon.

'Yes, he's one of my favourites,' called Stella from the kitchen. Stella appeared with a tray with a coffee pot and cups which she placed on the coffee table. She then sat down on the sofa next to Shannon and poured the coffee.

'Do you take milk and sugar,' she asked.

'Milk only please. I'm sorry that Tony was teasing you. He had had a lot to drink. He'll be embarrassed when he sobers up tomorrow.'

'It's not a problem, Tom.'

'He means well but sometimes it can get a little irksome.'

'Don't worry about me, Tom, I can handle the teasing. The RAF boys were always doing it but I knew it wasn't malicious.'

'Are you in a serious relationship at the moment?'

'No, there's no one special in my life.'

'I hope you don't mind me asking. I don't want to step on anybody's toes.'

'Are you making a pass at me, Tom Shannon?'

'No, I mean yes. I think I am, with the best of honourable intentions, of course.'

'I should hope so.'

'When I first met you I felt something. I was immediately attracted to you but there was something more. I felt almost as if I knew you, as if I'd known you for a long time. That sounds a little trite but I don't know how else to describe it.'

'I remember you holding my hand for a long time. It felt so right and I was comfortable with it. Then I saw Tony's face.' They both laughed.

'That's Tony. He doesn't miss a thing and he's teased me about it ever since. I think he was put on this earth to embarrass everybody.'

'When you were telling me about your loss I felt that those sad memories were flooding back into your mind. I could see the sadness in your eyes. If you ever feel the need to talk some more about it, I'm a good listener.'

Stella put her arms around him and gave him a hug. She was amazed that she had such strong feelings for this man whom she had only just met. This had never happened to her before and although she was comfortable with it, she felt she had to make a comment.

'That's the first time I've hugged a man I hardly know.'

'I'm glad I'm the first and I hope I'll be the second.'

'Now that definitely was a pass.' They both laughed again.

When they had finished their coffee they sat quietly for a while listening to a Kenny G CD. Shannon looked at his watch and was surprised to see that it was well after midnight.

'It's late,' said Shannon getting up from the sofa, 'I'd better go.'

They walked to the door.

'Thank you for the coffee.'

'Thank you for seeing me home.'

She kissed him on both cheeks.

15

It was the morning after Shannon had taken Stella home and he was happier than he had been for a long time. He was fairly certain that he was falling in love with Stella. He never thought that he could fall in love again and he felt on top of the world. He was getting out of the shower when the phone rang. It was McDonald.

'Shannon there's been a development. I need to have a chat with you. Come to The Priory at nine o'clock this morning.' McDonald rang off without further comment.

When Shannon arrived at The Priory he was met by Sergeant Dave Thomas, one of the military policemen, who checked his ID and booked him in. He made his way to the main office where he found McDonald and Clarke sitting at a desk drinking coffee. Sitting, as usual, in front of a computer was Peter Blake. As Shannon was helping himself to a coffee Stella arrived and indicated that she would like a cup too. They both joined McDonald and Clarke.

'Something has cropped up that may be of particular interest to you, Tom,' said McDonald, 'there's been a bank robbery in Belfast and they got away with fifteen million pounds. Sadly they murdered the Assistant Bank Manager and his wife and daughter.'

'That's not the sort of thing Ironclad is usually interested in. It sounds like a police matter.' said Shannon.

'True,' replied McDonald, 'ordinarily it wouldn't interest us. However, we have been informed by MI5 that Declan Brady, who is ex-PIRA, may have been involved in the robbery. He has been seen with Max Parker in the Norbreck Hotel in Blackpool. It's possible that they are going to team up to buy drugs and weapons. You had dealings with Brady when you were in Belfast. What can you tell us about him?'

'He's a very hard man and he would sell his mother if there was a profit in it. I would describe him as a ruthless, dangerous criminal. Dangerous because he is very clever and I know he wouldn't hesitate to kill without a second thought.' Shannon had discussed the discovery of the calling cards with McDonald. Brady was one of two men, outside Ironclad, who would know that Shannon was connected with these calling cards. Now it would seem that he was consorting with the Parker brothers. Was Brady responsible for arranging the planting of the cards? Shannon wasn't sure. He didn't think it likely that Brady could have got into the SAS Training Centre, placed a card in his holdall, and left without being seen. It would have been possible for Campbell to plant the card. Perhaps there was a connection between Brady and Campbell. Time would tell.

'The police believe that Brady is connected with this robbery and the brutal killing of the Carson family. Unfortunately they haven't got any concrete evidence,' said McDonald.

'What are we expected to do?' asked Clarke.

'This is where Tom comes in,' replied McDonald, 'he can approach Brady because of his previous connection with him and probably find out something. I know it's a long shot but we haven't got anything else to go on.'

'It might work if I can convince him that I'm looking for some action. He may wonder where I've been for the last twelve months or so but I'll think of something.' That's the problem thought Shannon. If Brady is responsible for the calling cards then he will know exactly where he has been.

'Good,' said McDonald, 'Tony can go with you for back up. Stella will fly you out to the Holywood army base so she too will be able to give you some back up. Before you go, Peter will arrange a secure communication system for you.'

'When will we be flying out there?' asked Clarke.

'Six hundred hours tomorrow morning. All the arrangements have been made at the Greenacre airfield and at Holywood army base. By the way, Tom, I forgot to tell you that Sergeant Campbell has been discharged from the SAS and has returned to his home in Northern Ireland. He refused the medical help he was offered. I understand he arrived in Belfast about the same time you arrived in Manchester.'

'I'll make a point of keeping out of his way.'

Greenacre airfield was previously an RAF training camp a few miles west of Manchester. It was now only used by Ironclad and other Secret Service organisations. The runway was short but ideal for light aircraft. It was an uneventful trip although the flight was delayed by fog. The rain was torrential and visibility was extremely poor when they arrived at the Holywood army base. Shannon and Clarke were amazed at Stella's skill at handling the Cessna. She landed the plane without a hitch in spite of the dreadful conditions. Arrangements had been made for them to be billeted at the army base so that they would have easy access to assistance and supplies should they need them. They were met by Captain Charles Cosgrove who had worked with Ironclad on previous occasions and was aware of the need for secrecy.

'Hello, Tony, nice to see you again,' said Cosgrove as he shook Clarke's hand.

'It's good to see you too, Charles. It's been a couple of months since we last met. How is your sister?'

'I'm afraid her health has deteriorated and she has been admitted to hospital. I'm trying to arrange a trip to Manchester to see her.'

'I'm sorry to hear that. I hope there is some improvement when you see her. I don't think you've met my colleagues,' and he introduced Stella and Shannon.

'Flight Lieutenant Bellamy, I've heard of you. Not only are you an excellent pilot but I believe you are something of a weapons expert.'

'Spare my blushes, Captain,' smiled Stella.

'And it's good to meet you, Tom Shannon. I hope you enjoyed the SAS course.'

'It was excellent.'

'I've arranged for a couple civilian cars to be available for your use. Let me know if there is anything you need. You know where my office is and lunch is in the officers' mess at thirteen hundred hours.'
They thanked him then dropped their luggage in their allocated rooms.

After lunch they met in a conference room Cosgrove had reserved for them to plan their next move.

'We know that Brady is often seen in the Red Lion in Tomb Street,' said Shannon, 'so tonight I'm going to pay that pub a visit. I suggest you two wait here until I contact you.'

'Tom, we're supposed to be your back up. How can we do that if we're on this side of the river Lagan?' protested Clarke.

'Okay, but I don't want Stella involved. Brady is an animal and I'm not sure how things may turn out.'

'I'm not an amateur,' said Stella, 'I've been in tight corners before. More importantly, if I'm with Tony we will appear to be a couple out for the night and so look less suspicious than Tony on his own.'

'We could be nearby looking like tourists,' said Clarke.

'Okay, but keep away from the Red Lion unless I call you.'

'Right, that's settled,' said Clarke, 'I'm going for a chat with Charles Cosgrove so I'll see you two later,'

After Clarke had left, Shannon and Stella helped themselves to the coffee which had been laid on for them.

'I'm sorry for my comments earlier,' said Shannon, 'I must have sounded quite patronising and I was certainly out of order. I've never worked with a woman before.'

'That's okay, I'm used to it but don't worry I can assure you that I have been highly trained.'

'I'm sure Colonel McDonald wouldn't have recruited you if you hadn't and Cosgrove said that you are something of a weapons expert'

'Tell me about this Provisional IRA man, Declan Brady,' said Stella choosing to ignore Shannon's compliment, 'Colonel McDonald said that you had some dealings with him. What did he mean?'

'Ah, so you haven't been brought up to speed about me. Perhaps it's because you are our latest recruit and Jim hasn't had time to brief you. It could be that he wants me to tell you myself. Where do I begin?'

'Try the beginning.'

'Okay. As you already know I was engaged to be married to Laura Blake. She was Peter Blake's sister. The year before we planned to be married, my parents were killed in a car crash. We decided to carry on with our plans to get married because my parents would have wanted that. Laura's parents also thought it was the right thing to do. My grandmother was my only living relative and she lived in Belfast so I took Laura to meet her. When we were out shopping in Belfast, Laura was killed in the crossfire by a British soldier. I completely lost it and swore vengeance. I hit the bottle for a few months and ended up wandering around Belfast in a drunken stupor. I was entirely out of my mind.'

'That's very sad, Tom. This was the loss you were telling me about the other night.'

'Yes, Sean Keane found me lying in the gutter and took me to his home and sobered me up. When he was younger he and his parents lived near my grandparents in Belfast. The family went through a bad time and my grandparents helped them out. Sean ran a PIRA cell and I persuaded him to let me join. He was reluctant at first because he knew my grandmother wouldn't have approved.'

'So how did you persuade him?'

'With great difficulty I can assure you. I told him that I didn't want to kill anybody. All I wanted to do was to disrupt the activities of the security forces. He agreed to feed me information but insisted that I worked alone. I used various disguises and there were only two people who knew my real name; Sean Keane and Declan Brady. Sean thought that that would give me some protection.'

'I'm shocked. I want to ask you so many questions. How do you fit in with Ironclad? How did Jim McDonald find you? Did you get caught?'

'No, I didn't get caught. Jim McDonald will be only too pleased to tell you about his efforts to catch me. One of the last things I did was to set fire to two army vehicles when I was disguised as a blind man. Nobody was hurt. The Peace Process started so I thought it should be given a chance so I told Sean I was quitting and I left for England.'

'I would have thought that Jim was taking a big risk recruiting an ex-PIRA man. I don't think that I would have recruited you.'

'I have to admit that I didn't want to join Ironclad. Jim McDonald said that the alternative was to ask for amnesty. However, he thought that because of my reputation, the police and the army in Northern Ireland would want their pound of flesh.'

'Then why didn't you take your punishment like a man?'

'I was prepared to do that but Jim said that my real name would be made public and there was a strong possibility that my grandmother's life would be threatened.'

'Obviously you must have told Colonel McDonald who you were. Why did you do that?'

'After Laura's funeral I returned to Northern Ireland. I was missing for a couple of years or so. Peter and I were very close so when I turned up I couldn't tell him a plethora of lies. I had to tell him the truth. Sometimes these things have a way of leaking out. If Jim ever found out who I was then Peter would be in big trouble.'

'So by joining Ironclad you and your grandmother were protected and I suppose Peter Blake too. What did Colonel McDonald think he was getting in return?'

'He said that he had taken a great deal of interest in my activities in Northern Ireland and at the time saw me as a challenge. He tried every trick in the book with the help of the police and the army but couldn't catch me. He knew where I'd been because I always left a calling card but I was always one step ahead of him. He wanted someone who could work alone; someone who could make himself invisible.'

'Invisible?'

'A bit of an exaggeration,' smiled Shannon, 'he was referring to me appearing and leaving a scene without anybody noticing.'

'I wish you'd told me this sooner.'

'I assumed you knew. Jim has told all the team about me.'

'My father was a soldier who was killed in the Falklands and here you're telling me that you were in cahoots with the PIRA who were killing British soldiers. I'm appalled that Colonel McDonald considers you fit to be a member of Ironclad.'

'I've no excuse except to say that I was out of my head. I'm sorry you're upset. If I could go back and change everything I would but I can't. I just have to live with it.'

'Well I don't have.....', Stella was interrupted by Clarke.

'Hello, hello, you two look guilty. What have you been up to?'

'We've been talking about my "previous life" and Stella is in a state of shock.'

'I thought Jim would have told her,' said Clarke, 'Stella do you have a problem with Tom's history?'

Stella looked uncomfortable and didn't answer.

'Stella,' said Shannon, 'if you want to opt out I will understand. We have two members of Ironclad who are working on this base: Paul Adams and Mike Jones. I'm sure that one of them will take your place.'

'No,' Stella now looked angry, 'I will do my duty which is catching terrorists even if I have to work with one'

Point taken thought Shannon.

Sometime later they went together to the mess for the evening meal. The atmosphere, however, was a little strained. Stella avoided speaking to Shannon. What little conversation she made was only addressed to Clarke. Shannon's thoughts turned to the evening he had spent with Stella in her flat. Now everything had been turned on its head and he couldn't see how their relationship could recover from this. She would always see him as a British soldier killer, even though this wasn't true. It would appear that any hopes he may have had for a serious relationship with her had been dashed. The major problem now was that her animosity towards him could have a serious affect on their work for Ironclad. If the problem couldn't be resolved then McDonald would have to be informed. After the meal they returned to the conference room and finalised their plans. It was agreed that Shannon would go to the Red Lion in Tomb Street in the hope of meeting Brady. Stella and Clarke would be in easy reach in case they were needed.

16

Shannon arrived at the Red Lion that evening at nine o'clock. In the far corner of the bar four men were sitting together. Shannon recognised Brady and with him were Martin Nolan and Michael Donovan who had been part of Sean Keane's PIRA cell. Shannon had met these two men when he was in one of his disguises so they wouldn't recognise him. The fourth man he didn't know. As he approached the table Brady stood up.

'Shannon, Jeez, it is yourself isn't it? Everybody thought you were dead.'

'You know what Mark Twain said "the report of my death was an exaggeration" or something like that.'

'I thought you were too much of a crafty bugger to be dead.' Brady began to laugh and Shannon remembered, as he watched him, that when he laughed or smiled, his eyes never joined in the fun. They remained hard and cold.

'So what have you been up to?' asked Brady.

'You know, a bit of this and that, banging a few heads together, a few assassinations, mostly abroad,' said Shannon thinking perhaps he had gone too far because Brady didn't look convinced.

'These are a few of my business associates,' said Brady turning to face the table, 'you know Martin Nolan and Michael Donovan from the good old days and this is Tim Doherty.'

'I don't think we've met, I can't recall your face,' said Nolan.

'I don't remember you either,' said Donovan.

'Of course you don't, you stupid buggers. He never had the same face twice. He was the blind man who destroyed the two army trucks and sorted out that policeman who beat up that youngster. He only reported to me and Sean Keane, that is, when he felt like it,' Brady looked a bit angry when he said this.

'Sean Keane, what happened to him?' asked Shannon. At this point Brady turned and nodded to the barman, who came over and drinks were ordered, after which Brady continued.

'When those bastard traitors, Adams and McGuinness decided to surrender to this bloody Peace Process, Keane said they were right and he quit. He runs a garage somewhere in Derry. I hear he's making a bloody fortune,' Brady looked a bit disgruntled.

'And are you making a fortune too?' asked Shannon.

'A little export and import, I manage to scrape by.'

'Ah, Declan, you're too modest. What about that lovely farm you own?' said Doherty, speaking for the first time and from the look he got from Brady, Shannon thought it could be his last.

'So what brings you back to Belfast?' Brady asked, a little too hurriedly, Shannon thought.

'Things got a bit too risky abroad and I wanted to check on my flat in Manchester and my parents' home in Cheshire. Then I read in the newspapers about the big bank robbery in Belfast and I thought it could be fun if some of the lads had got together.'

'Most of the lads I knew have gone legit like me,' said Brady, 'a few are still messing about with guns and explosives calling themselves the Real IRA, the cheeky bastards.'

'It seems I've wasted my time then,' said Shannon getting up from his chair, 'I was hoping to get in on some action. Anyway, thanks for the drink, perhaps I'll see you around sometime.'

'Sure, 'said Brady, looking somewhat relieved, Shannon thought.

Clarke and Stella had managed to get a window seat in the American Pie, an eating place on the opposite side of the street facing the Red Lion. They could see the entrance to the pub from the window.

'Tony,' said Stella, 'do you trust Tom?'

'Yes, why do you ask?'

'Because he was a member of the PIRA and he's in the Red Lion chatting with his old pals. They could be conspiring to wreck our assignment.'

91

'I think that's very unlikely. I've worked with Tom on a couple of assignments. He is an efficient operator and I know he is loyal to Ironclad.'

'You can't be sure. You've only known him a relatively short time. These men are his old PIRA pals and he may feel some loyalty to them.'

'One can never be sure about anything in this game but when you've worked closely with somebody you get a gut feeling. If I were in a tight spot I would hope that Tom was by my side.'

'Perhaps it's my background. Both my father and grandfather were senior officers in the army. They both experienced the treachery of double agents. How do we know Shannon isn't a double agent?'

'We can never be certain of anybody I suppose. Tom never killed anyone. Colonel McDonald can vouch for that. Jim spent many months in Northern Ireland trying to catch Tom but couldn't. Tom always left a calling card, a card with a red rose printed on it. I believe it was Laura's favourite rose. The bombs he left were hoax bombs. He would pour sugar into the petrol tanks of police cars and army vehicles. He played lots of tricks similar to that which fouled up the work of the security forces but he never killed anyone. Jim recruited him because of his experience with the way terrorists work and the fact that he could work alone and silently.'

Stella took a sip of her coffee without making any further comment. Clarke felt very uneasy. One member of the team not trusting another was bad news and could jeopardise a mission. He wasn't sure what he should do about it. Perhaps when Stella got to know Tom better she may change her mind. He thought they had become an item. If that was true then it looked as if it had gone belly up.

Back at Holywood Shannon met with Clarke and Stella in the conference room.

'I have a feeling Brady is up to something,' said Shannon.

'What makes you think that?' asked Clarke.

'It was pretty clear to me that Brady didn't want me to know about the farm he owns. He looked very angry when one of his pals mentioned it. Why would he not want me to know that he owned a farm? I didn't want to scare him off by asking too many questions so I didn't make any comments about the property.'

'If he is up to something, do you think it may have something to do with the farm?' said Clarke, 'if so, then we need to find out before we go back to Manchester.'

'I'm not sure. Brady told me that Sean Keane had left the PIRA and started a business in Derry. It may be useful if I paid Sean a visit, reminisce about the "old days" and see if the farm crops up in the conversation.'

'If you could find out the location of the farm, you could arrange to join Brady for a drink at the Red Lion. If you are able to keep him occupied for a time, then it would give me a chance to check it out,' suggested Clarke.

'It's worth a try,' replied Shannon.

Clarke was aware that Stella hadn't spoken during his conversation with Shannon. He was sure that Shannon would have noticed too. If he had, he had obviously decided to ignore it. Perhaps that was the best way to deal with it. Nevertheless, Clarke was worried. They could find themselves in a dangerous situation and they need to be absolutely certain then everybody was on board. He was considering raising the matter with Shannon but he had to wait for the right moment. He was sure that Shannon and Stella had become quite close; how close he didn't know. He was aware that they weren't very close now. Nevertheless, these kinds of relationships could change overnight. It was a delicate situation.

They left the conference room having decided to go to the officers' mess for a nightcap. Cosgrove was sitting at a table by himself doing a crossword.

'It's one of my obsessions,' he said as they sat down with him. Clarke went to the bar to get drinks for everyone.

'Charles,' began Shannon when Clarke returned, 'I have no doubt that you have heard of Declan Brady. Does he own a farm?'

'I know of Brady only too well. He's a bad lot but I didn't know he had a farm. Since the Peace Process began he has kept a very low profile and hasn't given us any trouble. He was suspected of being involved in the Belfast bank robbery and the murder of the Carson family but the police didn't have any concrete evidence against him.'

'What do you know about Sean Keane?'

'Keane seems to have done quite well for himself selling and servicing vehicles in Londonderry. He appears to be keeping his nose clean and he has a young family. I believe that he has turned over a completely new leaf.'

'Do you have his business address?'

'We should have it on file because we try to keep tabs on these ex-PIRA chaps.'

'Do you think you could let me have the address by tomorrow?'

'I can do better than that. I'll get it for you now,'

A few minutes later Cosgrove returned with a sheet of paper in his hand.

'This is interesting. The records have been updated since I looked at Keane's details. It seems that he has opened a rather big car showroom in Belfast. He trades under the name of Northern Motors. He is obviously really prospering. You may not have to make that trip to Londonderry after all.' Cosgrove gave the paper to Shannon.

'Thanks, Charles, if he's at his Belfast showroom that's going to save us a lot of time.'

'Well, I think I'll turn in,' said Cosgrove, 'I'll see you chaps in the morning.'

After Cosgrove left, Shannon said, 'is Charles an old friend of yours Tony?'

'I've known him for a number of years. I first met him when I joined the army.'

'He seems a nice guy,' said Stella, speaking for the first time, 'I think it's time I turned in too.'

When Stella had gone Clarke and Shannon sat in silence finishing their drinks. Clarke was mulling over in his mind whether he should bring up the problem with Stella. Shannon beat him to it.

'You're worried about Stella, aren't you Tony?'

'I think she's a problem. She doesn't trust you.'

'I know and I understand that. She's never worked with me before. Now that she knows my history she feels insecure.'

'What are we going to do about it, Tom?

'The only thing that I can think of is to avoid any situation where Stella and I have to rely on each other, particularly in a sticky situation.'

'That could be difficult.'

'Not really. I'm sure she trusts you with your SAS background. If we have to split up we will have to make sure that she partners you and not me. Can you think of anything better?'

'I'm afraid not.'

17

Next morning Shannon made his way into Belfast as planned. According to the information Cosgrove had given him, Northern Motors was on Victoria Street. Shannon found it easily and pulled into the car park. He was quite impressed. It was a two storey building, built mostly of glass and charcoal coloured brick. As he approached the showroom the doors opened automatically and he went in. He looked around at the cars for a few minutes and then suddenly he was aware that a salesman was standing near him.

'Can I help you, sir?'

'I was hoping to see Mr Keane.'

'Do you have an appointmen, sir?' Wow, thought Shannon, Keane has certainly gone up in the world.

'No, but if you tell him my name is Shannon, I think he will see me.' The salesman went into the office at the back of the showroom and picked up the phone. After a few minutes he came back and said, 'Mr Keane will see you shortly, sir.'

After a few moments the lift doors opened and Keane walked out.

'Tom, this is a surprise,' said Keane as he shook Shannon's hand, 'there have been all sorts of rumours about you. Some said you had been shot dead. How are you doing?'

'I'm good but it looks as if you are better than good.'

'Come up to the office and we will have a chat.'

Shannon was gobsmacked by Keane's office. There was a large desk looking very tidy with the usual accessories. Nearby was a purpose-built desk with a couple of computers and a fax machine. There was a conference table and chairs at one end of the room and in the space near the desk were two black leather sofas complete with coffee table. All sitting on what appeared to be a very expensive beige carpet.

'Wow!' gasped Shannon as he fell into one of the sofas, 'obviously you've been extremely successful.'

'True, but it's been hard work and I took a risk with the finance.' Before Shannon could speak the door opened and a young woman entered carrying a tray with coffee and biscuits which she placed on the coffee table and left.

'This is a bit different from the good old days, Sean.'

'They were the bad old days, Tom. There was a lot of injustice and we thought we could put it right. It's hard to believe now that up to 1969 not everybody in Northern Ireland had a vote. Our cause was right but our methods were wrong. Now there's a real chance of peace and stability and the Real IRA and the rest of them are trying to sabotage it.'

'I met up with Declan Brady the other day. He seems to be doing well. He told me he is in export and import and I believe he has a farm somewhere.' Shannon had decided to mention the farm straight away.

'I've seen very little of Brady over the last year and my advice to you is to give him a wide berth. You haven't told me what you've been up to since I last saw you. I had begun to believe that you were dead.' Shannon wondered if Keane had deliberately changed the subject. If that was so, then he would have to be particularly careful now.

'I've been abroad for a while waiting for things to settle down over here and hoping that nobody had grassed on me,' Shannon wasn't comfortable telling Keane a lie but he had to be on his guard.

'Most of the lads didn't know who you were so I suppose you were fairly safe. So what are your plans during your stay in Belfast?'

'Well the only two people I really knew from the old days were you and Declan Brady and I wanted to thank you both for never revealing my identity. I'm thanking you now. When I bumped into Declan by chance the other day, we got so carried away talking about the old days that I forgot to thank him. I would like to thank him before I leave Belfast. He has a farm but unfortunately I forgot to ask him for the address. I was hoping you could give it to me.' Shannon was hoping his lying was going to pay off although he didn't feel too confident. Keane may be wondering why Shannon wanted to thank Brady when they both knew that Brady disliked him, probably hated him.

'Tom, you know you don't have to thank us but if it is important to you then I may be able to help you. About six months ago Brady came to see me in Derry. He wanted to buy a car, of course, he wanted a big discount and I mean a big discount. He said it was for old times' sake but it seemed like a threat to me. I didn't want to upset him in case he tried to get at me through my family. I agreed to the discount on the condition that he went elsewhere for servicing and repairs. He's not been back since.' Keane turned to one of his computers and pressed a few keys and a print out appeared which he handed to Shannon, 'that was the address he gave me when he bought the car. I don't know if he is still there.'

'Thanks, Sean, I will drive over tomorrow.' Shannon stood up and they shook hands.

'Take care Tom, times have changed and so have people. Don't get involved with the Real IRA or the other splinter groups. They're criminals dealing in drugs and prostitution. Be particularly on your guard when you meet Brady. He's not to be trusted.' Shannon nodded and left.

Back at Holywood, Shannon met with Clarke and Stella in the conference room that Cosgrove had arranged for their private use.

'Brady's farm is in Woodhill,' said Shannon, 'it's about nine or ten miles north of Belfast with a motorway most of the way. Tonight we must try and find out if Brady is hiding something there. What we are going to do is high risk but if we keep to the plan then everything should be okay. So let's recap – I will go to the Red Lion, you two make your way to Brady's farm. When I have established that Brady is in the pub, I'll let you know. Tony, take care, Brady may have left someone in the farm keeping watch.'

Shannon arrived at the Red Lion at nine o'clock. He had a look in the bar and saw that Brady was at his usual table with Donovan and two women. They didn't see Shannon so he went outside and called Clarke with the go ahead. He went back into the pub and approached Brady's table.

'Jeez, Shannon, two visits in two nights. You're not beginning to fancy me are you?'

'You're not that good looking,' said Shannon, trying to sound friendly, 'I think I owe you a drink.'

'Pull up a chair. You know Donovan and these are two good friends of ours, Daisy and Violet. It sounds like a bloody flower shop.' Brady roared with laughter but it didn't sound sincere.

The barman appeared and Shannon ordered drinks.

'So when are you leaving this beautiful city of ours?' asked Brady.

'I'm planning to leave tomorrow. It sounds as if you're trying to get rid of me.'

'No such thing, we'd like to keep you here permanently, wouldn't we Donovan?' This comment produced another roar of laughter from Brady with Donovan joining in.

'That's nice,' said Shannon thinking that they were obviously sharing a private joke at his expense. The barman arrived with the drinks.

'Today is Daisy's birthday and you're invited to join in the celebration,' said Brady 'we're going to make a night of it.' As if on cue the barman arrived with a birthday cake, complete with one candle.

'There's only one candle Shannon. It's not because I'm a tight wad, it's because a lady's age should always be kept a secret.'

Shannon thought that "lady" wasn't a word he would have used. They both looked like street walkers with skirts that could be described as pelmets and necklines that plunged down to their navels. They had applied too much make-up and their hair seemed to have an addiction to peroxide. Probably in their early twenties but it was difficult to tell. The cake was cut and another round of drinks was ordered. Brady and his pals had had a start on Shannon and were now well and truly oiled. They began to sing "happy birthday" for the third time and Shannon was wondering how he was going to get through the evening with this motley crew, when his mobile rang.

Clarke and Stella arrived at Wood View Farm about nine-thirty. Clarke parked the car in a lay-by some two hundred yards from the farm entrance. They had agreed that Stella should stay in the car and watch the road for unwelcome visitors. The road appeared to be a cul-de-sac and so would be easy to check. They had assumed that the road was a cul-de-sac because cars using the area always turned around and returned the way they came. The lay-by was very large with a number of shrubs and trees. It was used by courting couples. They arranged that if Clarke didn't call after fifteen minutes, Stella would contact Shannon.

Clarke made his way to the farm not using his torch and so minimising the chance of being seen. It had been a dry day but a heavy cloud had persisted. Now there were some breaks in the cloud which allowed the moon to occasionally sneak a glimpse at Clarke's progress. From the farm gates he could see a white single storey building some hundred yards away. Because of the poor light and the unfamiliar surroundings, he was moving more slowly than he had anticipated. He proceeded cautiously, taking cover from the shrubs which followed the curve of the drive. He couldn't see any lights in the farm house but as he got nearer there appeared to be a glow permeating through a gap in the curtains in one of the windows. He moved silently up to the window. Through the gap in the curtains he could see what appeared to be a hallway. Opposite the front door was another door leading into a room with a tiled floor. This door was wide open and he could see a fireplace and, in an armchair, a man who appeared to be asleep. He wasn't able to see any more of the room. He could hear some music, probably a television, he thought. There was a car parked in front of the house but he couldn't see any other vehicle. It looked like he was in luck. He could now see a barn a short distance away from the farm house and he thought this would be the obvious place to store something. The moon continued to abandon him occasionally and this was now proving to be helpful by giving him cover when he moved. As he expected, the barn doors were padlocked and also in full view of the farm house. He decided to look at the other side of the barn to see if there was another entrance and where he was less likely to be seen. This was when his foot collided with something metal, probably a bucket he thought, and the sound seemed to echo around the farm yard. He stayed still for a moment hoping the sleeping man hadn't been disturbed. All appeared to be quiet so he made his way to the back of the barn. He was also conscious that time was slipping away. He decided to call Stella.

'Stella, it's taken me longer that I expected. I'm now going to enter the barn; I'll give you a call when I'm inside.' He switched off not giving her chance to reply.

Luck was with him. He found a door which was locked but he managed to open it without too much difficulty. He thought it was strange that there hadn't been any security lights anywhere on the property. When inside, he switched on his torch, and looked around. About a quarter of the space was taken up by bales of hay. No surprise there then. Also in the barn were two white Transit vans and a fork-lift truck along with a few tools here and there. He could see that the bales of hay had been placed to form a wall behind which there were a number of large wooden boxes. He looked around and spotted a claw hammer. Lady Luck was definitely holding his hand. The box he opened contained sub-machine guns and no doubt, thought Clarke, the other boxes would also contain arms. He replaced the lid as quietly as possible thinking that it was unlikely that the sleeping man would hear. That's when he felt the pressure of cold steel on the back of his head.

'Caught you, you bastard,' boomed a voice, 'on your bloody knees and your hands behind your head.' Brady will be pleased, thought Doherty, as he proceeded to search Clarke. He removed the Walther from Clarke's holster then struck him at the back of his head. As Clarke fell to the ground the torch fell from his hand, and rolled partially beneath him, plunging the barn into semi-darkness. He managed to quickly remove the commando knife from the sheath on his calf. As he staggered to his feet, Doherty rushed at him with his weapon raised, and he died with a surprised look on his face as Clarke's knife cut through his carotid artery. Clarke switched off the torch and listened. Only silence. Perhaps the guy had been alone so he took the risk of calling Stella.

'Stella, I'm afraid I've had to kill a guy. See if you can contact Shannon because I need to spend some time here covering up.'

'Are you okay?'

'Yes, I'm fine.' Clarke switched off.

This had all gone wrong, thought Clarke, the plan was to search and withdraw not kill somebody. There was blood everywhere. He picked up his Walther and replaced it in his holster. He cleaned his knife on one of the bales of hay and returned it to the sheath. He had to make it look like a burglary gone wrong. He went over to the vans and made a note of the registration numbers then fixed a bug underneath each vehicle. He moved quickly back to the farm house. He went inside and checked all the rooms. He opened drawers and cupboards and generally tried to make it look as if someone had been searching for something. He hoped he had done enough to convince Brady. He was grateful that the dead guy had been alone.

Shannon answered his mobile phone, it was Stella.

'Hello darling, is everything all right?' He turned to Brady, 'it's the girl friend.' He stepped away from the table.

'Shannon, things went wrong, we need to talk.'

'Of course darling, you must go to your mother right away and stay until she is feeling better.' Shannon returned to the table feeling certain that Stella would have bristled when he called her "darling." He would have to deal with that problem eventually but he wasn't sure how or when it was certainly not now.

'The girl friend's mother has taken ill and she wants to return home. I should get back and see how she is coping. Thank you for a great evening and happy birthday to you again Daisy.'

'Thanks, sweetheart,' Daisy slurred.

'Does that mean that you are going back to Manchester too?' asked Brady, hopefully, thought Shannon.

'There you go again, trying to get rid of me,'

Shannon stepped outside and called Stella who gave him the details.

'When Tony gets back stay where you are and check any comings and goings. I'll join you as soon as I can.'

About an hour later Shannon arrived at the lane near Brady's farm where Stella and Clarke were waiting in the car. Shannon slid into the back seat.

'Apart from Tony there has been no movement in or out of the farm,' said Stella.

'Okay, I've been in touch with Cosgrove and he's making arrangements for some of his men to take over the watch on the farm.' A car pulled into the lay bye and parked behind them. 'It looks as if they are here now so we can get back to Holywood.'

Back at Holywood Shannon met with Stella and Clarke in the conference room.

'Tony, what happened?' Shannon asked.

'I'm afraid I was taken by surprise. I had to kill him or he would have killed me.'

'Do you think it was a set up?' Stella asked.

'I don't think so. I must have wakened him when I walked into the bucket. It could be that he checked the area periodically and I was just unlucky. It was certainly an unlucky day for him.'

'Let's assume it was a setup,' suggested Stella, 'how would they have found out that we were going to search the farm?'

'Only from those who were privy to the assignment,' said Clarke.

'Who were they?' asked Stella.

'The team in Manchester and Charles Cosgrove knew,' said Clarke, 'Paul Adams and Mike Jones are part of Ironclad and are based here at Holywood but they were not given the details of what we are doing.'

'The three of us obviously knew,' said Stella, 'and, of course, Tom got Brady's address from Sean Keane. I know Keane and Tom have a history. It's possible that Keane warned Brady. You were the one who nearly got killed, Tony. We need to find out if there has been a leak.'

'I don't think we should jump to conclusions, Stella,' said Clarke, 'I'm convinced that I was just unlucky.'

Shannon had remained silent during the interaction between Stella and Clarke. A flicker in Clarke's eyes told him that he was thinking the same thing. Where was Stella going with this? They were both aware that she didn't trust Shannon. Was she now suggesting that Shannon was the leak and had sent Clarke into a trap? Was it time that this problem was brought to a head? Clarke was tempted to say something but decided that it was Shannon's prerogative. Shannon didn't exercise his prerogative but suggested a different angle.

'We mustn't forget that Brady has been in contact with Max Parker,' said Shannon, 'Parker knows who I am because Tony and I have been on his back for some time. If my name came up at that meeting then Brady will have been forewarned. He may have guessed why I was in Belfast and so may have been expecting me at the farm.'

'That makes sense,' said Clarke, hoping that this would convince Stella of Shannon's innocence.

'I still think that Keane could have warned Brady,' said Stella, 'so it would be wise to keep him in the frame.' Clarke could see that Stella wasn't convinced that Shannon was clean. Suggesting that Keane had warned Brady also implicated Shannon. Clarke was concerned that this mistrust could seriously jeopardise the whole mission.

'On the positive side,' said Clarke, 'we now know that Brady is in possession of illegal arms and we know where they are being kept. I assumed that the Transit vans will be used to move them so I have bugged them and made a note of the registration numbers.'

'We will have to contact Jim McDonald,' said Shannon, 'to find out if he wants us to remove these weapons or allow Brady to deliver them in the hope that the trail will lead to the Parker brothers.'

'If Brady returns to the farm tonight he'll find the body,' said Clarke, 'he won't be able to report it to the police because the barn will then become a crime scene and the police will find the weapons. He's going to have to move the body before he moves the weapons.'

'I feel sure that he will be too well oiled to return to the farm tonight,' said Shannon, 'and you're right, he can't hang on to the body too long because the police will want to know why he hadn't reported the death earlier. He will have to dump the body.'

'Charles' men are watching the farm,' said Clarke, 'and their brief is to watch and record any activity but take no action.'

'Their cars are fitted with tracking equipment,' said Shannon, 'so if the vans move off they will be able to follow.'

They decided that it would be a good idea if they turned in. Back in his room Shannon began to think about the events of the night. It was unfortunate that Stella suspected that he was a mole. If he had gone into the barn instead of Clarke, then perhaps she would have been less suspicious. However, they couldn't have played it any other way. He had to be the one to keep Brady occupied. Perhaps it would have been better if Stella and Tony had gone into the barn together. Stella could have watched Tony's back. It's easy to be wise after the event. If Stella's attitude didn't change then he would have a major problem on his hands. He began to think about the first time they met. They both knew immediately that there was a mutual attraction. He thought that their relationship had developed into something more meaningful. Now it appeared that she couldn't stand the sight of him. He decided that he had to put the problem behind him. It was important to keep focused on the mission they had been given because Brady was cunning and ruthless and he wouldn't be taking any prisoners.

18

Next morning Shannon and Clarke were having breakfast in the mess. Stella had gone to the gym so Shannon thought this was a good opportunity to talk to Clarke about Stella.

'Tony, as you know, I'm concerned about Stella's attitude towards me. It's not getting any better. I can understand it because she comes from a military background and her father was killed in action in the Falklands. I have to confess I don't know what to do about it.'

'It's a problem, Tom. At one point I considered challenging her but decided against it. I have pointed out to her that I have worked with you and trust you completely.'

'It was unfortunate that you were attacked in the barn.'

'I suppose I should have taken her with me as backup because her skill with weapons is outstanding. I decided she would be more useful as a lookout in case some of Brady's cronies turned up. Hindsight is a wonderful thing.'

'I think the best approach will be to complete this assignment and then if she.....'

Shannon was interrupted by the appearance of Stella. She obviously suspected that she had been the subject of their conversation. There was an awkward silence. She didn't speak. She placed her kit on the floor beside the table and went to collect her breakfast. She returned, however, with only a cup of coffee.

'Not hungry this morning?' asked Clarke. Before she could answer Shannon's phone rang.

'Hello, Peter, we are just leaving the mess and on our way to the conference room,' Shannon gestured to Stella and Clarke to follow him.

'Okay, Peter, we're in the conference room now, any news?' Shannon switched on the loud speaker on his phone so that Clarke and Stella could hear.

'If Brady moves the weapons, Jim wants you to follow him to see where he goes. If he attempts to ship the arms over here, you are to stop him. I thought you'd like to know that Raz Parker has flown to Pakistan today. His grandparents own some property there. I'll keep you posted. Good luck.' He rang off.

'Those bugs you placed on the vans, Tony, are going to make our job a lot easier,' said Shannon.

'If the vans move off,' said Clarke, 'then we will have to make sure that we follow with two cars, in case they separate and follow different routes.'

Stella looked as if she was going to say something when there was a knock on the door and Cosgrove came in.

'I thought I'd give you an update. There's been no activity at the farm during the night but at eight o'clock this morning Brady's car arrived. Within the hour two more cars arrived. One was Michael Donovan's and the other belonged to Martin Nolan. There were two men in each car so it looks as though things are beginning to happen.'

'Thanks, Charles,' said Clarke, 'we have assumed that the road leading into the farm is not a through road but a cul-de-sac. Can you confirm this?'

'Yes, that's true, Tony, Orchard lane is a cul-de-sac.'

'Charles,' asked Shannon, 'will it be possible for one of your men to join us to keep track of these vans if they move off?'

'I'm sure that can be arranged. I'll have a look at the duty roster and get back to you.'

The rest of the day was uneventful until it got to nine o'clock in the evening. They were enjoying a drink in the mess when Cosgrove came in. He told them that Donovan's car had been seen leaving the farm. As agreed his men hadn't followed. He suspected that they were getting rid of the body as there had not been any report of a homicide.

He had arranged for one of his men to join them should the vans move off. Cosgrove declined to have a drink with them saying he had to catch up on some paperwork. After Cosgrove left, Stella announced that she would turn in early. At midnight Shannon and Clarke decided to call it a day. There had been no more activity at Brady's farm and they concluded that Brady wasn't going to do anything that night.

The next morning things started to happen. They were in the mess when Cosgrove came in. He said that the vans had been moved out of the barn and parked at the end of the drive. He suggested that they had to assume the weapons were going to be moved. He had arranged for Bill Chapman to join them right away. He had two unmarked cars equipped with tracking devices ready to go.

After Cosgrove left, Clarke said, 'Charles is the salt of the earth and of the old school; a real gentleman.'

'Not like us rough necks then,' laughed Shannon.

'This could be a set up,' said Stella.

'What makes you think that?' asked Clarke.

'Why move the vans to the end of the drive where they can be seen?' replied Stella, 'If the weapons have been loaded then it would be logical to move off immediately.'

'A good point,' said Shannon, 'but if they move off then we have to assume that the weapons are on board and follow. Our orders are to only stop them if they try to leave the country. Cosgrove's men will continue their surveillance in case Brady has arranged some other transport.'

Bill Chapman arrived with Cosgrove, introductions followed and they left. The two cars headed for Brady's farm. Stella and Clarke were in one car and Shannon and Chapman in the other. They had agreed that Stella and Chapman would be the drivers with Clarke and Shannon manning their mobile phones. When they were about a mile from the farm, their satellite trackers told them that the vans were on the move and going in the direction of the B59, which could take them to Larne or Ballyclare. The vans didn't seem to be in too much of a hurry.

'Do you think they have a ship somewhere around Larne?' asked Clarke speaking to Shannon on his mobile.

'They've missed the turn off for Larne and appear to be heading for Ballyclare. They could still take the A57, I think, to Larne.'

The vans stayed on the B59 heading for Ballymena. After about fifteen miles it was clear that the destination was not Larne. When the vans reached the outskirts of Ballymena they turned west and continued along another B road. Ten miles later they pulled into a garden centre.

'This is weird, surely they've not stopped to buy plants,' said Clarke. Both cars pulled over on to the grass verge a hundred yards away from the entrance of the garden centre. There were other cars parked there so they weren't too conspicuous.

'We need to find out what they're up to,' said Shannon, 'It's risky but I think that Bill and I should go in and see if we recognise them. Let's hope they don't recognise us.'

Shannon and Chapman walked into the garden centre and looked around then suddenly Chapman pulled Shannon to one side.

'There are two guys heading for the cafe. One is a guy called Dave Connors and the other is Pat Daley. They've both been in for questioning in connection with the shooting of two soldiers but the evidence wasn't strong enough to hold them.'

'I don't know them so I don't think they'll know me. Is there any chance they'll recognise you?'

'No, the police dealt with the investigation but we like to be kept informed.'

'Right, let's pretend we're looking at the plants keeping the vans in view in case this is where they intend to do a switch of some kind.' After nearly an hour the van drivers left the cafe and made their way to the vans. No one had been near the vans in that time. The vans moved off.

'Let's get out of here,' said Shannon.

When they joined the others, Shannon said, 'I'm beginning to smell a rat but we are committed now so we'll have to follow it through.'

The vans continued travelling west and after ten minutes the two cars followed them.

'My guess, Tom, is that they're taking the weapons into the Republic, perhaps they have the necessary organisation there to ship them out more easily.'

'If that happens, Tony, we will have to inform the Garda and ask them to intercept them. Let's see what happens when they get to Derry.'

The vans proceeded into the centre of Derry and then turned into the Northern Motors car park.

'This is very interesting,' said Shannon, his voice coming over the mobile phone, 'this is Sean Keane's place.' Stella face had a look of "I told you so" which didn't escape Clarke's notice and he was glad that Shannon wasn't in the same car.

'I think that Stella and I should go in on the pretext of buying a car,' suggested Clarke, 'that will give us the opportunity to look around.'

'Good idea,' agreed Shannon, 'Brady and his thugs don't know either of you so it won't matter if they see you. I'll give Sean Keane a call just to test the waters.'

After Stella and Clarke left, Shannon called Keane's Belfast number. Within a few minutes Keane's secretary put him through.

'Hello, Tom, how are you?'

'I'm fine, Sean, I just wanted to let you know that I managed to see Declan Brady the other night.'

'It's strange but I hadn't seen Brady in a little over twelve months, then yesterday, out of the blue, I got a call from Michael Donovan telling me that he was Brady's business partner. He said they had two Transit vans, in good condition, which they wanted me to sell for them and I could keep a third of the selling price. It was more of a demand than a request and luckily we had had some enquiries for second hand

Transits at our Derry branch. He said they would deliver them to Derry on a sale or return basis.'

'Sounds like a good deal.'

'I could do without it, Tom, I don't trust Brady. I've told my Derry manager that when the vans arrive he must check that they've not been stolen. If there's the slightest problem, he must send them back to Brady. There's no doubt, the past does come back to haunt you but then in the past I would have had him sorted. That's not an option now.'

'Perhaps everything will turn out all right, Sean. Good luck.' Shannon rang off.

As Stella and Clarke were walking through the Northern Motors car park they saw the two van drivers getting into a car. The car appeared to have been waiting for them because it moved off immediately and left the car park. Clarke didn't know the man who was driving but he did see the registration plate and there was no doubt, it was Brady's car. The salesman saw them and walked over to them.

'Can I help you?'

'We were looking at those Transit vans and wondered if they were for sale?' said Clarke.

'They are but we do have a customer who is interested in buying them.'

'Would it be possible to have a look at them?' asked Clarke.

'No problem, sir. If you do wish to purchase them we would have to give our other customer first refusal. I'll go and get the keys.'

'This is very strange,' said Clarke, after the salesman had left, 'he's not going to open these vans if he knows what's inside.'

'Perhaps there's nothing inside, Tony.'

'Please don't tell me we've been chasing two empty vans across the countryside.'

'If he opens these vans then we probably have. On the other hand, the salesman may not be in on the act, in which case, we have another problem.'

'What problem would that be?'

'If the boxes are in the vans do we declare that we know what's in the boxes or do we play dumb and allow the vans to carry on with their journey and track them?'

The salesman returned with the keys and opened the vans.

Both vans were empty!

19

They returned to Holywood. Chapman resumed his normal duties and the trio met in the conference room.

'Brady seems to have anticipated our every move,' said Stella.

'Tom, do you think your name came up at Brady's meeting with Max Parker?' asked Clarke.

'I said it was a possibility. If it did, then that would explain a lot of things.'

'What do you mean?' asked Stella.

'Tony and I have been putting a lot of pressure on the Parker brothers over the past few months. If Brady is trying to do some sort of illegal deal with Max Parker then Parker would bring up the fact that he is being watched and by whom.'

'If he mentioned our names,' said Clarke, 'then Brady would recognise Tom's name.'

'That wouldn't explain how he has been a few steps ahead of us,' said Stella, 'I'm convinced it was a set up. The two vans were parked at the end of the drive for all to see. They must have known they were being watched. How did they know?'

'We don't know the answer to that,' said Clarke, 'and I think it is counter-productive to suspect each other.' Clarke felt that he needed to say that to discourage Stella from pointing the finger at Shannon again. There was an uncomfortable silence for a few moments, broken by Shannon.

'I think our first priority is to check the barn.'

'I agree,' said Clarke, 'and I think we should do it tonight.'

'All right,' said Stella, 'but this time I think we should all go.'

It was midnight when they arrived at Orchard Lane. They parked the car some two hundred yards away in the lay-bay they had used previously. Although the weather was dry and fairly warm, it was a very cloudy night and visibility was poor.

'Cosgrove's men aren't here,' said Stella.

'Perhaps he thought they weren't needed if the weapons were gone,' whispered Clarke.

They made their way silently towards the barn. They couldn't see any lights in the farmhouse and no security lights came on. There were no cars parked anywhere in the farmyard. They entered the barn by the rear door after Clarke had successfully picked the lock again. When inside they paused and listened. It was quiet, apart from their own breathing, so they decided to risk using their torches. Clarke walked across to the bales of hay where the arms had been stored. The area was empty.

'They've gone,' said Clarke.

'They must be here somewhere, perhaps they've moved them into the farm house,' said Shannon.

They searched the farm house thoroughly but found nothing.

'These old farm houses usually had earth or solid floors of some kind but no cellars,' said Clarke as he stamped on the floor.

'That's it,' exclaimed Shannon, 'it's been staring us straight in the face all the time.'

'What has?' asked Stella and Clarke almost in concert.

'Most of the barn floor was concrete but the part where the bales of hay stood was wooden. There may be a cellar underneath.'

After they had moved several bales of hay they found a trap door which opened to reveal wooden steps leading to a fairly large storage area. The boxes were there.

'That's a relief,' gasped Shannon, 'I think we should now ask Cosgrove if he will arrange for these boxes to be taken to Holywood, unless either of you have a different plan.'

'I think it's the only way to make sure that they don't fall into the wrong hands,' said Clarke.

'I agree,' said Stella, 'we shouldn't give Brady the chance to outwit us again.'

It was a little over an hour before the trucks arrived but Cosgrove's men worked very quickly and soon had all the boxes loaded and then they left.

When Shannon, Clarke and Stella arrived at the army base the boxes were being unloaded and taken into the armoury. Cosgrove was waiting for them.

'I've arranged for the weapons to be locked in the armoury for tonight. Perhaps tomorrow would be a better time for you to check them,' said Cosgrove, 'I've also arranged for some food for you in the mess.'

'Great.' said Stella, who was feeling quite hungry as well as tired.

'Thanks, Charles,' said Clarke, 'we'll go to the mess straight away and then turn in. We'll see you tomorrow and thanks for the help.'
They arrived at the mess to find a veritable feast of cold meats and salads and all the trimmings.

'I'm fairly certain now,' said Stella as she filled her plate, 'that we've been duped.'

'I think you're right,' agreed Clarke.

'It would certainly seem that Brady was prepared to sacrifice the weapons, perhaps for some greater goal,' speculated Shannon.

'He tricked us into chasing empty vans so it appears that he wanted us out of the way for a period of time, or could it be that he was genuinely trying to sell the Transits?' asked Clarke.

'Perhaps we'll never know,' said Stella, 'but at least we are in possession of the weapons and not the terrorists and so we have achieved one objective.'

'True,' agreed Shannon as he poured the coffees, 'but I would like to know why he hadn't moved the weapons before now. It seems as if he wanted us to find them.'

'I can't believe that,' said Clarke, 'he stands to lose a hell of a lot of money.'

'Perhaps he has a hell of a lot of money,' suggested Stella, 'he may have the several million pounds from the bank robbery. I think he's on top of the list of suspects for that crime.'

'I'm beginning to smell a rat again,' said Shannon, 'Tony, when you found those boxes, you opened one of them. Was there a reason why you picked that particular box?'

'It was on top of two other boxes and first in the row, along with the fact that the claw hammer was nearby and I wanted to work fast. It was the obvious one to open.'

'Of course it was, just about everybody would have chosen the same box.'

'What are you getting at, Tom?' Clarke asked.

'Come on let's open those boxes,' said Shannon, getting up quickly from the table.

It took about half an hour to alert Cosgrove and for arrangements to be made for the armoury to be unlocked. When inside Clarke picked out the box he had opened. He recognised it from the splinters of missing wood and the blood stains from when he was attacked. They opened it up and inside found sub-machine guns as Clarke had described. One of Cosgrove's armourers was on hand and he was examining the weapons. Shannon and Clarke began opening the other boxes.

'Sir,' said the armourer, speaking to Cosgrove, 'these weapons are faulty and only fit for scrap.'

Shannon and Clarke had opened several of the other boxes only to find scrap metal.

'You were right, Stella, we were duped,' said Shannon, 'They arranged it so that we would open that particular box hoping that we would believe all the boxes contained weapons. If we had arranged for Brady to be arrested, then the police would only find boxes of scrap metal. Brady had all the angles covered.'

'You said he was clever,' said Clarke.

Next morning Shannon was first to arrive in the mess for breakfast. A few minutes later Stella and Clarke appeared. They collected their breakfasts and joined Shannon. Outside it was wet and overcast, positively gloomy and that also described Shannon and his companions.

'Well, we're back to square one,' said Shannon, 'we haven't found any weapons and we haven't traced the stolen money.'

'To be perfectly fair to ourselves,' said Stella, 'that wasn't our brief. We were asked to find out what Brady was up to.'

'That's true,' said Clarke, 'Brady made us believe that he was gun running but we have no proof that he is up to anything. The run around he sent us on was obviously a distracter. He made us look the other way and we don't know why.'

'Brady always seemed to anticipate our every move,' said Stella, 'we must have a mole somewhere.'

Before anyone could speak Shannon's mobile rang.

'Hello, Colonel,' said Shannon as he turned on the loudspeaker on his phone, 'I'm afraid Brady took us for a ride.'

'Yes, I believe so; Peter gave me all the details. Tom, there have been some new developments here in the North West and a number of arrests have been made. I want all of you to return to Manchester as soon as possible. I'll fill you in when I see you at The Priory.' He rang off.

It was a little after midnight when a large truck moved slowly down Orchard Lane towards Brady's farm. It stopped at the entrance and two men jumped down from the cab. They were carrying high powered torches and they guided the truck as it reversed up the drive. The truck stopped at the farm house and a third man jumped down and went into the building. The two men with torches crawled underneath the truck and removed what appeared to be two fuel tanks. Later all three men carried bags which they loaded into the dummy fuel tanks. The dummy fuel tanks were refitted to the truck and the vehicle made its way back down the drive. Several hours later, and after a stop at a Belfast warehouse to pick up some items of furniture, the truck rolled off the ferry at Stranraer. It then made its way to the M6 and carried on south. Eventually the truck pulled into a car park at the rear of a warehouse in Manchester. The dummy fuel tanks were removed and their contents were taken into the warehouse.

20

Shannon, Clarke and Stella arrived at The Priory soon after lunch and went straight to the main office where Blake was working away at his computers.

'Hi Peter, is there anything interesting happening out in space?' asked Shannon.

'I'm picking up a lot of strange messages floating out in the ether. I haven't figured them out yet, probably aliens.'

'Is Jim in his office?'

'Yes. He wants us to join him in the conference room at fifteen hundred hours.'

Shannon went over to the drinks cabinet and poured himself a glass of Jameson's.

'I know it's early but I need this.'

'It's not too early for me, I'll join you,' said Blake.

'I'll not spoil the party, I'll have a Jameson's too,' said Clarke.

'Make mine a coffee. Somebody's got to be sober when we see the Colonel,' said Stella.

The door opened and McDonald appeared.

'Stella, can I have a word,' McDonald left followed by Stella.

'Very mysterious,' said Clarke, 'Jim doesn't usually talk privately with members of the team.'

Shannon wondered if McDonald had somehow found out about his problem with Stella. He was sure that Clarke wouldn't have said anything. Perhaps Stella had decided that she couldn't work with him and wanted out. He hoped that that wasn't the case because he wanted the chance to show her that he wasn't all bad. He suddenly realised that Laura was no longer foremost in his mind and he felt a little guilty about that. Peter Blake and his parents, however, had made it quite clear that he had to sort his life out and move on. He had hoped that he could have moved on with Stella. He again recalled his first meeting with Stella and he was certain that there was some chemistry between them. That was only a short time ago and now it would appear that Stella suspected that he was working for the terrorists. She didn't trust him and was probably at this moment asking McDonald to take her off the team. It looked as if his dream of a future with her was indeed just a dream.

Shannon was still thinking about Stella when McDonald came into the office and said he would like to start the meeting early in the conference room. Stella wasn't with him. Had she asked for, and been given, a transfer? The loss of Laura had nearly destroyed him. Now it would seem that he had lost Stella too. It certainly looked as if he wasn't going to get the chance to somehow make it right. On the way to the conference room Shannon came to the conclusion that Stella had asked for a transfer. Perhaps McDonald would inform them now. They all sat down and McDonald spoke.

'I have been informed that the threat of a terrorist attack has worsened. The government has declared that the Risk Assessment is now classified as Severe. MI5 have put into effect Operation Pathway. They have arrested a number of Pakistanis in Lancashire and the Greater Manchester area. The Half Moon Club has been raided and some arrests were made. Max Parker was arrested but released after a few hours without charge. Raz Parker is still in Pakistan.'

'So it would appear that MI5 are expecting something to happen here in the North West,' said Clarke, stating the obvious.

'Yes, so we need to check on Brady and the Parker brothers,' said McDonald, 'another name has cropped up in connection with the Parker brothers, an Irishman called Dooley. Paul and Mike will be joining us shortly and they will fill us in.'

The door opened and in walked Paul Adams and Michael Jones. They were the newest members of Ironclad. Their surveillance work in

Northern Ireland has proved very useful to Ironclad. They had been friends since they met at University.

'Sit down chaps,' said McDonald, 'and tell us what you know about this Dooley fellow.'

Jones explained that Brian Dooley had a furniture company in Belfast operating under the name of Celtic Furniture Limited. The furniture was good quality and was produced in a factory in Belfast. He had been very successful. He had a warehouse in Dublin and a few months ago opened a warehouse in Manchester. He shipped over his goods through Liverpool and Stranraer. Dooley had supplied furniture to the Parker brothers for their night club in the past. MI5 had suspected that Dooley had been dealing with the Real IRA for some time but hadn't found any concrete evidence against him. Jones said that he had moved around in the Republican area and knew that Dooley mixed socially with suspected terrorists. After he expanded into Manchester it looked as if he had overstretched himself. Jones's investigations showed that Dooley had a cash flow problem and his creditors had been pressing him for their money. Last week all the creditors were paid off. The word on the street, said Jones, is that Dooley had done a deal with Brady.

'We already knew that Brady had been in touch with the Parker brothers,' said McDonald, 'we also knew that Dooley had done some business with the Parker brothers which was presumably legitimate. Now there's a strong suspicion that Dooley is connected with Brady.'

'If Brady has bailed out Dooley,' said Clarke, 'then Brady will be able to put pressure on him to do his bidding. He will have access to Dooley's transport and storage facilities.'

'And a bit more bad news,' said Adams, 'is that Brady has got his hands on a quantity of Semtex.'

'If Brady has got his hands on some Semtex,' said Shannon, 'I'm certain that he will have found a way to ship some to Manchester.'

'If Tom is right,' said Clarke, 'and Brady has shipped some Semtex to Manchester, then the chances are that it is in Dooley's warehouse. I think we should check that warehouse.'

'It will be difficult to get a warrant without tangible evidence,' said McDonald, 'our only course of action is to resort to some illegal investigation,' and he looked knowingly at Shannon and Clarke.

'Tony and I will put our heads together and see if we can find a way to persuade Dooley to let us look around his warehouse.'

It was after midnight when Shannon and Clarke arrived at Dooley's warehouse which was situated on Great Ducie Street. The area was occupied mostly by commercial premises and Manchester prison, previously known as Strangeways, was nearby. At that time of the night the streets were very quiet. The sky was overcast occasionally spitting drops of rain. Clarke had parked the car in a nearby street and he and Shannon had walked a hundred yards or so to the warehouse. From the front of the building the place appeared to be in darkness. They decided to look around the rest of the building and check out any possible access point. To the rear of the building was a parking area surrounded by a nine feet high wire fence and a gate which was padlocked. Parked inside the fence were two container trucks. A street lamp, conveniently placed near the entrance gates, shone on the trucks and they were able to see that both trucks had Northern Ireland number plates.

'The whole place is in darkness so it looks as if it's not being manned.'

'There are bars on the windows on the ground floor. There are a number of security lights probably on sensors and a couple of alarm boxes. Perhaps they think that's sufficient to protect furniture.'
It was then that they heard a vehicle approaching. Shannon and Clarke moved back into the shadow and away from the street lighting. The vehicle turned into the street at the side of the warehouse. It was a white Transit van. They both kept perfectly still as the van approached

and stopped in front of the gates. A man got out of the van, opened the gates, and waved the van in.

'I do believe they're two of Brady's cronies,' said Shannon, 'and if I'm not mistaken they're Byrne and Doyle, the big, tough, blond cousins.'

'Do you think we've got it right this time,' said Clarke, remembering their last encounter with Transit vans, 'or are they just moving furniture?'

'I'm glad you see the funny side of everything,' smiled Shannon, 'but if it's furniture then I'm emigrating.'

'Let's assume that Brady has used Dooley's trucks to make a delivery of Semtex from Ireland, is it likely that they will risk taking it directly to the Parker brothers? I think we should fix a bug on that van in case they have a different destination in mind.'

'That's a good idea. It'll make it easier to follow them and if they lead to the Parker brothers then.....' Shannon began but didn't finish because Byrne and Doyle came out of the warehouse each carrying bags which they placed in the van. They loaded the van with several more bags and then went back into the warehouse.

'Keep me covered,' said Clarke, 'I'm going to fix a bug under the van.'

Clarke moved off and Shannon drew his Astra from his holster, a weapon given to him by Sean Keane in his PIRA days. He also carried a Bauer .25 auto pistol which was small enough to be secreted in an ankle holster, another gift from Keane. Shannon fitted a silencer to the Astra and followed Clarke. They both moved silently along the fencing keeping in the shadows where possible. When they entered the parking area, Clarke made his way to the van. He fixed the bug and as he was making his way back to Shannon, the warehouse door opened and Byrne and Doyle came out.

'Hey you,' shouted Doyle, 'what the hell are you doing here?'

'I'm just walking home from a party,' replied Clarke as he continued to walk away.

'Oh yea, and who the hell do you think you're kidding?' growled Doyle, who drew what appeared to be a pistol from inside his jacket.

'I had a few drinks and lost my way,' Clarke called out as he kept walking.

'Bullshit, stop or I'll shoot.'

Clarke began to walk faster. Doyle raised his weapon and fired. Shannon heard the dull thud of a silencer and Clarke went down. Shannon moved quickly in the direction of Clarke and began to shoot at the two men. Doyle went down immediately and Byrne ran for cover. Shannon was relieved to see Clarke getting up and he fired a few more shots to discourage Byrne from reappearing. They both quickly retreated through the gates.

'How bad is it?' asked Shannon when they were back in the car.

'It's my arm but it's only a flesh wound. I dived to make it more difficult for him to hit me again.'

'I'm taking you straight to The Royal so that Mark, or one of his staff, can take a look at the damage.'

'What about the van?'

'It'll keep, you've bugged it.'

21

'What the hell happened?' demanded Brady.

'Frank's been hit and it looks real bad, shouldn't we be seeing to him?' protested Byrne.

'You can't take him to hospital. All gun wounds have to be reported to the police,' explained Max Parker.

They were in the Parker brothers' private office in The Half Moon Club.

'What are we going to do then? He's been hit in the arm and leg,' said Byrne.

'Okay, okay,' growled Brady, 'I know he's a cousin of yours. What can we do Max?'

'I'll give Doc Greene a call. He's not a doctor any more. He was struck off a few years ago. He's done a few jobs for us. He'll be glad of the money,' said Parker as he picked up the phone. After making the call he told Byrne that Greene was on his way.

'That's taken care of, so tell me what happened,' insisted Brady. Byrne gave him all the details.

'Bloody hell, Peter, you've really dropped us in the shit. The fella you shot is going to have to get some hospital treatment and then the police will be informed,' said Brady.

'It was Frank who shot the fella, not me. What could we have done?'

'You could have chased him off. The thing that worries me is that they were armed. Who could they be?'

'One of the fellas did look familiar,' said Byrne, 'It was the second fella, the one who shot Frank. As he went through the gates one of the security lights caught his face. I'm sure I saw him in Belfast. Well I think I did, although I think it would be a strange place for him to be.'

'For Jeez sake,' screamed Brady, now at the end of his tether, 'either you saw him or you didn't. Was he in Belfast or wasn't he? Make your bloody mind up.'

'It was when you were in the Red Lion celebrating Daisy's birthday. Me and Frank were late and as we walked into the pub we saw this big, blond fella get up from your table and leave. I feel sure it was him.'

'That was Shannon who was a member, or supposed to be a member, of my PIRA cell. I never trusted the bugger. He came to the Red Lion pretending to be looking for a job but I knew the bastard was checking up on me.'

'Did you say Shannon?' interrupted Parker, who had been sitting quietly, listening to the exchange between the two men, 'if it was Tom Shannon then the other guy will probably be Tony Clarke, they usually work together. Both these men work for Colonel McDonald who is head of the counter-terrorism team in Manchester. They've been giving us a lot of aggravation.'

'I found out a little while ago that Shannon had signed up with the Brits,' said Brady, 'he's very clever and is used to working on his own. If his partner is only half as good as he is, then they will be a force to be reckoned with. I knew he was going to Belfast to investigate me so I planned a little diversion for him.'

'What do you mean by "diversion"?'

'After we did the bank job,' said Brady, ignoring Parker's question, 'the police brought me in for questioning. They accused me of nicking the money to buy arms for the Real IRA. They were just guessing, groping in the dark'

'You didn't tell me that the police had you in for questioning.'

'Well, nothing came of it so I didn't think it was important.'

'So what was this diversion that you planned?' Parker asked again.

'It was simple really. If the security forces were convinced that I was an arms dealer, then it would be easy to make Shannon believe that they were right. A few boxes filled with scrap and one box with sub-machine guns, which were knackered, was all I needed. I knew they would search the farm and find the boxes. My plan was to bugger them around for a while so I could move the Semtex and the drugs.'

'Was it during the search that Doherty was killed?'

'Correct, the stupid eejit. Anyway, one of my guys, pretending to be a dealer, got in touch with Northern Motors in Derry and said he was interested in buying a couple of vans. Later Donovan got in touch with Keane asking him if he would try to sell two Transits, on sale or return, and offered him a big percentage of the selling price. I knew that Shannon would follow the vans and so give me the chance to move the stuff. I was informed, however, that an army surveillance car was parked in the lay-by near the farm so we had to delay moving the materials.'

'If they searched the farm house why didn't they find the drugs and Semtex?'

'They were focused on the boxes. I knew they would eventually find the cellar and believe I was trying to hide the boxes for delivery later. I guessed they would take the boxes to Holywood as evidence and to prevent me from tricking them again. I was then informed that the surveillance team had been called off and we moved the goods.'

'You still haven't told me where you hid the drugs and Semtex.'

'The farm was used by the original IRA. There is a hidden room, which is accessed through the side of the fireplace, where the IRA hid men and weapons. That's where the drugs and Semtex were hidden. The Semtex is the type which is difficult to detect. The new stuff has something added to it. I think it's to make it smell.'

'It must have been risky bringing that kind of cargo into England.'

'Dooley, Byrne and Doyle brought it over in one of Dooley's trucks. We had a couple of dummy fuel tanks fitted underneath the trucks to house the drugs and Semtex.'

'I'm impressed. You must have an excellent intelligence set up.'

'I'm glad I have, particularly now that Shannon is on the case,'

'Shannon and Clarke didn't turn up at the warehouse by chance, Declan. Let's unload those bags before they pay us a visit. They obviously suspect Dooley so we will.....' Parker stopped speaking as the door opened and "Doctor" Greene came in.

'Hello Doc. I have a patient for you. Would you take him up to the first floor and have a look at him? You know which room to use.' Greene left with Doyle without speaking.

'Declan, I didn't see anybody following us,' said Byrne, 'I did a couple of detours and at that time of night it would have been obvious if somebody had been tailing us. I think the fella who was shot has gone to hospital.'

'You may be right but has it crossed your stupi mind that they may have been bugging the van when you caught them?'
Parker moved to the back of the office and pressed something on the wall. A panel opened revealing a space about three or four yards square. It contained six steel filing cabinets.

'We have our secret room too,' smiled Parker, 'there's plenty of room for the bags in here,' Parker then spoke to Byrne, 'go upstairs to the first floor, you will see a door marked "Staff" at the end of the corridor. Tell the guy sleeping in there to get his fat ass down here right away. His name is Ali.' When Byrne returned, the three of them began to unload the Transit van. By the time Ali had surfaced and got dressed, all the bags had been placed in the hidden room.

'Ali, I want you to take the van and dump it somewhere in Yorkshire. Byrne will follow you in my car and bring you back. Wipe everything clean so there won't be any finger prints,' said Parker.

'Won't the van be traceable back to you?' asked Brady.

'No,' answered Parker, 'we paid cash for the hire of the van and all the documents we used were forgeries. Some of these vehicle hire guys often don't ask too many questions.'

'Shannon's going to have a nice trip to Yorkshire,' sneered Brady, 'and when he gets back I'm going to take him out before he does us some real damage.'

Shannon and Clarke made their way to the hospital. Their tracking device showed them that the van was driving around the city in a haphazard way, sometimes doubling back. They were obviously making sure that they didn't have a tail. On arrival at the hospital,

Clarke was seen immediately and the doctor confirmed that it was only a flesh wound. When they returned to the car they checked the tracker. They could see that the van was stationary in the Whitworth Street area. As they made their way to Whitworth Street, the van moved off. The roads were fairly quiet at that time of the morning and so the van moved easily through the streets. Eventually the van turned onto the M62 on the eastbound carriageway. Shannon kept his distance but keeping the van in sight. After about an hour the van pulled into a service station followed by a BMW saloon car. There were only a few vehicles in the car park, mostly heavy goods vehicles. Shannon parked behind a large truck. The BMW parked next to the van and the driver of the van got out and into the BMW.

The BMW left at speed. Shannon quickly drove over to the van, opened the doors only to find it empty, déjà vu.

They followed the BMW out of the car park and back to Manchester. They were confident that nothing had been taken out of the van and loaded into the car. Neither had the van stopped anywhere on the journey to the service station. The bags must have been unloaded at The Half Moon Club.

22

Next morning in the conference room at The Priory, Shannon and Clarke gave McDonald the details of their fruitless night.

'We've been giving the Parker brothers a lot of hassle recently,' said McDonald, 'so we have to be careful. We don't want them to bring a charge of harassment because we haven't got any evidence to secure a conviction. Let's hope the police can find an excuse to get a search warrant.'

'If they have Semtex and drugs hidden in the club,' said Clarke,' is there any way we can make sure that they don't move them?'

'Peter has managed to access some cameras in that area. As from today we are able to watch the front and back entrances of the club. We will have to wait to see what their next move is.'

'Jim, I'm concerned about Stella,' said Shannon, who had decided to raise the matter with McDonald, 'she wasn't too happy when I told her about my time with the PIRA. I hope she hasn't resigned or asked for a transfer.'

'She didn't say anything about that to me.'

'I wondered if her absence had anything to do with me.'

'No, I've given her compassionate leave. Her brother, who was working undercover in Belfast, went missing three days ago. She's gone to see her mother for a couple of days.'

'I didn't know she had a brother.'

'His name is Ian. He's been working undercover for MI6 for about twelve months. What she doesn't know is that a ransom demand has been received. They want two million pounds or he will be garrotted. As you know the government won't deal with terrorists.'

'Garrotted,' exclaimed Clarke, 'that's a first.'

'Yes, indeed,' said McDonald, 'a bullet in the back of the head was the terrorists' usual method. It was rumoured some time ago that some bodies had been found in Northern Ireland which appeared to have been garrotted. I don't know how true that was but I never saw any.'

'Have they declared who they are?' asked Clarke.

'No, they haven't,' said McDonald, 'but we need to find out. Tom, I believe you may be the only one who has a chance to root out these criminals.'

'How did they make contact?' asked Shannon.

'Ian's own mobile phone was delivered to the police with a text message and a picture of Ian tied to a chair. Behind the chair there appears to be some kind of pole. Ian is tied to the pole with a cord around his neck.'

'What do you want me to do?'

'Go to Belfast and see what you can find out. Unfortunately I haven't got any information which could help you. I do have Ian's phone which the kidnappers will use to make contact in a week's time. Take it with you. I must point out, Tom, that this is not an order it is a request. If you don't want to do this, then that's okay. As you know the government won't deal with terrorists demanding a ransom. I hoped that we could do something unofficially.'

'Should I go with him as back up?' asked Clarke.

'No,' said McDonald, 'I need you here to follow up on Brady and the Parker brothers. Tom will be able to move around the area easily. If he finds that he needs help, I'll make the necessary arrangements. Remember, Tom, this is unofficial so don't take any unnecessary risks. If you need help let me know as you can see Tony is raring to go.'

The following morning Shannon was on a flight to Belfast Airport having decided to avoid Holywood army base. He thought that if there was a mole operating in the organisation, the fewer who knew about his mission, the better. He hired a car, using the false driving licence provided by McDonald, and then made his way to Connery Cottage.

He had inherited the cottage from his grandfather, Tom Connery, and he had used it during his activities with the PIRA. He had spent a lot of time with his grandfather when he was a child and everyone in the village called him young Tom Connery. The name had stuck and this had been useful in helping to keep his identity secret. It would be good to be back in the cottage again. He had spent many happy holidays with his grandfather when he was a boy.

Shannon arrived at the cottage a little before noon. The cottage had been in the Connery family for three generations. It was a single storey building, with white walls and a thatched roof, standing in about half an acre of land. There was also a detached garage which his grandfather had added some years ago. Shannon unlocked the garage door and removed the cover off the Harley-Davidson which was parked there. It had been his grandfather's pride and joy. He took his luggage out of the car boot and went into the cottage. He would have to go into the village to buy some provisions. Gerry Cunningham ran the village grocery as did his father before him. Gerry still referred to Shannon as Tom Connery. Everybody he met in the village was glad to see him. People waved from across the street. He felt very much at home here. He would have loved to introduce Stella to these lovely, friendly people but that was out of the question now. This was one of the penalties for his bad, mad time searching for revenge.

When Shannon returned from the village he was feeling quite hungry. He decided to have a meal first before he unpacked what few items of clothing he had brought with him. Later he gave some thought to how he was going to approach the problem of rescuing Ian Bellamy. Shannon understood why McDonald had asked him to do the job without Clarke. Shannon was born in Northern Ireland and lived there until he was ten years old. He could switch on the Northern Irish accent whenever it suited him and this would help him to move more easily in the area. He also knew the area very well and he was accustomed to working alone. He had some contacts in Northern

Ireland but he wasn't sure if he could rely on any of them. Sean Keane was probably his least risky contact but he may be unable to help or possibly not want to help. He would have to tread carefully. He had been informed that the kidnappers would make contact on the mobile phone in one week's time. He would have to be ready with a plan before that.

He began to think about Stella again. He still had strong feelings for her and was sorry that she now felt animosity towards him. He could understand that and he wondered if he would ever be able to convince her that he wasn't as bad as she believed him to be. When McDonald had asked him to investigate the possibility of a rescue he had readily accepted. He had great respect for Jim McDonald and was happy to accept any mission he was given. But in this case he wondered that if deep down he was using this as a way of seeking Stella's approval. They say *"all is fair in love and war."* Whatever the reason, Shannon decided, it must be right to try to rescue this man from the possibility of being garrotted. It was a barbaric and obscene method of murder and a terrible way to die. He only hoped that he could pull off the rescue although he didn't have much, if anything, to go on. All he had were a few letters on a mobile phone which didn't make any sense. He needed some help but where from? He was also aware that his time was limited. He had to take a risk and see if Sean Keane could help. Keane didn't know that he was now a member of an anti-terrorist team. On the previous occasions he had met Keane he had kept the information from him. He was now feeling guilty about that, particularly as he was going to ask his help with this rescue attempt. He would now have to tell Keane the truth and hope that he would understand.

Next morning he rang Sean Keane and arranged to meet him in his Belfast office at ten o'clock. Keane was waiting for him in the showroom and they both took the lift to Keane's office.
    'This is a pleasant surprise,' said Keane.

'It's good to see you again, Sean. I hope that when I tell you why I'm here you'll still want to speak to me. What I'm about to tell you is highly confidential and it's essential that no one ever finds out what we have been talking about. I want you to give me your word that you will keep it to yourself.'

'This sounds very serious, Tom, and of course, you have my word.' Shannon told him what had happened to him when he went back to England. He described his meeting with Colonel McDonald and explained why he had decided to join Ironclad. He told him that Brady was probably responsible for the bank robbery and the murder of the Carson family. He then went on to tell him what he was doing in Belfast.

'That's some story, Tom, but I thought .....' Keane was interrupted by the arrival of his secretary bringing coffee which Keane had requested earlier. After she left the room Keane continued. 'I thought you had planned to start up your own law firm. But I'm glad that you're not mixed up with Brady.'

'I was hoping, Sean, that you could give me some information. I will understand if you don't want to be involved. However, I promise you that your name will never be mentioned.'

'What I find interesting, Tom, is this threat of garrotting. It's not something that the PIRA did as far as I know. There was, however, a guy called Gary Ross. He was often referred to as Gary Garrotte or Garry the Garrotte because it was a method of torture he used to get information from his rivals or to eliminate them. He's a gangster and a very dangerous man. He deals in drugs and prostitution'

'Do you know where I can find him?'

'I've not heard anything about him for some time. He used to own a pub in Helen's Bay. It was rumoured that the pub cellar had a tunnel leading to the beach which was used by smugglers many years ago. I don't know how true that is. I think the pub is called the Smugglers Inn so I suppose the name of the pub supports the rumour.'

'I've got Ian Bellamy's phone which the kidnappers sent to the police. It has a picture of Ian sitting in a chair with a cord around his neck, fastened to a pole. The background appears to be a brick wall painted white but there is something written on it in red that's partly obscured by the pole. It's the only clue I have and I was hoping that someone would recognise it.'

Shannon handed the mobile phone to Keane. The picture was quite clear and Keane studied it for a few moments.

The letters written on the wall which could be seen on either side of the pole were:

Left hand side	Right hand side
LET	HATE
A	AS
T	AR

'I'm afraid they don't mean anything to me. I'll transfer this picture on to my computer and make a few enquiries.'

'Time is of the essence, Sean. In about six day's time the kidnappers will call on the cell phone to make arrangements for the ransom to be delivered. I don't know if they can be stalled but I don't want to take the risk.'

'I have a few favours I can call in. I'll move as fast as I can. If we can identify this place it will be too dangerous for you to affect a rescue on your own.'

'I'll cross that bridge when I come to it.'

23

Frank Doyle's two bullet wounds received, courtesy of Shannon, at Dooley's warehouse hadn't healed and he was in some considerable pain. Brady had refused to let Doyle go to hospital because he was afraid of bringing their activities to the attention of the police. In fact, Brady had insisted that they stay at the Half Moon Club and not return to their hotel. Peter Byrne had become very concerned about Doyle's condition and he decided that he would have to persuade Brady that he is taken to hospital. Brady came into the bedroom to check on Doyle's progress.

'Declan, we have to get Frank to hospital today,' insisted Byrne.

'Not possible. It's too risky.'

'He's running a temperature and that quack Greene is useless.'

'He's been struck off but he did qualify as a doctor so he must know what he's doing.'

'That's not good enough. Greene is not allowed to write prescriptions so Frank is only getting medication that anybody can buy over the counter. Frank needs antibiotics. At least get a proper doctor to come and examine him.'

'You know as well as I do, that if a doctor sees that he is suffering from bullet wounds, he will have to report it to the police. If that happens then we are all in deep shit and I mean all of us. That includes you, Frank. Do you want to go to prison for a very long time?' Brady retorted angrily.

'I know it's a problem but if we could get back to the hotel and call an ambulance they won't connect us with you.'

'That won't work. Shannon knows who you are and he will be on the lookout for you. That's one of the reasons we need to take him out. I'm going to the airport to pick up Connors and Daley. When they get here their first job will be to get rid of Shannon. So sit tight until I get back. Brady stormed out and slammed the door. These two had become a thorn in his side and they could jeopardise the whole project. The whole mess had been brought about by their own stupidity. He decided they would have to be taken care of along with Shannon. He knew they were two hotheads who rarely put their brains in gear. It was his mistake and he would sort it out. They would be two more hits for Connors and Daley and two fewer people to share the spoils.

Byrne was angry by Brady's response and he was very close to putting a bullet into him. If anything happened to Frank then he would make sure that Brady paid for it.

'How are you feeling Frank?'

'The pain's bad and I feel as if I'm on fire.'

'Then we have to get you to hospital.'

'I think Brady will have something to say about that. Don't forget we will be risking prison.'

'It's your decision, prison or death?'

'Why don't you drop me off at the hospital and then clear off. Once I'm in the waiting room at A&E someone will take care of me.'

'Can you stand up?' Doyle tried to stand up but his legs couldn't make it and he fell back onto the bed. The effort of trying to stand up had sapped what little strength he had left.

'Brady's gone to the airport so I'm going to call an ambulance and we'll take it from there.'

By the time the ambulance arrived Doyle seemed to be losing consciousness. The paramedics examined his dressings then fixed an oxygen mask on him and he was carried down the stairs to the ambulance. Byrne, who was now extremely concerned, went with him in the ambulance.

On arrival at the hospital Doyle was taken immediately into a treatment room and examined by a doctor. The doctor asked Byrne a few questions then asked him to accompany the nurse. Byrne left with the nurse who took down the details of how Doyle's injuries had occurred, his medical history and any medication he was taking. Byrne was angry with Brady for the delay in getting Frank to the hospital. Frank was his only remaining relative and he promised himself that if anything happened to Frank then Brady would be extremely sorry. After he gave the nurse all the information she asked for, he pointed out to her that Doyle had been treated by a doctor who had been struck off.

Byrne had been in the waiting room about fifteen minutes when two police officers came in and approached him.

'I'm Sergeant Hill and this is Constable Milner. Are you the man who brought in Mr Frank Doyle?'

'Yes,' replied Byrne seeing no point in denying it.

'What is your name, sir?' asked the sergeant.

'Peter Byrne,' replied Byrne, thinking it was no secret now because he had given his name to the nurse, along with the name of the hotel where he was staying, in case they needed to contact him.

'Do you know who did this to Mr Doyle?' asked the sergeant.

'No,' said Byrne.

'Where did the shooting take place, sir?' asked the constable. This was the question Byrne was afraid of and he was uncertain how to answer it. The two police officers noticed his hesitation.

'It's difficult to say,' stammered Byrne, 'I'm a visitor here and I don't know the names of the streets.'

'Are you saying, sir, that the shooting took place in the street somewhere but you don't know the name of the street?'

'Yes,' said Byrne but he could see that they didn't believe him.

'Can you explain to us, sir,' asked the sergeant, 'why it is that we have been told that Mr Doyle was brought here by ambulance from the Half Moon Club?'

Byrne had no answer for that so he sat in silence.

'All right, sir,' said the sergeant, 'you are obviously not telling us the truth so we will have to take you down to the station where you will have to make a statement.'

'Let me see if Frank is all right first.'

The constable left the waiting room to check and fifteen minutes later returned with the doctor who informed Byrne that Doyle was seriously ill and had been transferred to the intensive care unit. He couldn't allow any visitors at the moment. The doctor left and the two police officers escorted Byrne off the premises.

24

McDonald had arranged a meeting at The Priory at two o'clock in the afternoon. He had recalled Paul Adams from Holywood and Stella had returned from leave. Blake and Clarke were also at the meeting.

'Our first priority,' began McDonald, 'is to locate those bags which were moved from Dooley's warehouse and find out what's in them. We will have to move fast. We can't involve the police because we really don't have any specific evidence against Brady or the Parker brothers that would stand up in court. I want you to look at a way this can be done tonight.'

'I'm concerned that there may be a mole in the organisation,' said Stella, 'they always seemed to be one step ahead of us in Northern Ireland.'

'I think I may have some evidence of that,' said Blake, 'I've intercepted some calls sent to Brady's phone from public phone boxes in Belfast. The messages say "The watchers are here" or "The watchers have left" They were sent at the time Stella, Tony and Tom were searching Brady's farm.'

'This is a problem,' said McDonald, 'but I don't think it's anybody in the team. It's imperative, therefore, that all information about our activities is kept strictly within the team.'

McDonald's phone rang. 'Hello, Charles,' said McDonald, 'yes the line is secure.' He listened for a few moments and then said, 'thank you for the information, Charles, but I think whatever they were hiding in the farm has been transported to Manchester. We believe that the goods have been delivered to the Half Moon night club so Brady's farm is of no interest to us now. We are planning to raid the club tonight, unofficially of course. Okay, Charles, keep me informed.' McDonald closed his phone and said, 'that was Charles Cosgrove. He said two men turned up at Brady's farm this morning and are still there. He knows that they were members of the PIRA. Their names are Martin Nolan and Michael Donovan.'

McDonald left the team to try to formulate a plan to get hold of the bags which they felt certain were somewhere in the Half Moon Club.

'This is going to be a tough one,' said Clarke, 'we have to decide when to do the search and come up with a plan on how to do it.'

'Is it possible that the bags were dropped off somewhere when the van was taken to Yorkshire?' asked Stella.'

'I think that's unlikely,' said Clarke, 'when Tom and I arrived at the service station car park, we saw some guy get out of the van and get into Max Parker's car. They didn't take anything out of the van. We followed the car at a safe distance back to the Half Moon Club. The car didn't stop anywhere on the way back.'

'So how do we get into the club and bring the bags out without being seen, even if we can find them?' asked Paul Adams.

'A good question,' said Clarke, 'I think we should go to the club when it's in full swing. Raz Parker is still out of the country so Max will be managing the club by himself. We have to come up with something to distract Max so that a search can be made.'

'Parker doesn't know me,' said Stella, 'so I could distract him and you three could make a search.'

'It's an idea,' said Clarke, 'but it could be very risky for you.'
Before Stella could answer, the conference door opened and McDonald walked in.

'I've just had a call from the Assistant Chief Constable, Harry Simpson,' said McDonald, 'he tells me that two customers at the Half Moon were taken to hospital suffering from a drug overdose. One of them didn't survive. He now has a reason for a search so he's arranging search warrants so we will have to wait now until we hear from Harry before we can make a move.' McDonald left.

141

'We have to wait until the police have searched the club,' said Clarke, 'so I suggest that we should give some thought as to who is the mole.'

'Those messages that you intercepted, Peter,' said Stella, 'appear to prove that there is a mole.'

'Jim doesn't believe that the mole is someone in the Ironclad team,' said Blake, 'so who else could possibly know what we are doing?'

'I've always been suspicious of Keane,' said Stella, 'I still think he played a part in that wild goose chase in Ireland. He gave Brady's address to Tom and then the vans we were following turned up in the Northern Motors' car park owned by Keane.'

'Tom seemed to be satisfied that Keane had nothing to do with that,' said Clarke. Stella rolled her eyes in disbelief.

'Did you recognise the voice, Peter?' asked Adams.

'No, he used some sort of voice distorting mechanism. I'll just go to the computer room and bring you a recording. One of you may spot something that I may have missed.'

After a few minutes Blake returned with the recording. 'I've just picked up another call to Brady's phone, "Moon search tonight." I think we all know what that means and the mole got that information pretty quickly.'

Blake played the recording but no one had any idea who it could be.

'So now Brady thinks that we plan to search the Half Moon tonight,' said Stella, 'if we did, they would be expecting us and we would have egg on our faces.'

'Let's make a list of possible suspects,' said Adams.

'Everybody who was at the meeting today should be on the list,' said Clarke.

'Originally, I always felt that Keane was Brady's informer,' said Stella, 'but he couldn't have possibly known about our plans tonight. Of course, there could be more than one informer.'

'Charles Groves knew about our plans,' said Blake, 'and he is in Belfast. If you remember Jim told him about it on the phone earlier.'

'What about Mike Jones?' asked Blake, 'did anybody tell him anything?'

'He couldn't have known anything about tonight unless Captain Cosgrove told him,' said Adams.

'I think that's unlikely,' said Clarke, 'Charles wouldn't let anything slip.'

'The last call came from Belfast,' said Stella, 'and the only person who knew about tonight, who is in Belfast, is Charles Cosgrove.'

'I have a high regard for Charles,' said Clarke, 'I joined the army straight from University. When I was doing my SAS training he helped me quite a lot.'

'Is that all you know about him?' asked Stella.

'I kept in touch with him over the years,' said Clarke, 'he had a one off affair and his wife found out. She has given him a dog's life ever since. She upbraids him for not getting the promotion she thinks he is entitled to. She pushed him into buying a very expensive house. He'll do anything to pacify her.'

'If he's in financial trouble and is not happy about not being promoted,' Blake said, 'isn't it possible that he may be tempted to do something stupid?'

'I don't know that he is in financial trouble,' said Clarke, 'but I do know that his wife likes to spend money on expensive clothes and she makes several trips abroad with rich women friends. I started out to defend him but I feel as if I've put him in the dock.'

'I think we will have to put Charles on the list along with the four of us here,' said Blake, '

'What do we know about Mike Jones?' asked Clarke.

'I met him at University and we have been good friends ever since,' said Adams, 'we joined the SAS together and were eventually posted to Northern Ireland. We were recommended for Ironclad by Captain Cosgrove.'

'Mike was in Northern Ireland when Stella, Tom and I were searching Brady's farm,' said Clarke.

'That's true,' said Adams, 'but I trust him absolutely.'

'We've talked about two people who are not here to defend themselves, 'said Blake, 'we haven't talked about each other.'

'There's one other person we haven't discussed,' said Stella, 'and I think it's important that we do discuss him.'

'I presume you mean Tom,' said Clarke.

'Yes, he is ex PIRA and his buddies were Keane and Brady,' said Stella, 'he was in Northern Ireland with us and could easily have passed information to Brady.' Stella had become very heated which caused an uncomfortable silence. No one spoke for a few moments,

'He couldn't have known about the search of the Half Moon tonight,' said Adams.

'True,' said Stella, 'but, as I said earlier, there may be more than one mole and he could be one of them.'

'I don't believe that,' said Blake, 'that's a very serious accusation and he's not here to defend himself.'

'I think he should go on the list like the rest of us,' said Clarke, 'but like the rest of us we have to presume that he is innocent until proven guilty.' Clarke was very uncomfortable with Stella's attitude towards Shannon. She was, however, right in that he had worked with the Provisional IRA. Had he been turned by the PIRA? He felt guilty that he should be having such doubts about Shannon. They had worked together and Shannon had proved himself on more than one occasion.

'The point I'm making is that he is the only one on the team who has been fighting on the other side,' said Stella, 'can we trust him? Would we trust him with our lives?'

Stella had become very angry and Clarke wondered if her bad feelings about Shannon had been aggravated by the kidnapping of her brother. Then it suddenly occurred to him that she hadn't asked where Shannon was. She mustn't know that he was probably risking his life trying to rescue her brother. Would he be at liberty to tell her? Only he and Shannon were there when McDonald asked Tom to take on the task of a rescue. He couldn't mention it here; Tom's life could be at risk. He would have to wait for the right moment to tell Stella in confidence. She must be going out of her mind with worry about her brother. He felt she had a right to know that something was being done. A silence had fallen on the team again. It was obvious that everybody felt awkward. Blake broke the silence to everyone's relief.

'I wasn't sure what may develop this evening. I couldn't see us getting home for dinner so I ordered sandwiches. They'll be in the kitchen about now.'

Blake and Adams made for the door. Stella didn't move for a moment so Clarke sat down next to her.

'Stella, I know you have a lot on your mind at the moment. Please don't blame Tom for it. Tom thinks you are the best thing since sliced bread and I know he's hurt because you don't trust him'

'How can I trust him? How can any of you trust him? He's ex PIRA.'

'The girl he was going to marry was shot dead in front of him by a British soldier. It was an accident but the effect is the same. The previous year his parents had been killed in a car accident. The death of Laura was the last straw that broke him. I'm not defending what he did. It was wrong but you have to try to understand what he was going through. He must have......'

'Lots of people suffer during conflicts,' interrupted Stella, 'they don't become terrorists.'

'I'm not sure whether I'm out of order telling you this but I'll take a risk. Tom is in Northern Ireland at the moment. He's looking at the possibility of rescuing Ian. Jim asked him to go but emphasised that it was not an order but a request. He thought that with his connections in Northern Ireland he may be able to do something. He could be risking his life.'

Stella seemed stunned and didn't speak for several moments.

'Oh my God, I've been claiming that he's still a terrorist when he's risking his life trying to rescue Ian. What must you think of me? Tom must have been so hurt because I didn't believe him and I treated him so badly. He never once complained about my behaviour.' Stella began to cry and Clarke was unable to pacify her for some time.

'You didn't know, Stella. Tom understood how you felt about his PIRA connections and he couldn't think of a way of making you feel differently about him. He had hoped that the more you worked together the more you would begin to trust him. Let's hope he survives this mission because he has no backup. Only Jim and I know what Tom is doing so I will have to ask you to give me your word that you won't tell anyone else.'

'You have my word, of course, and thank you, Tony. That's a great relief to know that something is being done but now I have to worry about Ian *and* Tom. If anything happens to Tom I shall never forgive myself for the way I have treated him.'

'I've told you before; Tom is a resourceful and competent operator. I'm sure that he will pull it off.'

25

Shannon had just finished breakfast when his mobile phone rang. It was Keane. He had some information but didn't want to speak about it over the phone. Keane asked Shannon to meet him at his Belfast office. Shannon decided it would be a good opportunity to give the Harley-Davidson a spin. He arrived at Northern Motors at ten o'clock, parked the motorbike in the car park and went into the building. Keane was talking to one of his staff but broke off when he saw Shannon. They took the lift to Keane's office. As usual Keane's secretary arrived with coffee and biscuits and after she left Keane spoke.

'I've had a bit of luck. I managed to locate someone who had some dealings with Gary Ross. It's true he has a fondness of garrotting. Nothing has ever been proven because those who survived this torture are afraid of speaking. Those who didn't survive are buried God knows where. Ross is a dangerous criminal who deals ruthlessly with anyone who opposes him.'

'What about the picture Sean?'

'My informer, who obviously wants to remain anonymous, is fairly certain that the picture was taken in the cellar of the Smugglers Inn. The words are written in this order,' said Keane as he handed Shannon a piece of paper, 'I think you'll see that they fill the gaps caused by the pole.'

LET THEM HATE
AS LONG AS
THEY   FEAR

'Excellent. Now I will have to find a way to check on that cellar and if Ian is in there, try to get him out.'

'Tom, this is madness. Ross is certain to have a guard, perhaps more than one guard. You can't do this alone. You told me that Ian Bellamy's cell phone was sent to the police originally so why don't you involve them?'

'The police will have to get a search warrant and that will take time. If they search the place and Bellamy isn't there then Ross will know they're on to him. He then may kill Ian and hide the body. What about this tunnel that's supposed to run from the Inn to the beach?'

'I don't know if there's any truth in that rumour. My contact did me a hand drawing of where he thought the tunnel was,' Keane took a sheet of paper from his desk drawer and handed it to Shannon, 'he couldn't guarantee that it was correct.'
Shannon studied the drawing and said, 'It seems that the tunnel doesn't run to the beach. It looks as if it ends at a fort. Is there a fort in that area?'

'There is a fort there but it's a museum. I'm told, however, that there is also a ruin of some ancient fort so it could be that. I don't think it could be the museum but I'm not familiar with the area.'

When Shannon left Keane he made his way to Helen's Bay on his Harley-Davidson. It was a dry, sunny day ideal for bikers. When he arrived in the area he soon found the fort which Keane had said was a museum. It looked fairly modern. He moved along for several more minutes enjoying the scenery when he found himself in a wooded area. He turned down a footpath which seemed to be well trodden and probably led to the beach. Eventually he came to the fort Keane described as a ruin of an ancient fort. He was certainly right about that. A lot of the stone walls had collapsed. There was one tower-like building which Shannon could see at the far end of the site. He parked his bike and scrambled over the piles of stones. When he got near to the tower he could see that it was only the ground floor that had survived. There were stone stairs built in a spiral leading to nowhere.

This didn't look good. Perhaps the story about the tunnel was just a myth. He looked around the rest of the ruin but couldn't find anything which suggested the entrance to a tunnel. If there was a tunnel and if it did lead to this fort then it could be under all this stone and rubble. It would take weeks to excavate and he had less than a week. It looked hopeless and Shannon was now feeling desperate.

Shannon went through a gap in the wall adjacent to the tower which looked as if it were once a doorway. The ground here was mostly overgrown with a few stones from the fort scattered around. He wandered aimlessly feeling very disappointed. He had hoped to find the tunnel. He would now have to think of some other way to rescue Bellamy. He sat down on a large stone and stared into space. He suddenly became aware of a mound of earth almost hidden by shrubs and trees. It wasn't visible when he was standing up but from the sitting position he could just make out the shape. He crawled through the shrubbery and saw what appeared to be a hole in the mound. He was elated. Had he found the tunnel entrance? He clawed away at the earth, removed several stones and some of the vegetation. He could now see a wooden archway underneath the soil. This had obviously been built much later than the fort. If this was the tunnel he was looking for, it was patently obvious that it hadn't been used for long time.

He brought a high powered torch and a short shafted spade from his bike. With the spade he was able to remove some of the smaller shrubs which made it easier to enter the tunnel. He had to stoop in order to move along. He was surprised to see how well the tunnel had been constructed. Clearly good timbers had been used. There had been some small falls of earth which did slow down his progress but he came across one very bad fall which reduced the height of the tunnel by half. Using the spade he cleared some of the debris and scattered it about the floor of the tunnel behind him. It would have been possible for him to crawl through the gap but he didn't know what condition Bellamy would be in and they would probably have to make a quick getaway. If he was badly hurt then it would be problematic. He would have to try to clear some of the debris in the place where there had been a bad fall. After about an hour he came to an area where he could stand upright. His heart missed a beat when he saw a wooden door. He tried the handle but it wouldn't move. He noticed that the hinges had been fixed on his side of the door. There didn't appear to be any keyhole. He retraced his steps down the tunnel, removing some of the fallen earth and scattering it around as best he could. When he arrived at the bad fall it took some time to remove enough earth to make it reasonably easy to move along. He had to scatter the earth down the tunnel in both directions. If Bellamy was in bad shape then he would have had difficulty scrambling through the narrow gap. He hoped he had removed enough of the earth to allow Bellamy to move along easily. It was difficult, dirty work in a restricted area and Shannon was glad when he had completed it and arrived at the end of the tunnel. He gathered some bushes and covered the entrance to the tunnel. He then collected some stones and other debris and spread them about the area in an attempt to cover up his footprints. He was looking forward to a good, hot shower.

Shannon travelled up in the lift to Keane's office. He had been back to the cottage, had a shower and a change of clothing. Keane was expecting him. Shannon told him about the old fort and the tunnel.

'So what are your plans, Tom?'

'I think the best time to try to get into the cellar would be in the early hours of the morning. The pub will be closed and hopefully most people will be asleep.'

'Are you still going to do this alone?'

'Yes, but I will have to ask you for one more favour. I need a weapon. I obviously couldn't bring one with me on the plane.'

'I anticipated that,' Keane unlocked a drawer in his desk and produced a Walther, 'it can't be traced.'

'Thanks, Sean. I owe you.'

'When do you intend to make the rescue?'

'Tomorrow morning about three o'clock.'

'Be careful, Tom, Ross is a vicious criminal. Why don't you let me help you?'

'You've already helped me. I couldn't have got this far without you. You have a wife and children so I don't think you should take the risk.'

'Okay, you've got my number in your cell phone. If things go wrong give me a call.'

It was exactly three in the morning when Shannon arrived back at the door in the tunnel. He had brought a haversack with a collection of tools along with the Walther tucked in his belt. He tried the door again but it wouldn't budge. He took a screw driver and a spray can of multipurpose lubricant from his haversack and proceeded to try to remove the screws from the hinges. They were well rusted and difficult to move in spite of the lubricant. He had to take care that he didn't break the heads. Progress was slow. He stopped periodically and listened. There was no sound from the other side of the door. He first removed all the screws which were holding the hinges to the jamb. He then bent back the hinges and used them as handles to lift the door out. After a struggle he managed to remove it. He placed the door quietly against the wall of the tunnel. To his dismay he could see, a few paces away, another door. This door didn't have any hinges on his side of the door. Had he run out of luck?

He stopped and listened again. No sound. To his surprise the handle on the second door turned but the door didn't open. He could see a keyhole. He took out a set of skeleton keys from his rucksack. Clarke had taught him a trick or two about picking locks. It took him ten minutes before the lock turned. He switched off his torch and opened the door quietly. As his eyes adjusted to the dark he could make out a bed against the opposite wall. He approached the bed then switched on the torch but turned it away from the bed. The only other piece of furniture in the room was a chair. The pole he had seen on the cell phone picture was in the middle of the room and the writing on the wall confirmed that he was in the right place. He turned his attention to the bed. There was someone in it. He could see that the man had been badly beaten and he hoped he was conscious. He shook him gently. The man murmured. He shook him again. The man opened his eyes, he looked ill. One of his eyes was badly bruised and completely closed with cuts and bruises all over his face.

'Can you walk?' The man nodded. He raised himself up and sat on the edge of the bed.

'Who are you? Are you someone new to give me another beating?'

'My name is Shannon and I have come to get you out of this place. Are you Ian Bellamy?'

'Yes.'

'Okay, let's go.'

Shannon helped Bellamy to stand up. He didn't seem too steady on his feet but they made it through the first door. Shannon closed the door and then explained to Bellamy that they would have to travel along a tunnel in single file and there wouldn't be much head room. Bellamy nodded.

They moved very slowly through the tunnel stopping regularly so that Bellamy could rest. On one of the occasions when they stopped Bellamy said, 'I've just remembered that they check me every two hours. They wake me up and tell me the time. I'm sure that the reason was so that I didn't get a decent night's sleep.'

'So what time did they last check on you?'

'They said it was two o'clock but I couldn't be sure that they were telling the truth.'

'If they were telling the truth then they should be checking the cellar about now. They'll probably panic for a few minutes but eventually come to the conclusion that you've escaped through the tunnel somehow. We'd better get a move on.'

They tried to move a little faster but it was difficult for Bellamy who seemed to be in a lot of pain. Shannon could hear some shouting and then some movement coming in their direction along the tunnel.

'Ian, I want you to keep moving through the tunnel. I'll wait here and surprise them with a bullet or two. They won't be expecting any resistance.' Shannon gave him a pencil torch.

Bellamy crawled away and Shannon lay flat on the ground in the dark. As soon as he saw a torch light appear he fired two shots and two men fell to the ground and they didn't move again. He paused for a moment to make sure that they were not faking then he followed Bellamy. He caught up with him fairly quickly. They moved very slowly because Bellamy was weak and in pain. When they reached the end of the tunnel Shannon helped Bellamy out through the shrubbery.

'Well, well, what have we here? Two rabbits perhaps.'

Two men were standing near the entrance to the tunnel. Both men had weapons.

'Oh my God. It's Ross and one of his henchmen,' whispered Bellamy.

'And who's your friend, Mr Bellamy?'

'My name is Shannon.'

'Well we don't need you Shannon so kneel down. A bullet in the back of the head will make it look as if you've upset one of the Real IRA terrorists.'

'Don't be stupid,' said Shannon, 'you will add murder to the kidnapping. The police know we are here.'

'Good try,' said Ross, 'If the police knew you were here they would be here too. I see no police.'

Shannon was forced to his knees by the henchman and Ross pointed his gun at Shannon's head. Shannon thought of Stella. He had fouled up and now he and Stella's brother were going to die. A shot rang out and Ross fell to the ground. The other man turned and raised his weapon but didn't get a chance to fire as another shot rang out and he too fell to the ground. Out from the shadow of the trees stepped Keane.

153

'I thought you may need some help. I knew you were too stubborn to ask for it.'

'Sean, you're a sight for sore eyes.'

'I've got my car parked at the edge of the wood. I think I should take this young man to hospital.'

'I'll follow you on the Harley-Davidson.'

It was after six o'clock in the morning when Shannon returned from the hospital to the cottage. He had contacted McDonald to let him know that Bellamy was safe but in hospital. He showered and fell exhausted into bed. It was one o'clock in the afternoon when he surfaced. He went into the kitchen and made a coffee. He had left his mobile phone on the kitchen table and it was bleeping to let him know that there was a text message waiting for him. He opened it. It was from Stella, it read:

"Tom, you risked your life rescuing Ian. Mum and I will be forever grateful. Tom, I need to speak with you. I'm flying over to Holywood today. I should be there by 4pm. Please meet me there if you can. I'll understand if you don't want to see me. Stella."

26

Shannon arrived at Holywood army base at a quarter to four. As he was parking his car, Charles Cosgrove greeted him, 'Hello, old chap. Stella has arrived and is in the conference room. I have to dash to take care of some matter but I've arranged for coffee to be laid on for you.' Shannon smiled as Cosgrove "dashed" off across the parade ground. He was thinking of Clarke's words, 'Charles is the salt of the earth and of the old school, a real gentleman.'

Stella stood when she saw Shannon enter the conference room. She took a few steps towards him then stopped. She looked at Shannon, her big, green eyes filled with tears.

'Tom.....Tom I.....Tom please hold me.' Tears streamed down her cheeks. Shannon moved quickly towards her. He took her in his arms. She wrapped her arms around his neck and sobbed. Shannon was in heaven. He was going to hold on to her and never let her go. They held each other for several minutes until Stella calmed down.

'I think you need a good cup of coffee,' said Shannon as he brought the coffee pot and cups over to the conference table.

'Tom,' said Stella, drying her tears, 'I've treated you very badly and I've said some terrible things about you. What did you do? You suffered me in silence and then risked your life saving my brother. Can you ever forgive me?'

'There's nothing to forgive. You must have been shocked when you learned about my past. It must have made you feel very insecure. We have a dangerous job and it's important that we trust each other. I completely understand how you must have felt.'

'I didn't listen when Tony said that he would trust you with his life and he knew you far better than I did.'

'Wow, is that what he said?'

'He also told me that you said that I was the best thing since sliced bread. I've never been compared with sliced bread before.'

They both burst into laughter. The laughter took all the tension away and Shannon took both her hands in his.

'It's good to see you laugh, Stella. Let's go to the hospital now and see how Ian is getting on.'

At the hospital Stella cried again as she kissed her brother. Shannon had warned her that he had a couple of broken ribs so she refrained from giving him a hug.

'It's good to see you safe. Mum sends her love.' said Stella as she held her brother's hand.

'I'm safe because of this handsome guy standing beside you. I'm glad he's on our side.' Stella took Shannon's hand and squeezed it. Then Ian added, 'I'll never be able to repay you, Tom.'

'I had some help,' said Shannon.

'Yes, the mystery man. He appeared out of nowhere and disappeared again. I still don't know who he is. I think Tom would agree that he appeared in the nick of time.'

'He is a good friend but he wants to remain anonymous.'

'If you see him again tell him if I can ever help him, in any way at all, he only has to ask.'

'I think we had better leave now,' said Stella, 'we've been here too long and you are looking tired.'

Stella leaned over and kissed her brother. She was still holding Shannon's hand as they moved away from the bed. Ian spotted this and said, 'I hope you two are an item because I rather like the idea of having Tom for a brother-in-law.'

'You're far too cheeky,' said Stella, 'you must be getting better.'

27

After McDonald left the team in the conference room, ruminating over the possibility of a mole in their midst, he returned to his office. He was still there at ten o'clock that evening when his phone rang. It was the Assistant Chief Constable, Harry Simpson.

'Hello, Harry, I hope you've got some good news for me.'

'I'm sorry for the delay in getting back to you but things have been a bit hectic. I'm afraid it's a mixture of good news and bad. I'll give you the bad news first. We didn't find any trace of drugs or Semtex at the Half Moon Club.'

'That is bad news. I'm hoping the good news is very good.'

'It probably is. A man was brought into The Manchester Royal by ambulance from the Half Moon Club a couple of days ago. He was suffering from two bullet wounds. The man's name is Frank Doyle. He was accompanied by a man called Peter Byrne who claims to be his cousin. Are these names familiar to you?'

'Harry, you've just made my day. These two men were members of the PIRA and I would very much like my boys to have a word with them.'

'Frank Doyle is in the intensive care unit at The Royal. We've had Peter Byrne in custody for two days but we haven't been able to get anything out of him. If he is a suspect terrorist we could hold him for a few days longer.'

'Would you be prepared to hand him over to me?'

'Certainly, when do you want him?'

'It's a bit too late now so we'll let him sweat it out overnight. I'll send someone to pick him up tomorrow.'

Next morning Stella and Shannon arrived at the conference room at the same time. They were met with a standing ovation from Clarke, Blake and Adams. McDonald came in having heard the commotion and shook Shannon's hand.

'Well done, Tom.' He then turned to Stella, 'How is Ian?'

'He's safe thanks to Tom, that's the main thing. He took quite a beating but his body will mend in time.'

'Excellent. Well I have a bit of good news. Harry Simpson has Peter Byrne in custody and I want Tom and Tony to pick him up from the police station.'

An hour later Byrne was in the interview room at The Priory. Byrne was seated at a table opposite Clarke.

'What is this place? What am I doing here?' demanded Byrne.

'We ask the questions and you answer them,' replied Clarke.

'I've nothing to say,' retorted Byrne as he folded his arms and sat back in his chair.

'We know your name is Peter Byrne and the man in the intensive care unit, suffering from bullet wounds, is your cousin Frank Doyle. Am I correct?'

'No comment.'

'We also know that you and Doyle were members of the Provisional IRA.'

Byrne didn't speak. Shannon had been leaning against the wall behind Clarke listening to the interaction. He moved forward and placed both hands on the table.

'We know who you are,' hissed Shannon, 'you are one of Brady's men and you are going to go to prison for a very long time. In fact I'm going to make sure that you go to prison for life.'

'You've got nothing on me,' snarled Byrne.

'We can prove that you and Doyle were at Dooley's warehouse moving Semtex and drugs to the Half Moon Club.'

That piece of information seemed to unsettle Byrne but he kept silent.

'You will be surprised to know,' threatened Clarke, 'that we have the power to put you in solitary for the rest of your life. Nobody will know where you are.'

Byrne shifted in his chair and there was a hint of nervousness in his eyes.

'You and your cousin Frank are in big trouble,' said Shannon, 'but Frank is in worse trouble than you, isn't he? Your cousin Frank is in hospital in intensive care and he is not expected to live. Isn't that correct?'

Shannon realised that he had hit a nerve because Byrne was visibly shocked by this announcement.

'Who said Frank's dying?' Byrne jumped up from his chair and it took Shannon and Clarke a couple of minutes to get him seated again.

'Our information is that he was left for days without proper medical attention,' said Clarke, 'how could you do that to another human being?'

'We have also been told,' said Shannon, 'that if he had been brought in earlier he would have had a good chance to live. You wouldn't treat a dog like that.'

'What do you mean? If you know something about Frank, tell me. Are you saying that Frank won't live?' Byrne was getting agitated again.

'If you'd been a decent man, a decent cousin,' said Clarke, 'you could have saved his life.'

'It wasn't my fault. I tried to get him to hospital but I was prevented by....,' Byrne stopped speaking mid sentence.

'Who prevented you? Was it Declan Brady?' asked Clarke.

Byrne didn't answer.

'What were you doing at the Half Moon Club?' asked Shannon.

Byrne remained silent.

'We know that Semtex and other illegal substances have been delivered to the Half Moon Club and we know you and Doyle had a hand in it,' said Shannon.

'That's a bloody lie.'

'You and Doyle were seen at Dooley's warehouse loading a Transit van with the shipment from Northern Ireland. That's where Doyle got his bullet wounds. Isn't that correct?' asked Clarke.

'You can't prove that,' scowled Byrne.

'We'll give you a break now,' said Clarke, 'we'll talk some more this afternoon.'

Shannon moved away from the table and Clarke followed him to the door.

'You can't leave without telling me how Frank is,' screamed Byrne, 'is he going to die?'

'Just keep reminding yourself that his life is in danger because of you,' replied Clarke.

'Why should you care?' snapped Shannon, 'you'll never see him again.'

'You bastards,' screeched Byrne as Clarke and Shannon left the room.

After lunch Byrne was taken back into the interview room by Sergeant Dave Thomas. A few minutes later Clarke and Shannon joined them and Thomas left.

'I'm afraid I've got some bad news for you Peter,' said Clarke, 'your cousin Frank died about an hour ago.'

'You're lying,' screamed Byrne, 'you just want me to grass on my mates.'

'I'm sorry but it's true,' said Clarke, 'we are going to take you to the hospital shortly where you will be asked to formally identify your cousin.'

'All right,' said Byrne, 'take me to the hospital. I'll believe it when I see him because I don't trust you two bastards.'

When Byrne saw Doyle's body at the hospital he was shocked. Doyle had obviously suffered a great deal and it showed in his face. He had been convinced that Shannon and Clarke had been lying and were planning some sort of trick. He hadn't been prepared for this. He knew that Frank had died unnecessarily and Brady was to blame. Brady would pay one way or another. The big, hard man sobbed and almost collapsed. Clarke and Shannon had to help him into a chair. He sat with his head in his hands.

'Oh Frank, I'm so sorry, I'm so sorry,' Byrne moaned.

The return journey to The Priory was made mostly in total silence. Byrne did not respond to any attempt at conversation by Clarke and Shannon. It seem almost as though he was in some form of catatonic state. On arrival at The Priory, Byrne was taken up to his room by Sergeant Thomas. He made no protest nor did he ask where he was being taken. It appeared as if his mind had taken a trip to another planet. Clarke and Shannon joined Blake and Adams in the computer room. As soon as they sat down McDonald walked in.

'How did it go at the hospital?' he asked.

'It would be an understatement to say that Byrne was upset,' said Shannon.

'Yea, he's pretty shaken up,' added Clarke, 'and I don't think he's fit for any further questioning today. In fact, we were so concerned at his reaction to his cousin's death that we asked one of the doctors to check him over. We were told that he was okay.'

'Did you manage to get any information out of him?'

'I'm afraid not,' answered Shannon, 'but I think we've found his Achilles heel. It's the death of his cousin. I would guess that Doyle suffered a great deal before he died and I'm fairly sure that Byrne blames Brady. We are convinced that Brady prevented Byrne from taking Doyle to hospital.'

'I agree with Tom,' said Clarke,' if we leave him to stew overnight, give him a chance to think things over, he may be ready to talk in the morning.'

'All right,' said McDonald, 'that will have to do for now. Our investigation seems to have reached an impasse. The police couldn't find anything at the Half Moon and our cameras haven't picked up anything. Our only chance is Byrne. Let's hope you can squeeze something out of him tomorrow. There's nothing more we can do tonight so I'll see you in the morning.' McDonald left.

'Jim's right, we have reached an impasse,' said Shannon.

'There's something else you may be interested in,' said Blake, 'Connors and Daley arrived at Manchester Airport today and were booked in at the Grand Hotel.'

'They're two of Brady's hard men, 'said Shannon, 'something must be brewing.'

'I believe that you are on duty tonight, Peter,' said Shannon.

'That's true. No rest for the wicked.'

'What are your plans for tonight, Paul?'

'The Colonel has asked me to stay here tonight and help Dave Thomas to babysit Byrne and, of course, to help Peter drink his whiskey.'

'Okay, we'll see you both tomorrow,' said Shannon.

On the way out of The Priory Clarke said, 'I haven't seen Stella since lunchtime.'

'She's over at my flat.'

'Ah, a cosy night in, is it? Have you two become an item again?'

'It's early days yet. I wanted to take her out to dinner to celebrate Ian's rescue. She said she would prefer to cook a meal herself and you're invited.'

'Thank you very much. I hope Stella's cooking is good because I remember your skills in the kitchen were pretty much non-existent.'

'Don't push your luck, laddie.'

28

Brady picked up Dave Connors and Pat Daley from Manchester Airport. He booked them into the Grand Hotel and the three of them sat in the bedroom discussing the best way to get rid of Shannon. They eventually retired to the bar and after a couple hours they decided to have a meal in the restaurant. After the meal Brady left and returned to the Half Moon Club. He was met by Max Parker.

'What the hell's been going on here?' asked Parker.

'I don't know what you mean.'

'In the early hours of this morning two guys overdosed in the club. They were taken to hospital and one of them died. As expected the police arrived this afternoon with a search warrant. I knew they wouldn't find anything but I was concerned that Doyle was upstairs with two bullet wounds.'

'Jeez, so we're in deep shit.'

'That's what I thought but when the police left without a word I shot upstairs to check. Byrne and Doyle had disappeared.'

'That's all right then.'

'No it's not. The police were back here twenty minutes later. They wanted to know why I hadn't reported a shooting at the club. I explained that I had been away from the premises on business and so didn't know of any shooting. Luckily I was able to give them details of my business meeting.'

'How did you explain that a wounded man was in the club when it wasn't opened until later in the evening?'

'I said that I could only think that the cleaners had forgotten to lock the side door when they left and the man had got in that way.'

'Hang on a minute. I completely forgot. When I was driving back from the airport my mobile rang. I wasn't able to answer it.' Brady checked his voicemail. 'It was my informer telling me that the club would be raided tonight. The police obviously used the death of that smack head to raid it earlier.'

'It looks as if Byrne took Doyle to hospital. You can bet your shirt that Byrne is in custody and if anything happens to Doyle then he may spill the beans,'

'Byrne will keep his mouth shut,' growled Brady, 'he'll not want to lose his share of the proceeds.'

'You can't depend on that. Doyle and Byrne are family. If Doyle dies he'll blame you and don't forget he knows where the drugs and Semtex are hidden.'

'Then I'll have him removed along with Shannon. Did you get me the information on Shannon's flat?'

'Yes, a pal of mine owns a newsagents and he supplies newspapers to the flats. He gave me the code number for the main entrance door.'

'These informers of yours, are they reliable?'

'They'd better be, they're costing me an arm and a leg and I've got them on tape accepting my money.'

The phone rang and Max Parker answered it, 'Yes, they're okay. Show them up to my office,'

'It sounds as if Connors and Daley have found their way here.'

'Can you rely on these guys? Shannon is a very shrewd and dangerous operator.'

Before Brady could answer Connors and Daley walked in.

'Sit down fellas. This is Max Parker and he's done some very useful research for us. He's going to tell you about it now.'

'This is a map showing you how to get to St. John's Mews,' explained Parker as he handed them a sheet of paper, 'on the bottom of the sheet I have written the flat number and also a four digit number which is the code you will need to gain access to the building. In the entrance porch you will see a key pad on the wall, tap in the code and the door will open.'

'Before you top Shannon there's something I need to know,' said Brady, 'find out where Byrne and Doyle are being held. If Shannon's got them then there's a bigger risk that they may talk. I want to know if they've told Shannon where the Semtex and drugs are hidden. I think you know how to make them talk.'

'It'll be my pleasure, Declan,' said Connors.

'Do you have any questions?'

'How far is it from here?' asked Daley.

'I'm going to drop you off at the Science Museum,' answered Daley, 'it's only a few minutes' walk from there. When the job's done walk back to the Grand Hotel, I'll meet you there. It will be safer than using a car. Remember, do the job as quietly as possible and don't leave any fingerprints behind. Make sure nobody sees you entering the building and destroy the paper Max has given you.'

Brady and the two men left and Parker fixed himself a double gin and tonic. He had become a bit nervous about his association with Brady. The shooting at Dooley's warehouse was a big mistake and he began to feel that Brady's men were incompetent. Now it appeared that Byrne and Doyle were in the hands of the police. Connors and Daley were on their way to kill Shannon. He was doubtful they had the wherewithal to surprise and overcome Shannon. Brady seemed to be well organised and up to now he had managed to keep one step ahead of Shannon and the police. He certainly had some excellent informers but his men didn't seem to be up to it. He sat in a chair nursing his drink, full of doom and gloom, when the door opened and his brother Raz walked in.

'How was the flight?' asked Max.

'It was fine. Anything exciting happened here during my absence?'

'Sit down and I'll tell you all about it but I think you will need a stiff drink first,' said Max who was looking very tired. He poured them both a large gin and tonic then brought his brother up to date.

'I hope that Connors and Daley know what they're doing,' sighed Raz Parker.

'I'll drink to that because Shannon's no pushover.'

29

After the meal was over Stella made the coffee. Clarke had volunteered to load the dishwasher and Shannon organised the cognac.

'I'm sorry Peter couldn't make it tonight,' said Stella as she brought the coffee to the table.

'Both he and Paul are on duty. Peter is keeping a watch on the Half Moon Club with some help from Paul and, of course, we have Byrne as a guest.'

'Has Byrne given you anything yet?' asked Stella.

'No, it could be a long day tomorrow,' said Clarke.

'I suppose it depends on how cooperative Byrne is,' said Shannon.

'I thought the death of his cousin would have loosened his tongue,' said Stella.

'These are hard men we are dealing with, Stella,' said Shannon, 'they're in the business to make money and they don't have any scruples about how they do it. These are the kind of guys who jumped on the PIRA band wagon so they could indulge in criminal activities.'

'We're hoping that the death of Doyle will soften up Byrne but we're not sure. We'll have to see what other levers we can come up with,' said Clarke.

'Will you be able to offer him some sort of deal?' asked Stella.

'Jim's looking into that,' said Shannon, 'strictly speaking he's in police custody. The police are not usually too happy about making deals.' Clarke looked at his watch. 'Look at the time. It's ten-thirty and way past my bedtime. I'm also encroaching on your time together. Love birds need time together.'

'Ignore him, Stella. You know that Tony loves to switch into teasing mode. You'll get used to it.'

'Well, I must go,' said Clarke, 'what time tomorrow?'

'I think we should start about nine o'clock.'

'That sounds like a civilised hour,' replied Clarke, 'see you then. Thank you Stella for a wonderful meal and I shall be forever grateful that you kept Tom out of the kitchen.'

'Get out of here,' laughed Shannon as he threw a tea towel at him. After Clarke left, Stella and Shannon collected the coffee cups and took them into the kitchen. The door bell rang.

'Perhaps Tony's forgotten something,' said Stella.

'Or it could be Simon,' said Shannon, 'he's a pilot and when he's away I collect any parcels that may be delivered and keep an eye on his flat when I'm here. He pops in with a bottle of duty free now and then.'

'Does he usually call so late?'

'Not usually, perhaps his flight was delayed. I'll go see who it is.' Shannon opened the door. Connors pointing a hand gun, forced him back into the living room and then pushed him down into a chair. Stella, hearing the commotion, came out of the kitchen. She quickly took in the scene and reached for her handbag on the sofa.

'Naughty, naughty,' smirked Daley as he grabbed her wrist and pushed her against the wall. He picked up the handbag and emptied the contents on the sofa, 'what do we have here my darlin'? Oh it's a Walther. What's a pretty, little girl like you doing with a dangerous weapon like this? I prefer something like this.' He opened up his flick knife. 'Now be a good girl and sit on that chair next to your boy friend.'

'Where are you holding Byrne and Doyle?' asked Connors as he held his gun against Shannon's head.

'What makes you think I'm holding them?'

'Don't be a smart ass, just answer the question and make it easier on yourself.'

'I don't understand the question.'

'We know that Byrne and Doyle have been arrested and we also know that you've had a hand in it. Don't push your luck, Shannon, or you'll be sorry.'

168

'Who told you that I'm involved?'

'Brady, he's been keeping his eye on you.'

'Does he know that Doyle is in hospital?' asked Shannon, stalling for time and hoping that he could think of something to get them out of this predicament. Unfortunately, the old grey matter wasn't coming up with anything.

'He knows that Doyle has a couple of gunshot wounds.'

'You said that you knew that both of them had been arrested. I've told you where Doyle is so Byrne must be in the hands of the police.' Shannon could see that Connors was getting impatient and so he would have to bring his stalling to an end.

'What you obviously don't know is that Doyle has died from his gunshot wounds caused by neglect. Brady wouldn't let Byrne take him to the hospital for treatment. I can tell you that Byrne isn't very happy about that.'

'Tough, so where is Byrne?' asked Connors, 'we know he's not in the hands of the police.'

'I think it's time you started talking,' said Daley as he held his flick knife against Stella's face, 'unless you want me to make a mess of this pretty, little face.'

'Okay,' snapped Shannon getting concerned about Stella, 'what do you want to know?'

'I want to know where he is being held,' said Connors.

'He's being held in a high security unit.'

'Where is that?'

'It's on the south side of the city and it's heavily guarded so you won't be able to get in.'

'What has Byrne told you?'

'He's told us nothing.'

'Has he told you anything about....,' Connors hesitated. Not quite sure how to phrase the question.

'I've already told you, he's told us nothing.'

'I don't believe that,' barked Connors.

'Let me draw some pretty patterns on this pretty face,' sniggered Daley, 'that'll make him talk.'

'Hang on a minute, there's something else you don't know.'

'There ye are Dave,' grinned Daley, 'I knew the thought of this pretty face being rearranged would make him talk.'

'I've no idea what you think he may have told us but he has said nothing. In fact, since the death of his cousin he hasn't spoken a word to anyone. He's suffering from some sort of trauma.'

'What's trauma mean, Dave?' asked Daley.

'It's some sort of shock which sometimes affects speech, don't you know anything?' said Connors preening himself and feeling a little superior.

'That's right,' said Shannon quickly, wishing to reinforce Connor's definition, 'that's exactly it, like I said he hasn't been able to speak.'

'If Byrne can't speak, Brady will be satisfied with that,' said Connors, 'I don't think he'll want to break into a heavily guarded security unit.'

'You're right, Dave,' said Daley, 'if Byrne can't speak then he can't tell them anything. You deal with him and I'll take this pretty little thing into the bedroom.'

'You'd better be quick,' scowled Connors, 'I don't want to be hanging around here too long.'

Daley grabbed hold of Stella and began to drag her towards the bedroom. As she struggled Daley dropped his knife in an attempt to hold on to her. Stella turned quickly and taking Daley's wrist she twisted him over on to his back and then kicked him in the crotch. This distracted Connors who turned as if to help Daley. That was a mistake. This gave Shannon the opportunity to reach for his .25 Bauer pistol from his ankle holster. He pushed the pistol hard into Connors' ear.

'Drop the gun or your brains will be decorating my walls and that would make me very angry.'

Connors dropped his gun and Stella picked it up. Daley was still writhing on the floor.

'I'd forgotten that you specialised in the Martial Arts,' smiled Shannon, 'I'll ring the police. I'm sure they'll be able to find them a bed for the night or perhaps longer.'

After the police had gone Shannon made another coffee and they sat together on the sofa.

'Stella, I hope you weren't upset by Tony's comments about us being love birds. I thought you looked a little embarrassed. He was just teasing again.'

'I'm sure that Tony means well. He's a good friend of yours but I feel he is pushing you along a path you aren't ready for. I know you lost someone very dear to you in terrible circumstances and I'm sure the hurt is so deep that it is difficult to recover.'

'I'm very fond of you, Stella. When I first met you my heart missed a beat. I've never felt like this for a long time but my feelings are a little mixed up at the moment. I feel guilty about Laura's death and I feel guilty about my time with the PIRA. I'm damaged. I'm afraid that I may hurt you and I wouldn't want that to happen.'

Stella put her arms around him and gave him a hug. Her heart was breaking for the hurt she knew he was suffering and her cheeks were wet with tears. She wanted to hold him close and kiss away the pain but she wasn't sure he was ready for that yet.

'Let's drink the coffee before it gets cold,' said Stella, brushing away the tears with her hand.

'Now you're upset,' said Shannon seeing the tears.

'I'm okay. It's just that I can see the hurt in your eyes and there is nothing I can do to help.'

'You've already helped, more than you know.'

'I've given you a lot of grief ever since you told me you had worked with the PIRA. That couldn't have helped.'

'Your family has a military background so I understood how you felt.'
They finished their coffee and Shannon looked at his watch and then stood up 'It's late,' he said 'let me walk you home. It's been a very unusual evening. The fresh air will do us good.'

Stella linked Shannon's arm and they walked in silence through the Manchester City streets. It was a warm night. The sky was cloudless and the moon was full. They seemed to be completely oblivious of people passing by. When they arrived at Stella's flat Shannon waited until Stella was safely inside. Stella turned to Shannon and said, 'Thank you for seeing me home, Tom.'

'It's been my pleasure, Stella. Good night and I hope to see you tomorrow.'

'Tom' Shannon turned around and Stella put her arms around his neck and they kissed for the first time. It was a long, sweet kiss. Once again Stella's eyes filled with tears but this time for a different reason. As Shannon walked home to his flat his thoughts were full of Stella and he hoped that this relationship would last. He was convinced she was good for him. He hoped that he would be good for her because he had a lot of baggage. He would have to make sure that she didn't get hurt because of his ghosts from the past. They both had dangerous jobs and that worried him a lot. That was the downside.

30

It was nine o'clock the following morning. Shannon and Clarke were in the interviewing room at the Priory. Shannon had just finished telling Clarke about the forced entry into his flat by Connors and Daley, when Sergeant Dave Thomas brought Byrne into the room. After Thomas had left, Clarke pointed to the chair at the table and Byrne sat down. Clarke sat in the chair opposite. Shannon remained standing, leaning against the wall behind Clarke.

'Well, Peter,' began Clarke, 'you've had some time to think things over. Are you prepared to help us with our investigation?'
Byrne remained silent for a few minutes, his eyes focused on the table. Clarke began to wonder if perhaps Byrne had not fully recovered from the death of his cousin. He had taken it very badly and in hindsight it may have been wise to have given him some more time. Clarke also remembered Shannon describing Byrne and Doyle as two hard, ruthless men. He also realised that it was essential that they found the drugs and Semtex and the sooner the better. He decided to press on.

'Peter,' said Clarke, 'you must know now that Brady doesn't care a damn about you or your cousin Frank. If he did he wouldn't have let Frank die. You can't trust him.'

'I don't know you. How do I know that I can trust you?'

'I suppose you don't,' answered Clarke, 'but surely we must have the same goal, to put Brady away.'

'Everybody has an angle. Everybody looks after number one. I don't see that you are any different.'

'Well, you know what I want. I want to put Brady away for a long time. I thought that you would want to help us to do that.'

'You'll never get Brady.'

'What makes you so sure?'

'Brady is very clever and he has his informers all over the place. He knows what you're going to do before you do.'

'Are his informers that good?'

'Why do you think that you've not been able to catch him?'

'Perhaps our luck is changing,' suggested Clarke, 'we've got you and last night Connors and Daley were arrested for attempted murder.'

'You've got nothing on me and you've got nothing on Brady,' snapped Byrne.

Shannon moved across to the table.

'We've got enough on you to put you away for a long, long time,' said Shannon as he leaned on the table and pushed his face closer to Byrne, 'I think we should cut this crap and stick you in solitary and throw away the key.'

'So now we're playing good cop, bad cop,' smirked Byrne.

'We can prove that you were at Dooley's warehouse loading illegal substances into a white Transit van,' claimed Shannon.

'You can't prove that,' protested Byrne, 'where are these so called illegal substances?'

'We can also prove that you shot and wounded someone at the warehouse,' said Shannon ignoring Byrne's protest.

'That wasn't me. That was.....' Byrne stopped abruptly.

'You were going to blame Frank, weren't you?' said Shannon.

Byrne didn't reply and now looked very uncomfortable.

'Peter,' said Clarke, 'Brady was responsible for Frank's death and yet you're trying to protect him.'

This seemed to strike a nerve and Byrne shifted uneasily in his chair. He didn't speak.

'Right,' said Shannon, 'this is the situation. The police arrested you for not reporting a gunshot wound and being in possession of a firearm. If we hand you back to the police then you will get a long custodial sentence. When we get Brady, and rest assured we will, we will have evidence that you were involved in dealing with illegal substances because Brady's not going to save your neck. He'll do his best to get a deal for himself.'

'Don't forget Peter,' said Clarke, 'that Connors and Daley are in police custody. They may be thinking about doing a deal because they are facing an attempted murder charge. If they do then you will go down along with Brady.'
This seemed to have the required effect. Byrne now looked extremely nervous.

'What kind of deal will you give me?'

'If you cooperate with us,' said Clarke, 'we could put in a recommendation of leniency. It all depends on what you can offer.'

'Is that the best you can do? Brady's sure to find out that I grassed on him and then I'm a dead man.'

'Believe me,' said Clarke, 'if you help us we'll have enough on him to put him away until he is a very old man. He hasn't been able to move the drugs or Semtex. He obviously has a good hiding place in the Half Moon Club because the police haven't been able to find them.'

'I told you Brady was clever,'

'He's not going to sit on those drugs too long,' said Clarke, 'he'll want a return on his investment. When he does try to move them, then we'll have him.'

'He'll wait his time,' said Byrne, 'he can't be short of money. He's got millions from the bank robbery.' As soon as the words left his mouth, Byrne realised that he had made a mistake.

'Ah,' said Shannon, 'so you know about the bank robbery and the murder of the Carson family. Something else we can throw at you, accessory after the fact, probably before the fact too. I think you've added a few more years onto your sentence.'

'I had nothing to do with the bank robbery or the murder' shouted Byrne.

'Maybe,' said Shannon, 'but you knew of it and didn't report it to the police. An assistant bank manager and his family were terrorised by the robbers and then murdered. You have just confirmed, what we

175

have always suspected, that it was Brady and his cronies who committed the crime and we have it all on tape.'

'I advise you to cooperate,' said Clarke, 'if we hand you back to the police the bank robbery and murder will be added to the charges. Add to the fact that you are ex PIRA you are certain to go down for the maximum.'

'Can you offer me a better deal than leniency?'

'That all depends on what you can offer us,' said Shannon, 'can you tell us where the drugs and the Semtex are hidden? Do you know where Brady has hidden the money he stole from the bank?'

'Let's suppose I can do all that. I'm only supposing, mind you. What would the offer be then?'

'I would guess that you would get a very good offer. I should think that all charges would probably be dropped,' said Shannon.

'Probably is not good enough,' said Byrne, 'if I agree to give you all this information, then I want a copper bottom guarantee that all charges are dropped and more.'

'Let me put it this way,' said Shannon, 'if you can tell us where the drugs and the Semtex and the stolen money is hidden, then I'm confident that no charges will be brought against you. Brady will be put away for a long time.'

'Brady has a lot of friends. He could easily arrange to have me taken out when he's inside.'

'We can give you a new identity,' said Clarke, 'a new country if you wish. Nobody will be able to find you. What do you say? Will you help us?'

'Okay, this is what I want,' said Byrne, 'I want a guarantee that Brady or any of his buddies never find out that I grassed on them. I want all charges past and present dropped. I want a new identity and enough money to set me up in a business of my choice.'

'I think that's possible,' said Shannon, 'provided you can give us what we want. Can you?'

'I know where the drugs and Semtex are hidden unless they have already been moved. I have a fairly good idea where the stolen money, or what's left of it, is hidden.'

'Do we have a deal?' asked Clarke.

'We do when I see a legal document setting out all the conditions I have asked for. I want it signed, with witnesses, by the proper authorities.'

'We won't be able to arrange that before tomorrow,' said Shannon.

'What's another day?' said Byrne.

Shannon and Clarke informed McDonald of their progress so far with Byrne. McDonald was confident that the document which Byrne had insisted on was possible. He felt certain that when he gave the details to the police and the CPS they would be only too willing to agree. It was imperative that the drugs didn't get onto the streets and who knows what plans Brady and the Parker brothers had for the Semtex.

It was eight o'clock that evening and McDonald had invited the team to have a drink with him at the Midland Hotel. It was his favourite watering hole. He had arranged for two of the security men to man the cameras. He gave them instructions to let him know if they saw anything unusual happening at the Half Moon Club. Except for Stella everyone had arrived and McDonald ordered the drinks.

'You all know the score with Byrne,' said McDonald,' there's nothing we can do until he gives us the information he claims he has. We will, of course, check what he tells us before he receives any guarantees in writing.'

'I'm concerned about this mole,' said Blake, 'he seems to have thwarted everything Tom, Tony and Stella tried to do in Northern Ireland. From the message I intercepted it would appear that Brady was warned that we planned to raid the Half Moon Club the other night.'

The waiter arrived with the champagne and the conversation ended until he had gone.

'I ordered champagne in anticipation of Byrne coming up with the goods,' said McDonald, 'I hope I'm not tempting providence.' All the glasses were filled and the discussion continued.

'Some of the team discussed this problem of the mole and I'm afraid that we didn't come up with any concrete conclusion,' said Clarke, 'we were only able to speculate.'

'I seem to remember,' said Adams, 'that we all agreed that all our names should go on the list as possible suspects.'

'And I seem to remember,' teased Clarke, 'that Stella named Tom as number one suspect.'

'I think you will be in big, big trouble when she finds out what you've just said,' smiled Blake.

'And I'll be the one to tell her,' said Shannon shaking a finger at Clarke.

'Until we are able to solve this mystery,' said McDonald ignoring the banter, 'none of us will feel safe on any mission we are asked to do. After we've sorted out Brady and the Parker brothers, I will have to give this problem top priority.'

Another round of drinks arrived and the conversation moved away from work and the chatter got louder with each round of drinks.

'Where is Stella tonight?' asked Clarke looking at Shannon.

'She's gone to see a play at the Exchange theatre.'

'Has she gone by herself?'

'She's gone with a friend.'

'Hello, hello, sounds like competition to me,' teased Clarke.

'She's a free agent, Tony.'

'Do I detect a little bit of jealousy?' said Clarke, determined to wind up Shannon.

'Stop it Tony, or I'll give you.....

Before Shannon could finish, Stella walked into the room and joined them.

'Looks like you guys are having a good time.'

'What would you like to drink, Stella?' asked McDonald.

'A gin and tonic would be nice, thank you.'

McDonald beckoned the waiter and ordered the drink.

'Did you enjoy the play Stella?' asked Clarke.

'Yes, it was excellent.'

'Did your friend enjoy it too?' asked Clarke, taking a sneaky, glance at Shannon's face.

'She did.'

Clarke was crestfallen and Shannon's face contorted as he struggled to suppress his laughter.

'Are you two up to something again?' asked Stella.

'Ignore them, Stella,' said Blake, 'they've never been the same since Brady had them chasing an empty van all over Yorkshire.' This prompted some laughter and funny comments.

McDonald interrupted them, 'I'm going to order one last round.'

'Don't include me, Colonel,' said Stella, 'it's time I left.'

'I'm leaving too, Jim,' said Shannon.

McDonald called the waiter and Stella and Shannon left.

'It's a beautiful night,' said Shannon, 'may I walk you home, young lady?'

'Yes, that would be lovely, kind sir,'

Shannon and Stella made their way to Stella's flat. The night wasn't beautiful as Shannon had claimed. The sky was heavy with cloud and a light drizzle began to fall. By the time they arrived at Stella's flat the rain was torrential and a cold wind wasn't helping.

'I think it's a night for hot coffee,' said Stella as she made her way to the kitchen.

'Sounds good to me,' said Shannon as he followed Stella into the kitchen. He put his arms around her and gently kissed her on both cheeks.

'I missed you today,' he said as he began to kiss her neck.

'Of course, we could skip coffee,' suggested Stella.

'And have it for breakfast instead.'

'That's a great idea.'

'There is one problem though. You only have one bed and I think I'm too big for the sofa.'

'That's not a problem. I'd love to share my bed with you,' she said as she wrapped her arms around his neck and kissed him, then she took his hand and led him into the bedroom.

They were madly in love and they were alone. The atmosphere was electric with exciting anticipation. They fell into each other's arms and their kisses were warm and sweet. They embraced and kissed passionately until their need for each other became so intense that a new urgency possessed them. This would be their first time but their passionate love for each other washed away any inhibitions they may have had. The passion reached a new height and they could wait no longer. Afterwards they lay in each other's arms and they both felt that they were now complete.

31

At the time that Byrne was being interrogated by Clarke and Shannon, McDonald and Blake were meeting in McDonald's office. McDonald had given Blake the task of looking into the background of all the members of Ironclad as part of his plan to ensure that there was no mole within the team.

'I know you're not very comfortable with the task I've set you, Peter, but it has to be done.'

'I understand, Jim, the security of Ironclad comes first.'

'So what have you come up with?'

'Nothing totally conclusive but, nevertheless, some interesting information has turned up which we will have to consider.'

'All right, give me the interesting bits first.'

'The first surprise was Mike Jones. We knew, of course, that he left Manchester University with an excellent degree in electronics and then joined the army. What we didn't know about him, was that when he was nine or ten years old, his father committed suicide. There's nothing on his records either, with the army or with Ironclad, and it was never mentioned at any of the interviews.'

'Suicide in the family is something which most of us would not want to talk about.'

'That's true, Jim. However, it would seem that his mother had an affair with a British officer and his father couldn't live with it.

'It happens sometimes, Peter. I'm not sure that makes him a threat.'

'The next one is Paul Adams. Adams met Jones at University. They became good friends. Joined the army together and were eventually posted to Northern Ireland. Paul's aunt and uncle were killed in their home by a bomb. The local community thought that this was the work of the police. It was suspected that his uncle was associated with terrorists but this was never proven. Also his cousin was badly beaten by a police officer. I thought you would like to know that this police officer was badly beaten and a calling card with a red rose printed on it was tucked into his shirt.'

'Do you think that was Shannon? It was the card he used during his activities in Northern Ireland.'

'I don't know. It could have been a copycat.'

'Do you think Adams and Jones are working together to help Brady and his crew?

'I have no evidence of that but they both may have reason to want to wreak revenge upon the security forces. More interestingly, is their connection with Captain Charles Cosgrove.'

'What do you mean?'

'As you know all three of them are based at Holywood army base and all the calls from the mole came from the Belfast area. Cosgrove also recommended Adams and Jones to you as excellent candidates for a post with Ironclad.'

'So what are you saying?'

'I understand that Cosgrove was cajoled by his wife into buying a large, expensive house. She apparently has expensive tastes too. It's possible that Cosgrove is in financial difficulties although I have no evidence of this. Cosgrove has apparently received a large amount of money from somewhere. It could be from Brady, who we are almost certain, has the money from the bank raid. Adams and Jones both have motives to seek retribution. There could be some sort of conspiracy but I have no proof.'

'Okay, what else have you got?'

'Stella Bellamy and Tony Clarke both come from good, solid backgrounds. Stella's father was a colonel in the army and was decorated many times. He was killed in the Falklands. Tony's father was a major in the army and he died from a heart attack a few years ago. They have no connection with Northern Ireland and I haven't found anything which suggests they are a risk.'

'This brings us to your friend, Tom Shannon.'

'Yes, we both know his background and the role he played in Northern Ireland. The question is, has he gone back to his old ways? I don't think so but then I'm his friend. Nevertheless, he had the opportunity to betray us like everyone else.'

'He's done some good work since he joined us. Rescuing Ian Bellamy was no mean feat although he claims he had help from some chap who wishes to remain anonymous. That person may be a member, or a past member, of a terrorist group and Shannon may feel obliged to him. If that is so then that could be a problem. I think we should keep him in the frame for the time being. What are your feelings, Peter?'

'I think we have three possible suspects; Cosgrove, Adams and Jones.'

'Who is your number one suspect?'

'It would have to be Cosgrove because of the large cash deposits he has received in his bank account.'

'I'm inclined to agree. We will have to think of some way of catching him,' McDonald smiled and sat back in his chair and added, 'what about McDonald and Blake can they be trusted?'
Before Blake could comment there was a knock on the door and Shannon appeared.

'Come in, Tom,' said McDonald and Blake quickly closed his file.

'I gave Byrne the document he asked for this morning,' said Shannon, 'he claims he knows exactly where the Semtex and drugs are hidden in the Half Moon Club. He's certain the money is hidden in Brady's farm, in a secret room behind the fireplace, but he's not sure how to gain access. Tony's taking a statement from him now. I've told him that when we find all the items then the document will be signed.'

'Excellent, sit down, Tom,' Shannon took a chair up to McDonald's desk, 'Peter has been looking at the possibility of there being a mole in the team. To this end he has been carrying out some investigations into everyone's background. He's come up with the most likely suspect. He thinks it could be Charles Cosgrove.'

'Are you sure about this, Peter?'

'I believe he had the motive and the opportunity but I can't prove anything. We will need more evidence before we can take any action.'

'Because we haven't got any evidence we're going to have to test him and at the same time ascertain how accurate Byrne's information is,' said McDonald.

McDonald explained that they had to be sure that the information Byrne was giving them was correct. It would be a disaster if the police did another search at the Half Moon Club and found nothing. It would be embarrassing for the police and Ironclad. The Parker brothers would have good reason to complain of harassment. If the money from the bank raid was found at Brady's farm, then that would prove that Byrne was telling the truth. The police could then be given the go ahead. He believed that Brady must be running short of men. Doyle and Doherty are dead and Byrne, Connors and Daley are in custody. The last time that Cosgrove had made contact he said that Nolan and Donovan had turned up at the farm. McDonald wanted to check if these two men were still at the farm before he could put his plan into operation.

McDonald picked up the phone and punched in a number, after two rings there was an answer.

'Hello, Charles, and how are you? Yes, I'm fine. Charles, there's been a development with the Brady problem. I don't have all the details yet but I'm trying to assess how much manpower Brady has here in Manchester. It would be useful if you could let me know if Nolan and Donovan are still at Brady's farm.' McDonald listened for a few moments, 'well thanks for that. Keep in touch.' He rang off.
'He said that Nolan and Donovan caught a plane for Manchester about an hour ago. He said he was on the point of giving me a call.'

'How are we going to play this, Jim?' asked Shannon, 'Brady's farm is about fifteen miles north of Holywood. If Cosgrove is the mole, we will have to get there before he has time to get to the farm and move the money.'

'As far as we know all Brady's men are in Manchester,' said McDonald, 'so if Cosgrove tries to move the money himself, how long would it take him to get to the farm?'

'I think between twenty and thirty minutes depending on the traffic,' said Shannon.

'All right,' said McDonald, 'Stella will fly you and Tony over to Holywood army base. When you are about ten minutes from touchdown give me a call. I will then let Cosgrove know that you are approaching the base and ask him to have a car waiting for you. If he is the mole then he will only have ten minutes to arrange a car for you and get to the farm and move the money.'

'Won't he be suspicious of the late notice?'

'I'll spin some yarn about pressure from the top insisting on another search of the farm in case there are some weapons there. He knows that the police are convinced that Brady is a gun runner.'

When the trio arrived at the Holywood army base Cosgrove was waiting for them. After the usual greetings, Cosgrove handed the car keys to Clarke.

'This is a surprise,' said Cosgrove.

'A surprise to us too,' replied Clarke, 'Colonel McDonald suddenly decided that we had to give Brady's farm a thorough going over. We've had no success in Manchester so it's possible that Brady has some weapons or perhaps drugs or Semtex hidden on the farm.'

'I believe he has had some pressure from the top brass,' said Cosgrove, 'you've already checked it over two or three times and found nothing. Are you sure you're not wasting your time?'
Shannon got the feeling that Cosgrove was attempting to delay them. Perhaps he had managed to arrange for the money to be moved by someone else. If all Brady's men were in Manchester who could it possibly be? Perhaps they had got it wrong and Cosgrove wasn't the mole.

'You know how it is, Charles,' said Shannon, anxious to end the conversion, 'orders are orders. Ours is to do or die.'

'Let me know if you need any help,' said Cosgrove, 'Paul Adams returned yesterday. I could make him available.'

'Thanks, Charles,' said Clarke as he got into the car.

When they arrived at Wood View farm it was dusk. Clarke parked the car in the lay-by they'd used on previous occasions. It was possible to see Brady's farm from this spot.

'Stella, I want you to remain in the car,' began Shannon, then seeing the frown on her face, he added quickly, 'I'm not doing this to protect you. If we can't find an easy way to get into this, so called secret room, then we may have to break into the wall and that could be very noisy. We probably won't be able to hear if someone approaches the farm. We need someone on the outside to warn us. I'll call you at intervals of fifteen minutes so that you'll know we're okay.'

'All right, that makes sense.'

Shannon and Clarke made their way up the drive leading to the farm house. There didn't appear to be any lights on in the building. As expected the door was locked. That was no problem to Clarke who was a very competent at picking locks. Within a few minutes the door was open and they went in. They were familiar with the layout of the building. A corridor ran the length of the farm house with four doors leading off into different rooms. The door immediately opposite the front door led into a large kitchen which also served as a dining room. They checked all the other rooms and were satisfied that there was no one in the house so they decided to take a risk and switch on a light. The kitchen was the only room with a fireplace. The fireplace was a rectangular alcove fitted with a wood burner which was obviously a modern addition. They tapped the inner walls of the fireplace but they appeared to be solid. There were no apparent levers or hooks which may have suggested a means of opening a hidden door. The rest of the room was clad in wooden panelling right up to the front of the fireplace. The panelling was decorated with carvings of various flowers and animals. It looked as if they had reached a dead end. They began to wonder if Byrne had told them a pack of lies. Perhaps Brady had fed all his men this line about the hidden room in case they were tempted to betray him.

Clarke had walked around the room examining all the panelling. He then noticed that one of the carvings on the side of the fireplace was that of a rat.

'Look at this, Tom. I hate rats. Who would want a carving of a rat in the kitchen?' He then hit the offending carving with his fist. A panel flew open and almost simultaneously Clarke received a blow to his head with a hand gun. He fell to the floor unconscious. Before Shannon could reach for his weapon the assailant had him covered. It was Sergeant Campbell.

'Well, well,' said Campbell, 'we meet again. I'll wager I'm not what you expected to find in the secret room.'

'It was a rat that revealed the room and it was a rat that came out of it.'

'It's not a time to make jokes. Take your weapon out very slowly and place it on the floor, then kick it away.' Shannon did what he was told. 'Now reach slowly down to that ankle holster, take out the Bauer and do the same with that.'

'I can see that you are well informed,' said Shannon, after he had removed the second weapon.
Clarke began to moan and it appeared that he was coming round.

'Tie him to that chair with the rope on the table and make it quick,' said Campbell as he gave Shannon a push. Shannon helped Clarke to his feet and tied him to the chair. Campbell checked the ropes to make sure they were secure, at the same time keeping his gun trained on Shannon.

'So what's your stake in this game?' asked Shannon.

'I have a score to settle with you and make a lot of money at the same time.'

'I don't believe that you can possibly have a score to settle with me. The first time I met you was at the SAS training camp. I could argue that I had a score to settle with you considering the way you treated me.'

'Okay, let's cut the crap. Kneel down.' Campbell forced Shannon to his knees. Shannon's mind was racing, trying to think of some way to postpone what was obviously going to happen. No doubt it was going to happen to Clarke as well. Clarke would be in the unenviable position of watching his friend take the first bullet.

'If you're going to kill me at least give me the reason.'

'Don't play the innocent with me. I know you worked with the PIRA. You were the bastard who left a calling card with a red rose printed on it when you carried out your dirty deeds.'

'Let's assume I am that person. How does that affect you?' Shannon was doing his best to stall for time and also trying to think of some way to escape. At least his hands hadn't been tied so that was one advantage. He wouldn't be able to do anything unless Campbell could be distracted. At the moment that didn't seem likely. To make a move on Campbell now would be fatal.

'You will remember Len Perkins.'

'Ah, Len Perkins, the police officer who terrorised a young boy then beat him senseless. He was also suspected of throwing a bomb through the window of the boy's home killing both his parents.'

'Len is my cousin. You terrorised him and then beat him up. He never recovered from that. His nerves were shattered. My young brother was murdered by you terrorist bastards so this is for him too. I got boozed up one night in a pub and met your old friend Brady.'

'And he told you all about me and that explains the calling card which was in my kit when I returned from the SAS Training Centre.'

'Yes, that was me. I wanted to let you know you were not safe anywhere. Cosgrove was also useful. He's fed up with the way the army has treated him and has thrown in his lot with Brady. Okay, enough of this time wasting. You are going to get what you're due.'

'So this is revenge.'

'Call it what you like, Shannon, but tonight is your last night. If you're a praying man, now's the time to pray.'

Campbell stood behind Shannon and pointed the gun at his head. Shannon could see Clarke struggling to get out of the chair but Campbell had checked the ropes and Clarke had no chance of breaking free. Shannon knew that Campbell wouldn't take the risk of leaving Clarke alive. He wasn't going to leave a witness and Clarke would have realised this too. There was nothing either of them could do. Campbell was a sadist. He would enjoy knowing that Clarke would also suffer, seeing his friend murdered and know that he was next.

'So you haven't got the guts to look me in the eyes when you murder me.'

'It's because I don't want to see your bloody, ugly face. This is not murder. You are being executed for your terrorist activities.'
So this is it thought Shannon, this is where it all ends for him and his good friend. His grandmother's warning is now going to become reality. It would appear that he would be in his grave very soon. Unfortunately so would Tony Clarke. There was silence for what seemed like a lifetime to Shannon and then the silence was broken by the noise of a gunshot. Shannon heard Campbell's body fall. He turned to see some of Campbell's brains splattered everywhere and a pool of blood was slowly spreading across the tiled floor. He stood up and looked at the kitchen door. Stella was standing there, her Walther in her outstretched hands, looking calmly around the room.

'Thank God,' shouted Clarke, 'the cavalry has arrived.'

'He always has a joke for all occasions, no matter how serious,' said Shannon, 'you wouldn't believe that minutes ago he was going to be murdered.' Both Shannon and Clarke laughed. Stella felt that the laughter was caused by relief rather Clarke's sense of humour. Shannon untied the ropes holding Clarke and Stella became aware of the blood on Clarke's head.

'Are you all right, Tony?'

'I will be when this pounding in my head stops. It feels as if my heart is trying to get out through my ears and eyes.'

'So what happened and who is this guy I just shot?'

189

'It was my old friend Sergeant Campbell,' said Shannon, 'It's lucky you turned up when you did.'

'Your fifteen minutes were up and you didn't call so I guessed something had gone wrong.'

'It's a good thing you're quick on the trigger and a crack shot,' smiled Shannon.

'Is the money here?' asked Clarke.

'Good question,' said Shannon, 'I haven't checked the hidden room yet.'

'Let's do it then,' said Clarke as he stood up and found that he was a little unsteady on his feet and the pounding in his head worsened, 'I'll have to sit down,' and he flopped back into the chair.

Shannon and Stella went into the room and were surprised to find that it had been fitted with furniture. There was a bed and one or two other pieces of furniture. Screened off in the corner was a toilet and wash basin. Under the bed they found two holdalls which were full of money. They brought the holdalls out and showed Clarke.

'Bingo,' said Clarke, 'a result at last.'

'We need to take care of Campbell's body,' said Shannon, 'I'll get in touch with Jim and tell him what has happened.'
Shannon told Stella what Campbell had said about Cosgrove.

'Tony, I'm really sorry. I know you had a high regard for him,' said Stella.

'Yes, I'm sorry too and very much surprised. I still can't believe it.'

'What are we going to do about Cosgrove, Tom?' asked Stella.

'We'll let Jim take care of that. I think he'll arrange for the military police at the Holywood base to arrest him. There's one thing that puzzles me, why did Campbell want to discredit Cosgrove? If he wanted to get Cosgrove into serious trouble then why tell us? He was going to murder us so we weren't going to tell anyone.'

'Perhaps it was the sadist in him,' said Clarke, 'it may be that he wanted us to die knowing that Cosgrove was a mole and we were helpless to do anything about it.'

'When I think about how he treated me at the SAS Training Centre,' said Shannon, 'I can quite believe that.'

32

The following afternoon McDonald arranged a meeting at The Priory for all the available Ironclad team. Stella, Shannon, Clarke and Blake were present.

'Last night after I got your call,' said McDonald, looking at Shannon, 'I passed on to the police the information given to us by Byrne. The police raided the Half Moon and found the Semtex and the drugs hidden behind the panel exactly as described by Byrne. Harry Simpson is delighted. However, they are concerned that one of the Semtex bags had been opened and it's possible that some has been removed.'

'What about Charles Cosgrove, Jim?' Clarke asked'

'He was arrested last night and is being held at Holywood for the time being. I'm sorry about Charles, I know he is a friend of yours but because of him all three of you could have been killed.'

'What happed to Brady?' asked Shannon.

'He was arrested along with the Parker brothers, Donovan and Nolan.'

'Campbell's involvement was a complete surprise,' said Blake, 'his relationship with Constable Perkins wasn't picked up. More importantly, his connection with Charles Cosgrove didn't come to light either.'

'We were all surprised by Campbell's dramatic arrival on the scene too,' said Shannon, 'and but for Stella, Tony and I would be dead and the knowledge of Campbell and Cosgrove's involvement would have died with us.'

'There's something else we need to be concerned about,' said Blake, 'Byrne tells me that there was an Asian man who was living at the Half Moon Club. He was apparently the Parker brothers' dog's body. He's disappeared. His name is Ali Azim. He's an illegal immigrant who escaped from the Dover Removal Centre about two months ago. He's suspected of having connections with terrorist groups. The police have been alerted.'

'How did we miss him?' asked McDonald.

'He was stopped and searched on a number of occasions. He was never in possession of anything illegal. He claimed he was part of the kitchen staff at the Half Moon Club and the manager confirmed that. We had no file on him at the time so we had no reason to suspect him of anything.'

'If he's a terrorist,' said Stella, 'then he'll be looking for a densely populated area.'

'Are there any scheduled visits of the Queen, the Prime Minister or other VIPs in the area?' asked Shannon.

'We're looking into that,' said McDonald.

The phone rang and McDonald answered it, 'Hello, Harry,' he listened for a few moments and then rang off. 'That was the Assistant Chief Constable. They have arrested Ali Azim at Piccadilly railway station. He wasn't in possession of any Semtex. He was trying to get out of Manchester because he guessed that his identity had been discovered.'

'So we still have the problem of the missing Semtex,' said Stella.

'I have a very uneasy feeling,' said McDonald, 'I feel as if we've missed something. Who could possibly have this missing Semtex? All the suspects are either dead or in custody. The Semtex must be somewhere.'

'I think we've missed something too,' said Clarke, 'because I can't believe that Cosgrove is the mole. I know that.....' Clarke was interrupted by McDonald, 'I can't believe that either, Tony. Peter, where did you get all this information about Cosgrove's finances?'

'I didn't get it. Mike Jones supplied it,' replied Blake, 'you will remember that Mike did some research into Dooley's finances. During his research he came across details of a number of people, including Cosgrove, so he lifted the lot. He put the information in a report to me but at the time we were only interested in Dooley. I kept all the rest on file. When you asked me to find evidence of a possible mole I accessed the file and used the information.'

'Because Jones had produced it, you naturally assumed it was bona fide.'

'All the information he gave me on Dooley was absolutely correct. I had no reason to doubt the details in the rest of the report. He's a brilliant hacker.'

'What are you thinking, Jim?' asked Shannon.

'I'm thinking of a couple of possibilities. One, for me, is almost unthinkable.'

'I'm assuming this is to do with Mike Jones,' said Clarke.

'Peter,' said McDonald, not acknowledging Clarke's comment, 'Mike Jones was on your list of possible moles. What if Jones has fabricated the details about Cosgrove because Charles is still protesting his innocence.'

'That's possible but I haven't had any reason to check his information. As I said everything else he has produced has been accurate.'

'Does Mike have a motive?' Stella asked, 'is there anything in his background which suggests that he would do something like this?'

'He was on the list,' replied Blake, 'because he had the opportunity to send messages from Belfast to Brady. He may blame the army for his father's death. His father committed suicide after finding out that his mother was having an affair with a British officer. The whole matter was covered up.'

'Oh my God, what a stupid fool I've been,' said McDonald, 'how the hell did I miss it?'

'What is it, Jim?' Blake asked.

'Peter, are Jones and Adams still at Holywood?' asked McDonald, ignoring Blake's question.

'Yes, they're still working on the new communication system.'

'Get in touch with them. Make some excuse about checking on the progress of the modifications. I want to know if either of them is missing.'

'I know they are both due to be off for a long weekend but they should both be on the base today.'

'All right but check it out and find out what Mike's mother's first name is.'

Mike went over to the computer station looking puzzled.

'Jim, what's going on?' asked Clarke, 'do you think Charles is innocent?'

'What's Mike's mother got to do with this?' asked Shannon, before McDonald could answer Clarke's question.

'To answer you both, I'm not sure.'

'Jim, we're all intrigued,' said Stella, 'can't you tell us anything?'

'I'm sorry, I know I've always encouraged openness in the team but I would rather wait until Peter gives me the information I've asked for. We all have skeletons in our cupboard, things we'd rather forget. I'm no different. I'm praying that my gut instincts are wrong this time.' Blake returned and McDonald looked at him anxiously.

'I spoke to Paul,' said Blake, 'he tells me that Mike has gone AWOL. He recently bought a new Audi TT. He left for Dublin to catch the ferry. He said he was going to Wales, Abersoch to be precise. It's the anniversary of his father's death and he says it's time the guilty ones were punished. Paul says that Mike was quite agitated, almost manic and he was unable to persuade him not to go.'

'Do we know where Mike is now, Peter?' asked McDonald.

'Paul thinks he should have arrived in Liverpool by now.'

'Did you find out what Mike's mother's first name is?'

'Josefina Angelica.'

'All right,' said McDonald, 'we have to get to Abersoch before Mike. Peter, I want you to stay here and keep in contact with Paul, in case Mike changes his mind and goes back to Holywood. The rest of you are coming with me to my cottage in Abersoch. I'll explain on the way.' Clarke volunteered to drive so they all got into his BMW. On the way McDonald began to explain himself.

'It's general knowledge in the team that I have a cottage in Abersoch. Everybody also knows that my wife, Kate, spends August there and I visit whenever work permits. She has lots of friends there and on occasions our daughter stays there too. Kate and our daughter are there now.'

'Is it something to do with your wife?' asked Stella.

'No, it's something that happened before I was married. It's something of which I'm not proud. It spoiled the lives of a number of people and I pushed it to the back of my mind, hoping to forget it. These things have a habit of turning up when you least expect them to.'

'Jim,' said Stella, 'if this is something painful and private then you don't have to tell us.'

'I may have to ask you to risk your lives in order to save the lives of my wife and daughter, although I'm hoping it won't come to that. I think you are entitled to a full explanation.'

'Are you telling us,' asked Shannon, 'that Mike Jones is going to harm your family?'

'I'm not sure but I think it's probable.'

'Before we left,' said Clarke, 'Peter had calculated that it would take Mike about two hours thirty minutes to get to Abersoch from Liverpool. Our estimated time from Manchester is two hours fifty minutes. Mike has driven from Belfast to Dublin. He would have had a rest on the ferry and probably had a meal. Stopping for fuel would be the only reason he would have to break his journey from Liverpool to Abersoch.'

'Let's hope he has to stop for fuel then.' said Stella.

'Jim,' said Shannon, 'why don't you give your wife a call and warn her?'

'There is no land line at the cottage. Kate will have her mobile phone with her but the signal there is almost non-existent.' McDonald tried the mobile without success.

'Jim, why don't you inform the police?' said Clarke.

'I'd thought of that but if Mike is a bit off his head, the sight of the police may just push him over the edge. I'm hoping that I can calm him down.'

196

'Jim, why would Mike want to harm Kate and Fiona?' asked Shannon.

'About sixteen years or so ago I was having an affair with his mother. His father, George Jones, and I were serving in Northern Ireland and we became good friends. That's how I met his wife Josie. She liked to be called Josie. She was beautiful, probably still is. Josie's mother was Spanish and she had inherited her olive skin and big brown eyes. For me it was love at first sight. The affair went on for several months and then one night George walked in on us. He was devastated and more or less collapsed in front of us. After that he went into a deep depression and a month later he committed suicide. Mike would have been about eight or nine at the time and I know it broke his heart. I haven't seen his mother since.'

'How sad,' Stella said.

'I've been a fool. I should have realised that Mike was George Jones's boy but I didn't. Josie always referred to him as Miguel so naturally I thought that was his name. I've met a number of men since with the surname Jones so when Mike Jones turned up, I didn't make the connection. When I found out that his mother's name is Josefina Angelica, I knew immediately who he was.'

'Why would he want to harm Kate and Fiona?' asked Clarke, 'I would have thought that you would be his target.'

'I imagine he wants me to feel what it's like to lose someone you love. His father was his hero. With his computer skills he has managed to dig up the story of what happened. The army agreed to cover up the truth for the sake of the relationship between Mike and his mother. Both Mike's grandmothers were alive at the time. The truth would have destroyed the relationship between the three women. So it was claimed that the suicide was a result of the stress of working in Northern Ireland.'

'Let's hope we get there before he does,' said Shannon.

'I don't want him harmed, if that's possible,' said McDonald, 'he's suffered a great deal and he now believes that he will get some relief if he can make me suffer as well.'

'Revenge is not all it's cut out to be,' said Shannon.

They were now approaching the cottage and they could see an Audi TT parked outside. Clarke stopped the car about twenty yards away and they all got out. McDonald asked Stella and Clarke to go to the back of the cottage and enter through the kitchen. McDonald and Shannon walked up the front path. The door was unlocked and they went in quietly. They could hear Jones talking. In the living room Kate and Fiona were tied to chairs and Jones was in the process of gagging them. He must have heard them come into the room because he turned suddenly and faced them, a small device in his hand.

'Don't come any nearer or I'll detonate the bomb,' screeched Jones. His eyes were wild and his face was contorted with anger and hatred.

'Mike, it's me you want,' said McDonald, 'let them go, they haven't done you any harm.'

'I want you to live,' sobbed Jones, 'I want you to live and suffer like I did. I want you to feel the pain each and every day for the rest of your life. When you realise that you won't see your wife and daughter ever again, you will really understand what pain and sorrow feels like.'

'Mike,' said McDonald, 'if you do this you will have to live with it for the rest of your life. You may find that all you have done is to add further to the pain that you are already suffering. Your mother will suffer too because she will blame herself.'

'Get out, both of you,' Jones shouted, becoming more agitated, 'I'll detonate the bomb and then we'll all be dead.'

'Mike, please don't do this,' pleaded McDonald, 'stop now and let's talk calmly. I'll arrange for you to have some counselling. If you go through with this you will go to prison for a long time and that will kill your mother.'

'She deserves to suffer too,' snarled Jones.

'You don't mean that,' replied McDonald, 'she made a mistake and she's paid for it. Don't make her pay again. Your father's death almost destroyed her. She only kept on living for your sake.'

This seemed to make Jones hesitate and he stared at McDonald for a few seconds. It was then that the kitchen door opened and Stella and

Clarke came in. Jones swung around his mood changing at the same time.

'Stand back Stella and you too, Tony. I have a detonator in my hand. I will use it if you all don't get out. I don't want to hurt you but I will if I have to.'

'Mike, listen to me,' said Shannon, 'please stop this now. Believe me I know how you feel. I've been there. This isn't justice, this is revenge. Revenge nearly destroyed me and it certainly destroyed Campbell and it will destroy you. You know my history. It's similar to yours in a way. Don't make the same mistake that I made.' Shannon had been talking softly and quietly and walking very slowly towards Jones. When he got within an arm's length of Jones, he stopped but continued speaking, 'I was given another chance, a chance to move on. If I had continued with my vendetta then not only would my life have been destroyed but also the lives of everyone close to me. For your own sake you have to learn to forgive.'

Jones was standing with his arm outstretched and still holding the detonator. Shannon reached out slowly and calmly and took the detonator out of his hand. Jones looked at him with a tear stained face and then collapsed.

33

Next day after lunch the Ironclad team met in the conference room at The Priory.

'I've been in touch with Charles Cosgrove,' said McDonald, 'and given him my apologies. He was very understanding.'

'It's a great relief,' said Clarke, 'to know he's innocent.'

'What will happen to Mike Jones?' asked Stella.

'That's a difficult one,' said McDonald, 'he has agreed to undergo psychiatric treatment and today I will be sending a letter recommending leniency. I will do everything I can to help him. I owe him that.'

'On the positive side we did get a result with the arrest of the Parker brothers and Brady and his thugs,' said Clarke, 'which reminds me, what happened to Dooley?'

'Dooley was arrested yesterday,' answered McDonald, 'the police found dummy fuel tanks with traces of heroin in them on his vehicle.'

'There are so many unanswered questions that I don't know where to start,' said Stella.

'You're right, Stella,' said McDonald, 'so let's start with Charles Cosgrove and I'm sure that Peter will be happy to elaborate.'

'You all know that Mike Jones's report stated that Charles had some serious debts,' said Blake, 'he also reported that the debt had been cleared. It was perfectly true that Charles was in financial trouble and it is equally true that he is now solvent. The money came from his sister. His sister was a wealthy widow with no children. Her health had not been good for some time and she died a few weeks ago leaving everything to Charles.'

'Let's look at Mike Jones next,' said McDonald, 'Mike was determined to destroy my family and me for reasons you already know. As Peter will confirm, Mike is a very competent hacker. He found out that I was the man who caused so much damage to his family. In his undercover work he would have come across Brady or some of his cronies and then the plan for my downfall began. Paul Adams rang me this morning and said that he had done a thorough sweep of Holywood and found a lot of expensive state of the art bugging equipment all over the place. Brady would have financed that and that's how he was able to keep tabs on us.'

'How did Sergeant Campbell get involved in all this?' asked Shannon.

'He told you that he met Brady in a pub,' said McDonald, 'it was then that he found out who you were and saw an opportunity for revenge. Brady was also anxious to get rid of you so he saw Campbell as a useful tool to that end. He must have also thought that Campbell would be a splendid contact. He was living in the area and would be above suspicion. When Jones was at The Priory he could inform Campbell of anything he thought would be useful to Brady. Campbell would then inform Brady. That's why all the calls always came to Brady from Belfast. Jones has confirmed all of this.'

'I can understand that Campbell wanted to get rid of me because of what I did to his cousin,' said Shannon, 'but why did he tell all those lies about Charles Cosgrove?'

'I think I know why he wanted to discredit Charles,' said Blake, 'Cosgrove's wife is Campbell's *half* sister. Her surname was Browne so I didn't connect her with Campbell. Campbell would have known about Charles's affair and seen his sister's distress. Perhaps his hatred was such that he wanted to destroy Charles. I can't explain why he wanted to tell Tom and Tony.'

'I think Tony put his finger on it,' said Stella, 'when he said perhaps he wanted to make them feel more wretched. They were going to die believing that a friend had betrayed them and they couldn't do anything about it. And from the way he treated Tom at the SAS camp he was obviously a sadist.'

'I suppose that Campbell was at the farm,' said Shannon, 'in order to remove the money.'

'I'm sure that that was the reason,' said McDonald, 'the men who went to remove Campbell's body found his car in the barn and that's why you were surprised by him. You didn't see any vehicles and so assumed there was no one in the farm. He obviously heard you arrive and was prepared for you.'

'We now know that Brady gave Mike some of the Semtex,' said McDonald, 'that's how he was able to make the bomb. I hope that nobody else has any. We have no way of checking.'

'If there are no more questions,' said McDonald, 'then I think we should celebrate our success.'

Everyone was in agreement with that and Shannon began to pour the champagne.

'Cheers everyone,' said McDonald, 'and let's not forget Paul who can't be with us today.'

'That'll be an excuse to have another celebration later,' grinned Clarke.

'It's a good feeling to know we've rid the streets of those dangerous thugs,' said McDonald, 'the public will never know how you risked your lives to bring that about.'

McDonald's phone rang and after he dealt with the call he spoke to the team.

'That was Harry Simpson,' said McDonald, 'a bomb exploded a couple of hours ago in the Arndale Centre. Two people have been killed and several badly injured.'

'Is it never going to end?' asked Stella.

'Has anybody claimed responsibility?' asked Clarke.

'Not yet but they did find a third dead body a little distance away from the explosion. They think he committed suicide and he had in his hand a piece of paper which had the words "Allah Akbar" written on it.'

'What does that mean?' asked Stella.

'I think it means God is great,' said Blake.

'I think we can be fairly certain that he is, or was, the bomber,' said Clarke.

'I don't suppose we will ever know whether he used some of Brady's Semtex,' said Stella, 'or even if he had any connection with Brady.' Nobody had anything to add to that.

Shannon was sitting quietly thinking about his time in Northern Ireland when he was attacking army and police vehicles. Civilians too were terrorised by his activities. His hoax bombs in shopping areas had caused panic and confusion and innocent people had been hurt, even though no one was killed. He remembered how he was focused on only one thing, *revenge*. Nothing else mattered. Perhaps this man, who had committed suicide, had also been ravaged with grief and hatred and the need for revenge. What a waste. He recalled how upset his grandmother had been. How she had pleaded with him not to go down that road but he had ignored her pleadings and her distress. His thoughts were interrupted by Stella.

'Are you all right, Tom?' asked Stella as she became aware of his silence.

'I was thinking about the bomber. He did dig a grave for himself.'

'I called your grandmother and told her what you did for Ian,' said Stella and then she added with a smile, 'I also promised her that the next time she gives you advice, I'll make sure that you take notice.'

'I'll bet that made her laugh.' They both laughed and then joined the other three. They were all making so much noise that they almost missed the ring of McDonald's phone.

'Hello, Harry,' said McDonald at the same time motioning to the others to quieten down. He listened for a few minutes then, 'do you have any information about the prisoners?' another pause, 'I see, thanks Harry, let me know if you hear anything else.' He rang off. McDonald didn't speak for a moment but he had the undivided attention of all three of the team.

'As you probably guessed that was the Assistant Chief Constable. Bad news I'm afraid. There's been a serious accident on the M602 Motorway. A lot of vehicles were involved. One or two vehicles are on fire and bodies are strewn all over the place. The police van taking our prisoners to the Remand Centre was involved.'

'Are there many dead?' asked Clarke.

'Harry couldn't say. As you can imagine it's chaotic. All the services are there trying to sort it out.'

'Did Harry have any information about the prisoners?' asked Stella.

'Information is a bit sketchy yet. The bad weather conditions are making it more difficult for the services. Apparently there are bodies everywhere and traffic piled up across the lanes. Harry thinks that it may be difficult to identify some of the bodies.'

'I suppose with police, medics, and no doubt the fire service staff, along with the walking wounded it will be difficult to sort people out,' said Stella.

'It must be a nightmare,' said McDonald, 'so we'll have to wait until we get some more reliable information.'

Next morning the weather had improved a great deal. There was still some cloud in the sky but there was some evidence that the sun would make an appearance. The dark blue Ford Focus moved at a steady speed down the A580 travelling west towards Liverpool. The driver was careful not to break any of the speed restrictions and gave the impression that this was a pleasure drive with no need to hurry. The occupants of the car were three nuns. Two nuns were in the front seat and the third nun was sitting in the rear. The third nun was holding rosary beads in her hands but her eyes were closed and it was difficult to tell if she was asleep or deep in prayer. The nun driving the car saw, in the rear mirror, a police car approaching and informed the other nuns. The police car began to overtake and as it got level with the Focus, it slowed down and the officer in the passenger seat checked on the passengers. He was apparently satisfied because the police car continued travelling down the A580. Sometime later the

Focus was being driven up a ramp and onto the ferry at the Liverpool port. The ferry was bound for Dublin. On arrival in Dublin the Focus headed north out of the city. The nun in the rear seat was now wide awake. The rosary beads had disappeared and she was drinking something from a plastic cup. When the nuns arrived in Belfast they didn't go to a convent or even a church. They stopped outside a block of flats and opened the boot. Each took out a suitcase and went into the building.

The day after the news of the Motorway accident and about the same time that the Ford Focus was travelling along the A580, Stella and Shannon returned to The Priory. McDonald, Blake and Clarke were already in the conference room.

'Do we have any more news about the crash on the M602, Jim?' asked Shannon.

'I'm afraid not. Harry said he would let me know as soon as he had anything.'

'Let's hope none of them escaped and.....' Stella began but was interrupted by McDonald's phone.

'Hello, Harry,' said McDonald and after listening for a few minutes he reached for a pen and note pad and began to make some notes, 'that really is bad news, Harry. The bad weather and all the chaos made it easier for them. All right, let me know if you get any more information on them. We'll put our heads together and see what we can come up with.' He rang off.

'Sounds like bad news, 'said Clarke.

'The worst,' said McDonald, 'Raz Parker is dead. Max Parker and Dooley have been taken to hospital seriously injured. I am afraid that Brady, Donovan and Nolan have disappeared. Their bodies haven't been found so it's assumed that they've escaped.'

'It would have been an ideal time to escape,' said Clarke, 'the ambulance crew, the fire service and the police would have been fully occupied helping the victims.'

'I don't think they could have planned the crash,' said Stella, 'although stranger things have happened. I think it's unlikely because they didn't know when they were going to be moved.'

'They'll need transport and money,' said Shannon, 'do we know if they have any contacts in that area?'

'Not according to our records,' said Blake, 'Brady always used hotels or the Half Moon Club when he was in Manchester.'

'He's very clever,' said Shannon, 'I feel sure that he would have a bolt hole somewhere and he would have siphoned off some of the bank money in case of emergencies.'

'Do you think he will try to get back to Northern Ireland?' asked Stella.

'I think that's very likely,' said Shannon, 'he may have contacts there who may be prepared to help him out.'

McDonald's phone rang.

'Hello, Harry, have you got some good news for us?' After listening for a few minutes he ended the call.

'Is it good news, Jim?' asked Clarke.

'Harry says that a red Vauxhall Corsa was stolen in the Worsley area last night. Worsley is quite close to the M602 so it is possible that Brady and his crew could have taken it. The police have the registration number so they will be on the lookout at sea ports and airports.'

'There is a very good motorway network in the Worsley area,' said Blake, 'the M61, the M62 and the M6 which goes all the way to Scotland. There are other options too.'

'I'm sure the police will be covering a wide area,' said McDonald, 'Harry has arranged for regular bulletins to be sent to Peter's system. We'll have to wait and see what develops.'

34

Shannon's grandmother, Martha Shannon, had just finished watching one of her favourite late afternoon television dramas. It was dusk and so she reached across from her armchair and switched on the table lamp. It was time for her to prepare something for her evening meal. She was approaching the kitchen when the door bell rang. It must be Kate, she thought, probably run out of sugar again. She opened the door as far as the safety chain would allow. There was a man standing there.

'Are you Mrs Martha Shannon?' he asked'

'Yes and who are you?'

'I'm Chief Inspector Dalby,' he replied, waving his warrant card at her.

'What do you want? Has something happened to Tom?' Martha had become very concerned.

'No, your grandson is fine. Mrs Shannon, I need to speak to you in private which I can't do out here.'

Martha was uncertain about letting a stranger into the house. She reasoned, however, that he had shown his warrant card and he knew that Tom was her grandson. It looked as though he was genuine. She released the safety chain and then showed him into her living room.

'Would you please sit down,' he said.

'That usually means that there is some bad news to follow,' said Martha as she sat in her armchair.

'We have reason to believe that some terrorists may try to kidnap you.'

'Why would they want to do that?'

'They have recently escaped from police custody. Your grandson helped to have them arrested so we think there's a possibility that they will be looking for revenge.'

'Oh dear, what am I going to do?'

'Don't be alarmed. We are going to take care of you. If you pack a few items of clothing, which you may need for three or four days, we will take you to a safe house now. A police sergeant is waiting in the car outside.'

'I'll go upstairs and do that now.' As she was leaving the room she spotted her mobile phone on the bookcase near the door. She picked it up. 'I think I should ring Tom and let him know where I will be.'

'It's not safe to speak on a mobile phone. The terrorists may be listening and then they will know where you are. I think it would be in your interest if you give me the phone.'

Some fifteen minutes later Martha had packed her case and was ready to go.

'I need to make sure that the back door is locked,' she said.

'I've checked everything down here. If you give me your keys I'll make sure that the front door is locked before we go.'

A few minutes later they left the house and got into the car. Her case was put in the boot and Martha sat in the rear seat next to another man. She was feeling very nervous. The man turned and smiled at her. 'Everything is going to be all right, Mrs Shannon.' She didn't feel reassured.

The car moved off and disappeared into the darkness.

In Martha's house the telephone was ringing.

35

It was seven o'clock and the Ironclad team were still at The Priory. No more information had come through regarding the three missing prisoners. The police had watched all the sea ports and airports and the men hadn't been spotted. Brady and his men seemed to have disappeared into thin air. The stolen red Vauxhall Corsa still hadn't been recovered and none of the police patrols had reported a sighting. The police were beginning to think that the men were still in the country. The Ironclad team were particularly angry and frustrated after all the time and effort they had spent bringing these men to justice. They discussed all the possibilities. They accepted that it was, of course, nobody's fault. A traffic accident could not have been legislated for. The police van carrying the prisoners was damaged almost beyond recognition. It was amazing that the three men who had escaped had survived at all. The question is where are they? What happened to the red Vauxhall Corsa car? They are dangerous men and if they find themselves cornered then they could become extremely dangerous. If they have left the country, how did they manage it without being seen? The answer must be that they had another means of transport. They all concurred that Shannon's guess was probably right; they had a bolt hole somewhere with a car and cash. They thought it would be foolish of Brady to return to his farm so that was unlikely. Shannon didn't know if Brady had another property in Northern Ireland but, of course, he would have fellow criminals who may help him. They decided there was nothing they could do until there were more clues. Perhaps the police would have a break through. McDonald said they should call it a day and wait and see what tomorrow brings.

McDonald announced that his wife and daughter were visiting relatives in Scotland. He didn't fancy cooking and dining alone so had decided to dine at the Midland. He wondered if anyone would care to join him. Blake declined because his parents had invited him for dinner that evening. The rest of the team said they would be delighted. When they arrived at the Midland they were given their usual table. Drinks were ordered and everyone quickly made a choice from the menu.

'I'm worried about my grandmother,' said Shannon.

'Why is that?' asked Stella.

'I usually call her at least a couple of times a week. I've been trying this evening since about six-thirty. She doesn't answer her land line and her mobile phone is switched off.'

'She may have gone to see a friend or perhaps she's gone to the cinema,' said Clarke.

'If she's gone to the cinema,' said Stella, 'then she would switch off her mobile.'

'I spoke to her yesterday evening but she didn't mention going to the cinema.'

'Perhaps she changed her mind,' said McDonald, 'call her later this evening and check.'

The meal arrived and the conversation weaved from one subject to another and the disappointment of the day took a back burner. Clarke was on good form and provided the party with lots of funny stories and a good time was had by all. It was during one of Clarke's funny stories that Shannon's phone rang. He opened it up and saw that it was a call from his grandmother. He took a few paces away from the table, 'Hello, I've been worried about.....' then he paused and listened and after a few moments, 'let me speak to her. If you harm her.....' the caller rang off.

'Tom, what is it?' asked Stella when she saw that the colour had drained from Shannon's face.

'It was Brady. He claims he has my grandmother but he wouldn't let me speak to her.'

'Perhaps he's bluffing.' suggested Clarke.

'He was using my grandmother's mobile phone so he has either got her or somehow stolen her phone.'

'If he contacts you again,' said McDonald, 'insist that he lets you speak to her.'

'This proves that he has managed to get to Belfast,' said Clarke. Shannon rang his grandmother's mobile phone to check. It was switched off.

'He'll ring again,' said McDonald, 'he must want something, probably money.'

The news about Shannon's grandmother cast a shadow over the team. Shannon was hoping that it was money that Brady was after because he would scrape it together somehow. He had a sinking feeling that Brady was planning something more evil than a ransom. If anything happened to his grandmother he would never be able to forgive himself. He would hunt Brady down and when he caught him, Brady would wish he had never been born. McDonald suggested that they wrapped up the evening and met at eight-thirty the next morning at The Priory. He told Shannon that he would inform Blake of the development. He also insisted that Shannon call him at any time if he heard from Brady.

Brady didn't ring again that night.

As arranged everybody turned up at The Priory next morning at eight-thirty prompt. Blake set up all his equipment ready for when Brady made the call. It was hoped that Blake would be able to trace the call although the consensus was that Brady was too cunning to use the mobile phone. He would probably use a public phone box and one which would be outside his location. The only information Blake would get would be the location of the phone box.

At approximately ten o'clock Shannon's phone rang. As expected the call wasn't being made from Martha Shannon's mobile phone.

'Hello,' said Shannon.

'Listen and listen good,' said Brady, 'I want two million pounds in used notes delivered in two days.'

'How am I going to raise two million pounds in two days? I can't....'

'That's your problem,' interrupted Brady, 'I'll ring again in two days to tell you where to drop the money.'

'I want to speak to my grandmother. How do I know you've got her? If you have, how do I know she's alive?'

Brady rang off.

Blake was able to locate the public phone box but they knew that this information would be useless.

'We must decide how we are going to play this,' said McDonald.

'What do you mean?' asked Clarke.

'I think I can arrange to get the money together but the question is should we hand it over.'

'I would have a problem with handing money over to Brady,' said Shannon.

'I think it's important to be in Northern Ireland,' said McDonald, 'and run the operation from there and I'll come with you, Tom, and we'll go first thing tomorrow morning.'

'I want to be included, Jim,' said Clarke.

'If you think you boys are going without me, you're mistaken,' said Stella.

'All right,' said McDonald, 'but I think Peter should stay here and keep this place ticking over.'

By ten o'clock the next morning the foursome had arrived at the Holywood army base. Cosgrove had arranged a conference room for their exclusive use. Shannon hadn't received another call from Brady and Martha Shannon's mobile phone remained switched off. They would have to wait until the two days were up when Brady said he would ring again. The waiting, not knowing, was difficult but they were helpless to do anything else. They didn't know where Brady was except that he was somewhere in Belfast. They couldn't be certain that Nolan and Donovan were with him. He could be working alone although they thought that unlikely.

Shannon had a key to his grandmother's house so he and Clarke paid a visit. Having checked through the house they saw no signs of a struggle. There was no evidence of a break-in. They came to the conclusion that Martha had let her kidnappers in voluntarily. They must have told her a very convincing story, thought Shannon, to get her to leave her house. Shannon was hoping that she had come to no harm and that Brady's motivation was the money and not revenge. Deep down he knew that Brady wasn't the type to forgive easily. Brady was a thug and a killer devoid of any decent human feelings. They spoke to some of the neighbours but no one had seen Martha.

They would have to wait one more day before Brady would call again. McDonald pointed out that they needed the time to arrange the transfer of the two million pounds from a special account in the Bank in England. The Irish bank had agreed to put together two million in used notes. This money would be available as soon as the transfer had been complete.

'We will have to think of a way of avoiding handing over the money,' said McDonald, 'we will, of course, have to let Brady see the money or he won't play.'

'If Brady is on his own,' said Shannon, 'then we have a chance but I feel sure that Donovan and Nolan will be with him.'

'I agree. Their bodies weren't found at the scene of the accident so I think they're with Brady,' said Clarke, 'we will have to separate him from Nolan and Donovan somehow.'

Next morning at ten-thirty Brady called.

'Have you got the money?'

'We're hoping it will arrive this afternoon.'

'Hoping, hoping, that's no good, Shannon, either it will be there or it won't.'

'These things take time. The money is being transferred.....' Brady interrupted, 'I'll ring again this afternoon.' He rang off.

'He's avoiding being on the phone too long in case we are tracing the call,' said Stella.

'I'm sure he will be very conscious of that,' said Clarke, 'he will also be on the lookout for anyone tailing him.'

'He'll be hard to catch,' said Shannon, 'we will have to manipulate him into a situation where my grandmother and the money are in the same room at the same time.'

'You're right, Tom,' said McDonald, 'if we don't see Martha then the money remains with us.'

'If everything goes okay and we hand the money over to Brady,' said Clarke, 'what happens then?'

'Good question,' said McDonald, 'that's what we have to work out.'

At four o'clock an armed guard with the two million pounds in used notes arrived. At five o'clock Shannon' phone rang. A silence fell on the room and there was an air of anxiety.

'Have you got the money?'

'Yes.'

'Is it in used notes?'

'Yes.'

'Bring it to the Red Lion in Tomb Street at nine o'clock. No police or any of your slimy friends and no weapons. If I see anybody except your ugly face the deal's off. You know what will happen next.'

'I need to know that my grandmother is alive. Let me speak to her.' There was a pause then, 'Tom, don't come. He's going.....' The phone went dead.

'Was that your grandmother's voice?' asked McDonald.

'Yes, I wonder what she was trying to tell us.'

'She obviously doesn't trust Brady and is concerned for your safety,' said Stella.

'We have four hours before Tom has to deliver the money,' said McDonald, 'we have to have a plan by then. We may have to have a Plan B as well.'

'He'll definitely be on the lookout for anybody shadowing Tom,' said Clarke, 'if he sees any of us then the game will be up.'

'I'm not sure about that,' said McDonald, 'we recovered a large proportion of the bank's money. I don't think he will give up the opportunity of getting his hands on two millions. He must be short of cash. I'm not suggesting that we should take risks though.'

'What do you have in mind, Jim?' asked Shannon.

'I understand that there is an eating place opposite the Red Lion. I think it's called the American Pie or some such name.' Stella and Tony said that they had used the place on a previous occasion. McDonald suggested that they go there about eight o'clock and order a meal. They could then keep an eye on the pub.'

Stella and Clarke arrived at the American Pie at a little before eight o'clock. They asked for, and were given, a table near the window which gave them a perfect view of the Red Lion. They took their time looking at the wine list and the menu. They had almost finished the main meal when they saw Shannon enter the pub carrying a case. They knew that he wasn't armed but they were. They continued to act the part of a couple enjoying the evening, trying not to make their surveillance obvious. They had both agreed that Brady had chosen a strange place to do an exchange, if that was what he intended. It would be interesting to see how he was going to bring Martha Shannon to the pub, do the exchange and make his getaway. Whatever he planned they would be ready.

Shannon's adrenalin was flowing as he entered the Red Lion. There were about a dozen people in the pub mostly men. He couldn't see Brady or any of his men so he went up to the bar and ordered a Jameson's. He found an empty table facing the door and sat down. He had brought with him a local evening newspaper and he pretended to read it as he kept a watchful eye on the door and around the room. After half an hour there was no sign of Brady. The barman delivered another Jameson's and Shannon was wondering if something had gone wrong. He had just finished his second whiskey when he heard his phone ring. He opened it up.

'Are you enjoying your whiskeys, Shannon?'

'Where's my grandmother, you bastard?'

'Ah, getting a bit anxious are we? We can't rush these matters. This was a test to make sure that you didn't have someone tailing you and you've passed with flying colours.'

'If you've harmed as much as one hair on her head Brady.....'

'You're not in a position to make threats,' interrupted Brady, 'tomorrow I'll call you again to make arrangements for the exchange.' The phone went dead.

Back at Holywood the team were disappointed to find that they were back to square one.

'I have to admit,' said Shannon, 'that I couldn't see Brady making the exchange in the pub. It was too public. He will find a private place where he can be in complete control.'

'Let's hope that he now believes that you are going to do this alone. He will feel secure and that's when he'll make mistakes,' said McDonald.

'I think he will rent somewhere just for the day,' said Shannon, 'perhaps even a room in a hotel.'

'Let's assume that he does book a room in a hotel,' said Clarke, 'we have to put together a plan whereby we can protect Tom and his grandmother. When the money is handed over that's when they will become vulnerable.'

'Let's not forget that Donovan and Nolan must be helping him,' said Stella, 'so it's not just Brady we have to worry about.'

'That's true,' said Clarke, 'Tom is the only one who knows them but we have their photographs so we will have to keep our eyes open.'

The team spent another anxious night wondering what Brady's next instruction would be. Shannon was worried about his grandmother. This was taking longer than he had anticipated and the stress his grandmother must be suffering concerned him. This wouldn't have happened if he hadn't set out to seek revenge for the hurt he was feeling a few years ago. His grandmother had warned him and now she is suffering as Brady uses her to inflict his revenge on him.

Next morning the team set about discussing a possible plan of action. At eleven o'clock Shannon's phone rang, he switched on the loudspeaker. 'This is it. Be at Jurys Inn Hotel on Great Victoria Street at three o'clock this afternoon. No police and no slime ball friends and remember no weapons. When you arrive at the hotel give me a call on your grandmother's mobile phone. I will then tell you which room we're in. No tricks or you'll know what will happen.' The phone went dead.

'That's perfect,' said McDonald, 'the manager is a friend of mine and I know he'll help us to put our plan into operation.'

McDonald contacted the manager of Jurys Inn Hotel and explained what he wanted. The manager said there would be no problem and he would arrange everything right away. It was a little over an hour when a van arrived at Holywood from the Jurys Inn Hotel. All the supplies were checked and McDonald was satisfied that everything he had asked for had been delivered. Now that they were certain that the exchange was going to take place in a hotel, they were able to firm up the plan and fill in all the details. At one-thirty all of them, with the exception of Shannon, left for the hotel. They were all confident about the roles they were about to play.

Shannon arrived at two-fifty five. He called Brady who answered on the second ring.

'Bright and early, that's what I like to see, keenness.'

'Cut the crap and get on with it.'

'We're a bit stressed are we?'

'Stop wasting time.'

'I'm in room number one zero two on the first floor. Use the lift not the stairs,'

Shannon, who was standing at the reception desk, wrote something on a piece of paper and handed it to the receptionist. The receptionist immediately picked up the phone and as she was speaking Shannon made his way slowly to lift. He didn't press the button right away but kept his eyes on the receptionist. After about two minutes she looked at him and nodded. He called the lift.

On the first floor Donovan was waiting outside the lift. He was nervous. He was only too familiar with Shannon's reputation. He checked his holster for the third time to convince himself that the weapon was still there. He had checked the corridor as he had stepped out of the bedroom. On his left he could see a chambermaid working her way along, pushing a laundry trolley. To the right a waiter was standing outside a bedroom holding a tray. He could feel a bead of perspiration roll down his face as he heard the lift arriving. He reached for this weapon as the doors opened.

'You took your time, Shannon. I thought....' He didn't have time to finish his sentence as a blow to the back of his head silenced him. The waiter and the chambermaid tied and gagged him and placed him in the laundry trolley then covered him with a sheet.

McDonald appeared dressed in a maintenance man's uniform, 'That's one in the bag.' He turned around and knocked on the door of room 102 and waited. After a few moments the door was opened by Nolan.

'Sorry to disturb you, sir. I'm the hotel's maintenance supervisor. We have a water leak coming from this floor. I need to check your room. It will only take a few minutes.'

'It's not convenient at the moment.'

'I'm very sorry, sir, but I have to check. If it gets any worse then we could have a big, expensive job on our hands. If you don't let me check, the security men will have to be informed.'

'Okay,' said Nolan as he stepped aside, 'but be quick about it.' McDonald went into the room and made his way to the en suite. He went through the motions of checking the shower and the washbasin and the lavatory. He came out of the en suite and looked around the bedroom.

'Everything seems all right in here, sir. Sorry to have disturbed you.' Nolan was sitting on a chair near the window. He didn't speak. When McDonald came out of the bedroom he beckoned to Shannon. They walked along the corridor and met with Stella and Clarke.

'What happened?' asked Clarke.

'Nolan was the only one in the room,' said McDonald.

'Either Brady's been very clever and anticipated our moves,' said Shannon, 'or he intended this all along.'

'It doesn't make sense,' said Stella, 'he's exposed his two men.'

'Brady's not concerned about them,' said Shannon, 'he's still got his hostage and if he gets his hands on the money he doesn't have to share it with anybody.'

'Let's take Nolan into custody,' said McDonald.

36

After handing Nolan and Donovan over to the police, they all returned to Holywood more despondent than ever. Nolan and Donovan refused to give them any information even though it was pointed out to them that Brady had set them up so that he could keep all the money. It was also made clear to them that the charges they would be facing meant that they would be in prison for a very long time. Having checked with the hotel manager and staff, no one could recall seeing a man with an old lady entering the hotel that day. The receptionist had no record of anyone answering the description she was given. It looked as if Brady and Martha were never in the hotel.

The team discussed all the possibilities. What was Brady up to? He had sacrificed his two men probably because he didn't want to share the spoils with them. Wouldn't this make it more difficult for him to operate? When he was making his phone calls from the public phone boxes where would Martha be? Who would be taking care of her or more realistically who would be making sure she didn't escape? Brady couldn't use his farm because Cosgrove had it under surveillance. Did he have another place where he could stay? Shannon's greatest fear was that his grandmother was being left gagged and tied up all day in some miserable rented flat.

They came to the conclusion that, short of a large scale police hunt, there was nothing they could do until they heard from Brady again. They were all in the conference room after having dinner in the mess, although all of them seemed to have lost their appetites, when Shannon's phone rang. When he heard Brady's voice he put his phone on loudspeaker.

'You didn't do as I asked did you, you bastard.'

'What do you mean?'

'You brought your slime ball friends to the hotel.'

'You didn't turn up at all.'

'I didn't turn up because you broke our agreement.'

'I had the money you asked for. I knew you would have armed men at the hotel. I wasn't armed. Did you expect me to face them without back up?'

'This is your last chance. Any more slip ups and I'll disappear and you'll never see your granny again.'

'Remember this Brady; if my grandmother is not returned unharmed, you won't be able to hide anywhere on this planet. I'll hunt you down like the animal you are and you won't die quickly.'

'Now I'm really scared. Now listen to me. Meet me with the money at eight-thirty this evening in the Botanic Gardens. Enter the gardens from the Botanic Avenue entrance. Find yourself a seat. I will find you and approach you when I'm sure you're not followed. When you hand over the money I'll tell you where your grandmother is. Don't be late the gardens close at nine o'clock.'

'That's not good enough. I need to see my grandmother before I hand over the money.'

'Tough. That's the deal and it's non-negotiable.' The phone went dead.

There was silence in the room for a couple of minutes as the team digested what Brady had proposed. Shannon was feeling trapped. He would have no choice but to go through with it. The danger was that they could lose the money, and more importantly, his grandmother may not be found alive. If he didn't meet Brady as arranged then he was certain that he wouldn't see his grandmother again. Brady was a killer and Shannon had a feeling that this wasn't just about the money, it was always about revenge.

'This is not good, Tom,' said McDonald, 'Brady has complete control. Once he's got the money he doesn't have to keep to his side of the bargain.'

'That's true, Jim, but he's calling the shots. As he said it's non-negotiable.'

'There is one thing we can do,' said Stella, 'we can fix one of Tony's bugs to the case. If Brady clears off we will be able to find him.'

'I've been giving this some thought,' said Clarke, 'Tom has previously pointed out that Brady is a very clever criminal. He's certainly given us the slip on a couple of occasions. He will suspect that we will fix a bug to the case so I'll bet my shirt that he'll bring his own case.'

'I've got a feeling that you've got something up your sleeve, Tony,' said Shannon.

'Well, I noticed that the bank had made a good job of bundling up the used notes. They are all in neat, tidy bundles secured with strong paper wrappers. We can try and outfox Brady by fixing a bug in the middle of one of these bundles. If he does bring his own case then he will believe that he is   bug free.'

'Brilliant,' said Stella.

Shannon arrived at the Botanic Gardens at eight-twenty. As Brady had instructed, he entered the gardens from Botanic Avenue. He found a bench not too far away from the entrance and sat down, keeping hold of the case. He was armed this time. He had his Walther and also his Bauer .25 in his ankle holster. If Brady got the opportunity and was foolish enough to try and kill him, he would be ready. Stella had checked the road map and said there were two other entrances to the gardens as well as Botanic Avenue. It was assumed that Brady would have a car parked somewhere. He had specifically asked Shannon to enter the gardens from Botanic Avenue. Was this because his vehicle was parked in that area and he could make a quick getaway? Or could it be that Brady wanted to give the impression that he had left his vehicle on that side of the gardens? He could then leave by one of the other exits making it more difficult for anyone to follow him by car.

222

McDonald was in one car parked in Botanic Avenue. They only had one other car so it was decided that Stella and Clarke choose one of the other exits and park their car there. If it happened to be the wrong exit then they still had the bug to rely on.

At exactly eight-thirty Brady arrived carrying a large black holdall. It was half an hour to closing time so there weren't many visitors remaining in the Gardens.

'I hope the money is in that case.'

'Where is my grandmother?'

'Let's see the colour of your money first.'

Shannon opened the case and Brady had a quick look at the notes. He opened the holdall and, after looking furtively around, he quickly emptied the notes into his holdall. He zipped up the bag and then stood up as if to leave.

'Where's my grandmother?'

'She's at home.'

'Then before you leave I'll give her a call to check.'

'She won't be able to answer because she's tied to a chair.'

'You bastard, how long have you had her tied up?'

'That's the last of your worries. There a bomb under the chair your grandmother is sitting on. You have half an hour before it goes off.'

'You evil bastard. I should shoot you now.'

'That would be a big mistake. I'm leaving now and in ten minutes I will give you a call and give you the code that will defuse the bomb. If I were you I would get to your grandmother's house as quickly as possible.'

'How do I know you are telling the truth?'

'You don't but can you afford to take a risk?'

Brady walked off into the gardens. He was obviously taking one of the other two exits. Shannon quickly left by the Botanic Avenue exit where McDonald was sitting in a car waiting for him. They moved off quickly in the direction of Martha Shannon's home. Shannon called Stella and

Clarke and told them what had happened. They arrived at Martha's home in fifteen minutes. Brady hadn't called. They were now faced with the prospect of the bomb going off and they would be helpless to do anything. Perhaps this is what Brady had planned. Shannon knowing that his grandmother was going to die and he would have to stand by and watch it happen. Shannon felt that Brady was hoping that he would die too trying to defuse the bomb.

Shannon unlocked the door to his grandmother's house. He opened the door slowly, his heart was racing. He went in and McDonald followed. No booby traps on the door, so far so good. His grandmother was sitting in a chair; her head slumped forward onto her chest. She was gagged and her wrists were tied to the chair. It was difficult to ascertain if she was alive. They had to approach her slowly and carefully in case Brady had fixed a trip wire or some such device. Shannon and McDonald moved carefully around searching for any device that looked like a bomb. McDonald had had some experience at defusing bombs but he was no expert. Brady still hadn't called and twenty minutes had elapsed so perhaps his plan was to kill Shannon along with his grandmother or else there was no bomb. They couldn't see anything resembling a bomb near or under the chair. After searching the rest of the room they were confident that the room was bomb free. Shannon called for an ambulance then he and McDonald removed the gag and untied Martha. She was breathing but seemed to be unconscious or had Brady drugged her? They searched the rest of the house but didn't find anything.

The ambulance arrived. The paramedics examined Martha then placed her on a stretcher. After giving her an injection they told Shannon that it appeared as if she had had a heart attack. After they left Shannon locked the door and he and McDonald followed the ambulance to the hospital. After some time waiting in the waiting room a doctor appeared. She told Shannon that Martha had been admitted to the intensive care ward and it was too early to give a reliable prognosis.

She wouldn't be allowed visitors today so she advised him to go home and call tomorrow. If there was any significant development she would give him a call.

When they left the hospital Shannon rang Stella and Clarke to tell them what had happened. They said that they followed Brady at a safe distance to a block of flats at the edge of the city. They didn't enter the flats but were waiting outside in case Brady came out again. They were parked a short distance away from the front of the flats. McDonald asked them to stay there and they would join them. Clarke gave him the address and it was almost nine-forty five when they arrived. The flats looked quite dingy in the street lighting and probably look worse in the daylight. Brady had obviously not found the bug because the signal was still coming from the flats.

When Shannon and McDonald arrived they got in the car with Stella and Clarke.

'We don't know where he's parked his car,' said Clarke, 'when we arrived we saw him entering the flats carrying a black holdall.'

'Perhaps there is a parking area at the back of the flats,' said McDonald.

'How do you want to approach this, Jim?' asked Shannon.

'We know he's in there so let's try to locate which flat he is in. One option is to knock on the door and if he doesn't open it break it down. We have to consider, however, that members of the public are in the vicinity. We can't put them at risk.'

'Another option may be.....' began Clarke.

'There's someone coming out of the flats,' interrupted Stella. An elderly man, with a walking stick, was holding the door open for a nun. They walked down the path together and then stopped. The man raised his hat to the nun then he turned left and walked off. The nun walked away in the opposite direction.

'What was your other option, Tony?' asked McDonald.

225

'We could knock on his door and if he answers tell him we're looking for say a Mr Whitehead.'

'I could do that,' said Stella, 'he doesn't know me and a woman is less threatening.'

'If he doesn't answer then I can pick the lock,' said Clarke.

'It seems a bit lame but let's try it,' said McDonald, 'if he does open the door, Stella, you must stand aside quickly and we'll rush him. Shannon's phone rang.

'Hello, doctor,' Shannon listened for a few moments, 'thank you doctor. I'll come to the hospital tomorrow morning.' He rang off. 'My grandmother died without regaining consciousness.'

'I'm so sorry, Tom,' said Stella as she took hold of his hand. Her eyes were filled with tears. Both men offered their condolences.

'Okay, let's go get him,' said Shannon as he began to get out of the car.

All four of them went into the flats. There was a main porch with a lift and stairs. At the side of the lift was a door leading to the ground floor flats. The tracker device was indicating that the bug was somewhere on the ground floor. They went through the door into a corridor. The lighting in the corridor was poor and some of the numbers on the doors were missing. There was an unpleasant smell of stale food. The tracker directed them to flat number thirteen. Stella knocked on the door. The men kept out of view on either side of the door. No answer. Stella knocked again still no answer. Clarke took a leather wallet out of his pocket, opened it up and took out two metal objects. He placed them into the keyhole and he soon had the door opened. They had all drawn their weapons and they went cautiously into the flat. After a few minutes they had searched the place but there was no sign of Brady. The bug which had been with the money was on the bed.

'Would you recognise his car?' asked McDonald looking at Stella and Clarke.

'It was a dark blue Ford Focus,' said Clarke.

'I wrote down the registration number,' said Stella as she handed him a piece of paper.

'Let's check if there is a car park,' said McDonald, 'and if the car is there, then perhaps he's still around somewhere.'

As they were leaving a number of people were approaching the flats. There must have been at least a dozen men and women chatting and laughing.

'Looks like some sort of celebration,' said Stella.

'Stella and Tony will you check to see if there is a car park?' said McDonald, 'Tom and I will check the street for Brady's car.'

'Jim,' said Shannon, 'didn't you have a photograph of Brady which was taken when he was arrested?'

'Yes, you're right and I've got a copy with me.'

'It's a long shot but I wonder if any of these people would recognise him?'

'It's worth a try. It may turn up something.'

Shannon waited in front of the flats and McDonald walked down the street hoping to find Brady's car. The revellers were still quite noisy when they arrived at the entrance to the flats.

'Excuse me,' said Shannon, 'I wonder if you could help me?'

'Hush you lot,' said a woman, 'this fella is trying to say something. What do you want sweetheart?'

'Now Alice,' shouted another woman, 'you shouldn't be asking strange fellas question like that.' This brought raucous laughter from the rest of the crowd.

'I have a photograph here,' said Shannon when the laughter died down, 'I was wondering if you recognised this man?'

'Let's go into the porch. There's a good light in there,' said a man who seemed to be more sober than the rest of them.

They all crowded around Shannon peering at the photograph.

'He's an ugly bugger,' shouted one man.

'I'm glad I didn't meet him in the dark,' laughed a woman.

'Wait a minute,' said a man wearing a bright red sweater, 'come on you lot, don't you remember who he is?' More chatter broke out and some began to shake their heads.

'I'll give you a clue,' said red sweater, 'three nuns.'

'Aye, I know who you're talking about now,' said a woman with purple hair.

'This fella lives on the ground floor,' said red sweater, 'and he.....'

'He lives in number thirteen. Isn't that right Alice?' interrupted purple hair.

'The reason we remember him,' said Alice, 'is because about a week ago three nuns arrived and went into flat thirteen. Not the sort of people you see in these flats. The strange thing was that they weren't seen again. The fella in the photo and two other strangers are living there now.'

'We think these three fellas have eaten the nuns,' said a man with a cigarette dangling from his lips. Everybody laughed and purple hair gave him a slap on the arm and told him not to be silly.

'Thank you very much,' said Shannon, 'you've been very helpful.' As he left, the chatter and laughter started again as they pushed open the outer door and entered the main inner porch. McDonald was walking up the path shaking his head.

'I haven't seen Brady's car on that side of the street,' said McDonald, 'I'll check the other side.'

'Forget it,' said Shannon, 'Brady's gone.'

'How do you know?'

'The nun who we saw with the old guy was Brady.'

'There's no sign of his car in the car park,' said Clarke as he and Stella returned, 'was it parked anywhere on the street?'
Shannon told them how he believed Brady had escaped.

'He's obviously used the car to get away,' said Shannon, 'he must have thought that everything had gone too smoothly. It would have made him suspicious so he checked the notes and found the bug.'

It was after eleven o'clock when they returned to Holywood army base where McDonald contacted the police and asked for a check to be set up on all sea and airports. The duty officer arranged for some coffee to be delivered to the conference room. McDonald announced that he would have to return to Manchester in the morning because he had a meeting with the Home Secretary in the afternoon.

Next morning there was still no news of Brady. It seemed as if he had disappeared into thin air. It was unlikely that he would have returned to his farm but the police searched it anyway. All exits from the Province were being checked by the police. The Garda had been alerted in case he had fled to the Republic.

37

After Shannon's grandmother's funeral was over, the Ironclad team returned to Manchester. Shannon was given leave to deal with his grandmother's affairs. He had decided to sell her home but keep his grandfather's cottage which had been in the Connery family for about three generations. He was happy that his relationship with Stella had improved and he hoped that they had a future together. After a couple of weeks, Shannon had sorted out most of his grandmother's affairs and found a good estate agent and solicitor to take care of the sale of the house. Before he returned to England he decided to visit his grandmother's grave. He called at a florist and chose some flowers then made his way to the cemetery. He placed the flowers on the grave and his eyes filled with tears. 'Well Gran, you warned me but this is not the grave I expected to see. It should have been mine. It should be you looking at my grave. Remember *"dig two graves – one for yourself"* I'm the bad guy, not you. I'm so sorry Gran, so sorry. It's not fair; it's just not fair. This is worse than my worst nightmare.' Shannon hadn't realised that he had been speaking out loud. He suddenly felt two arms surround his waist and he heard Stella's voice, 'I love you, Tom Shannon.' He turned and held her for a few moments. If only his grandmother could have met this beautiful girl. He felt as if his heart was going to burst with grief. Life can be very cruel.

'What are you doing here?' asked Shannon.

'I thought you had been alone too long so I asked Colonel McDonald to let me fly over to see how you were coping. It's strange but I guessed you would be here.'

'Let's go to Connery Cottage. They can manage without us for a couple of days.'

Next morning after they had finished breakfast, Shannon poured two more fresh coffees and sat down at the table facing Stella.

'Stella, I'm not going back with you.'

'You have to; you are a member of Ironclad. It's your duty.'

'I don't mean I'm never going back. I'm going to find Brady.'

'You can't do that, it's too dangerous without backup. Brady has two million pounds and he has probably found himself a safe haven and recruited some guys to protect him.'

'Maybe but I promised him that if anything happened to my grandmother he wouldn't be able to hide anywhere on this planet because I would hunt him down.'

'Tom, this is madness. You don't know where he is and if you did find him what will you do? Take the law into your hands.'

'No, I'm not going to kill him. I will hand him over to the police. I just don't want him to get away with it.'

'Tom, please discuss this with Colonel McDonald first. He may have some ideas. The police are watching out for Brady. It will be difficult for him to leave the country,'

'Jim's up to his ears with problems in England. Military personnel are being murdered on the streets. He will be expected to find out if there is some organised movement behind these atrocities.'

'I know and he will need your help.'

'I'm sorry, Stella, but I have to do this. I will let Jim know and I'm sure he will understand.'

'All right, I guessed that you would be determined to do this and I knew that once you had made your mind up I wouldn't be able to change it. I came here in the Cessna to Holywood army base and so I was able to bring your Astra and Bauer .25. I don't want you to go after Brady without any firearms.'

'Thanks, Stella.'

'Please don't take any risks because you don't have any back up. I'd feel happier if you would promise me that when you locate Brady you will inform the police and let them arrest him.'

'That's my intention.'

Shannon contacted McDonald and he agreed to extend his leave by two weeks. McDonald made it clear that it was a concession and could be withdrawn if he was needed for some other mission. Stella left for Holywood army base and the flight to Manchester. Shannon made some fresh coffee and sat down at the table with a view to formulating a plan of action. Brady was wanted in Northern Ireland for the murder of the Carson family, the bank robbery and, no doubt, the police would have other criminal charges against him. Logically, it would make sense for him to leave the Province and find somewhere in the Republic where his capture may be less of a priority. He could be unlucky there, however, because the Garda would be looking out for him. To attempt to go abroad or to England would be very risky. Shannon was very much aware that Brady was extremely clever and he wouldn't be surprised if he had changed his appearance and was still living in Northern Ireland. The more Shannon thought about it, the more he began to believe that the task was too big for him. Stella was right, he needed backup. He decided that he would have to eat humble pie and go back to England. It was at this juncture that his mobile phone rang. It was Sean Keane. He said that he had some information for him but was not prepared to speak about it on a cell phone. Shannon said that he would meet him at his Belfast office that afternoon.

Shannon arrived at Keane's office in the middle of the afternoon. Before Shannon could speak Keane's secretary brought the usual tray of coffee and biscuits. When she left he could contain himself no longer.

'Sean, is the information you have something to do with Brady?'

'Yes, but let's not get too excited.'

'Why not? This is what I've been hoping for.'

'Let me explain. An old friend of mine was on a fishing holiday in Cloghan in Donegal. He called in The Ramblers Inn and standing at the bar was this guy drinking a Guinness. He felt certain it was Brady. He said he looked thinner than he remembered and he had a beard, a full set. He didn't know Brady that well so he could be mistaken.'

'But you think it was him, don't you Sean?'

'Well, I know that Brady is a keen fisherman. When he was a teenager his uncle often took him fishing in that area. It's famous for wild salmon fishing and hunting and lots of hikers frequent the area. My friend also said that this guy had very cold, blue eyes which made me think that it was Brady.'

'I'll go and check the area to see if it really is him.'

'I'll go Tom. If he sees you then he will know you are looking for him.'

'No, I can't let you do that. You have a wife and a young family. He won't see me. As you know I'm pretty good at changing my appearance.'

'I heard another piece of news the other day. I believe that Peter Byrne has bought a farm in Donegal. I couldn't believe it because I thought he had been arrested and sent to prison.'

'The bloody fool,' exclaimed Shannon, 'he may be one of the reasons why Brady is in Donegal. It could be the main reason.'

'What do you mean, Tom?'

'Byrne blamed Brady for the death of his cousin Frank Doyle; as a consequence he spilled the beans on Brady and his fellow criminals. On his evidence it was possible to convict Brady and all his cronies. Of course, he wanted a deal for himself which was granted. He was given a new identity and a shoal of money. He should have gone to live abroad, staying in Ireland is a big mistake. If Brady has found him it may be payback time.'

'The other possibility, Tom, is that Brady may be using Byrne's farm as a hideout. With the two million pounds you say he has he can afford a lot of protection. With a couple of guys on his payroll he could terrorise Byrne into letting him use the farm.'

'We're speculating, Sean. We don't know what he's up to but I'm going to find out.'

Back at Connery Cottage, Shannon changed the colour of his blond hair with a brunette dye and fixed a fake, full set beard. After a few more cosmetic touches, he checked himself in the mirror and gave a satisfied nod. He had kitted himself out with hikers equipment from a woolly hat through to good walking boots. He was now ready to play the role of hiker. He hired a car and headed out in the direction of Donegal hoping to get there in time to find some accommodation. The light had faded when he arrived in Cloghan but it had been a good trip and the weather was warm and dry. He made his way to The Ramblers Inn just in time to book the last single room. After a shower, he changed into smart casuals and made his way to the bar. It was too late for dinner but bar snacks were being served and he ordered a chicken and salad sandwich along with a coffee. There were quite a number of people in the bar, they were mostly men. No sign of Brady or anybody who looked like Brady. He had finished his sandwich and coffee and decided to go over to the bar for another coffee. After the barman had served him his drink, he turned to have another look at the people in the bar. He then noticed that there was another door at the far end of the bar. He thought that it may be the non-residents' entrance. Something else which he hadn't noticed earlier was that beyond the door was an alcove big enough to take a table and four chairs. Three men were sitting at the table. One man, who was clean shaven, was facing the bar and could be easily seen. The other two had beards, rather vulgar beards Shannon thought. This made him smile because his false beard could be described as vulgar. It was difficult to see the bearded men because of the way they were sitting at an angle to the bar. He had just decided to move down the bar to take a better look, when the door opened and Sean Keane walked in. One of the men sitting at the table beckoned to him and he went over to them. Shannon saw this as an opportunity to move nearer to see if he could hear what they were saying. As he got nearer, he picked up a little of the conversation, '....so I thought I'd do a bit of hiking, 'Keane was saying. Another voice said, 'So you've left the wife and kids at home to look after the business.' Shannon recognised that voice

234

immediately, it was Brady's. Shannon was unable to see his face properly but there was no mistaking the voice. He heard Keane tell Brady that his wife had gone to Dublin with her mother and the children to do some shopping. He also added that his staff were competent enough to take care of the business for a few days. Brady then invited him to join them. Keane went to the bar got a drink and rejoined them. Shannon was wondering what was going on. Was Keane here as back up for him even though Shannon had refused his help? Or was he here for some other reason? Shannon had stayed alive in the past by being suspicious of everybody and everything. But Keane, surely he wasn't in cahoots with Brady. He felt certain that he wasn't. He decided not to reveal himself until it was clear what Keane was here for. If he tried to take Brady now, he could be up against four men and also he didn't want to risk the lives of other people in the bar. He would have to wait. After about half an hour Brady and the other two men left. Keane made his way through the bar to the reception area. He passed Shannon but didn't recognise him. Shannon followed him after a short interval. Keane was at the reception desk where he was given a key. Shannon had been given the last single room which, in fact, was the last room available in the inn. So, obviously Keane must have booked earlier but how much earlier?

Keane went up to his room to call his wife to check that they had arrived safely in Dublin. After the call he sat on the bed considering his next move. He hadn't seen Shannon anywhere and when he was parking his car he didn't see his Harley-Davidson in the car park. His room overlooked the car park and he could see that Shannon's motorbike still hadn't turned up. Of course, he could have come by car or he could be staying somewhere else. Reception had not been able to confirm that a Mr. Shannon was staying at the inn but it was unlikely that he would use his own name. Keane knew, however, that Shannon's disguise skills were amazing and it was quite possible that he was sitting in the bar. He decided to go back to the bar. It was getting late and there was a chance that most of the non-residents may have left and so making it easier to identify Shannon.

Shannon was sitting at the bar enjoying a Jameson's whiskey, considering whether to turn in, when Keane came back into the bar. A number of the residents were fishermen, planning to be up early and so had gone to bed, leaving about half dozen people in the bar. Shannon guessed that Keane had been looking for his Harley-Davidson and may have assumed that he wasn't staying at the inn. He was mistaken. Keane had realised that it was almost certain that only the non-anglers would be in the bar at this time of the night. Keane looked around the bar then made his way straight to Shannon.

'May I buy you another whiskey? Is it Jameson's?' asked Keane.

'How did you know it was me?'

'I didn't but you were the only one drinking whiskey so I thought I'd take a chance.'

'Ah, my Achilles heel,' smiled Shannon.

'Looking at you close up, I'm still not sure it's you except for your voice.'

'Tell me, what are you doing here? I know you aren't a fisherman.'

'I know you won't like it but you need back up.'

'I know you won't like it but go home.'

'Tom, Brady has two roughnecks with him. You are outnumbered. You need someone to watch your back.'

'I'm not going to kill him. My intention is to bring him in and let the courts deal with him.'

'That will be very dangerous and something which will be very difficult to do by yourself.'

'I admit it will be difficult but I have to do it. I must remind you again that you have a wife and young children so you shouldn't be taking this kind of risk.'

'Tom, together we can take them. I know you have had special training but I've kept myself fit and I am more than capable. I also have an advantage over you.'

'What's that?'

'I can keep in touch with Brady and find out what he's doing here, and more importantly, find out where he is staying. You would find that difficult, if not impossible. I couldn't ask him too many questions earlier because it would have made him suspicious.'

Shannon was silent for some moments thinking it over. It did make sense and he knew that Keane was a good man to have on your side. He was still worried about his family commitments though.

'Okay,' Shannon eventually said, 'but I don't want you taking unnecessary risks. We do everything together. Agreed?'

'Agreed, however, there is something that I have already arranged and it would be foolish to cancel because it would make Brady suspicious.'

'What's that?'

'I'm meeting Brady near The Finn River tomorrow. I told him that I was looking for some interesting places to do some walking. He claimed to have a map showing a number of excellent trails for hikers.'

'I'm not happy with that. Brady is a very cunning bastard and probably has some hidden agenda. I'll follow you and perhaps together we can bring him in.'

'I think that's a bad idea. Brady said his cronies would be with him and I feel sure they will be armed. Also I understand that it is a popular spot for fishermen and ramblers so any attempt to overcome Brady may result in members of the public being hurt.'

'Good point. Make sure you have your mobile phone with you but we will only use them in case of emergency. Sean, what were we doing associating with scum like Brady way back when?'

Keane was silent for several moments.

'I've always believed that Partition was wrong, I still do. I believe passionately in a united Ireland. What set me on this journey were the atrocities suffered by the minority in the Province. I'm sure that a great number of people would see me as scum too, perhaps they are right. But at the time I couldn't see any other way forward. Eventually, I began to realise that if you want to persuade people to your way of thinking, the last thing you should do is to give them a bloody nose. When the Peace Process was launched I was relieved. I hoped that it would work. I hoped that it would be an opportunity for both sides to arrive at some compromise. I was sick and tired of the conflict and there didn't appear to be any chance of either side winning. What's your reason or excuse?'

It was Shannon's turn to be silent. After what seemed like an age Shannon told Keane about Laura and his insane quest to seek revenge.

'I'm really sorry, Tom. Now I can understand why you were drinking so heavily. Your grandmother was right about revenge, look what it's done to Northern Ireland.'

'Whatever else I do I must get Brady,' said Shannon, who appeared to be thinking out loud.

38

Next morning, Shannon caught a glimpse of Keane leaving as he went into the dining room for breakfast. Keane had said that he planned to return by lunch time, hopefully with Brady's address. Keane hadn't returned by lunch time and there was no sign of him when dinner was served. The previous day Shannon had had a bar snack instead of going into the dining room for lunch. He had spent a lot time chatting to the barman in the hope of learning about the area and the men who frequented the bar. He had done the same today. Adam, the barman was fond of having a chat particularly during the afternoon when it was quiet. They talked mostly about different interesting places in the area. Shannon had never even hinted that he was looking for someone but he felt it was time to see if Adam knew anything about the three men. After dinner he went into the bar and asked for a Jameson's. As the barman was serving the drink, Shannon decided to try to glean some information, hopefully without raising any suspicions.

'Adam, last night there were three men sitting at that table at the far end of the bar. They didn't appear to mix with any of the other anglers. They are not here tonight but there was something odd about them and I can't quite put my finger on what it is.'

'It's interesting that you should say that, sir,' smiled Adam, ' for a few weeks the blond one with the beard used to come in by himself. He would have a beer or two then leave. In those days he always wore a baseball cap pulled down over his eyes. Then two or three weeks ago the other two guys turned up. The blond guy with the cap became agitated when he saw them. As they sat down at the table, the blond man appeared as if he wanted to leave but the other two pushed him back in his seat.'

'Do they come in every night?'

'Usually they do but it looks as if they are giving it a miss tonight.'

'I assume that they must live locally?'

'I guess they do but I don't know where. I know some of the locals but I don't know them. Some visitors stay here and some stay in rented accommodation.'

'Is there much rented accommodation around here?'

'Some locals do bed and breakfast and there are three new chalets which have been built recently at the edge of the wood. They're available for rent and are very popular.'

'It sounds as if the area is doing okay if they've started building chalets. It must be good for business.' Shannon decided to leave it there, hoping that he hadn't asked too many questions about the three men.

It was getting late now and he was getting more worried about Keane. He wondered if he had gone straight to his room because they had agreed not to meet in public. He decided to check Keane's room. He knocked on the door a number of times but got no response. The barman had told him where the favourite fishing spots were so he decided to check them out. As he made his way there he began to feel that this was a waste of time but he had a need to do something. He was sure that all the anglers would have packed up and gone by now. He arrived at a clearing near the river and he could see that a car was parked. He got out of his car and looked around the area. There was no one in sight. He rang Blake and gave him the registration number of the car. Shortly Blake returned his call and informed him that the car belonged to Keane. He and Keane had agreed not to use their mobile phones except in emergency. Shannon decided that this was indeed an emergency. He called Keane's number, after a couple rings it was answered.

'Hello, Shannon,' it was Brady's voice, 'I was wondering how long it would be before you rang. So what are you and Keane up to?'

'What makes you think we're up to anything?'

'I'm not stupid. You are here on a mission and Keane is helping you. I think that Keane is very sorry he was involved now. He's probably thinking that he is never going to see his family again. Right now I don't think they would recognise him. His face has been rearranged a little.'

'Let him go Brady. It's me you're after. Let me know where you are and we'll do an exchange.'

'That's very tempting. To get you off my back would be a real bonus. Let me think about it.'

'Don't think too long because if I inform the police that you are in this county they'll swamp this area with armed men.'

'If there is even a whisper of police then Keane is a dead man. One more dead man won't make any difference to me.'

'Let me have your address and I'll come now.'

'Nice try, Shannon, but I'm not going to let you know where I am. I'll try to find a neutral meeting place and call you back in a couple of days.'

'Keane had better be....' Shannon didn't finish because the phone was disconnected.

Next morning, after the barman had given him directions, Shannon made his way to look at the new chalets at the edge of the wood. He thought that Brady may have rented one. The sun was shining in a blue sky and it was quite warm. In the garden of the first chalet an elderly couple were sitting on a bench enjoying the sunshine. Outside the second chalet a young man was washing his car and a young woman was coming out of the chalet with two cups of tea or coffee. Two down and just one to go. In the garden of the third chalet, two little blond boys were playing in the garden. Shannon stopped in his tracks. What a fool he had been. Peter Byrne and his deceased cousin Frank Doyle were blond and one of the three men in the bar was blond and could easily have been Byrne. Keane had said that Byrne had bought a farm in this area and if Keane knew then it was quite possible that Brady had also found out. Adam, the barman, had said that Byrne appeared to be alarmed when he saw Brady. If the blond man is Byrne then he has reason to be afraid. Brady will know that he had betrayed him because he wasn't arrested with the rest of them. Shannon felt certain that Brady was holding up at Byrne's farm but where is that farm?

When Shannon got back to the inn he phoned Peter Blake and asked him if he knew where Byrne was living. Blake pointed out that that was classified information but felt sure that Colonel McDonald would have the necessary clearance. He promised to find out and phone back as soon as possible. Shannon impressed upon him that it was urgent because Brady may be planning to kill a couple of people. Blake was true to his promise and within fifteen minutes he gave Shannon the information he asked for. Shannon switched off immediately and took out his map of the area. Blake had told him that the farm was called Kingarrow Farm and was about half way between Cloghan and the town of Kingarrow. That would mean that the farm was about three or four miles away. Of course, it wasn't necessarily true that Brady was staying at Byrne's farm. The barman had said that when Byrne first saw Brady he looked scared and appeared to want to leave the bar but was restrained by the other two men. On subsequent evenings, Byrne had returned to the inn with Brady and his companion. If Byrne was scared of Brady why was he apparently hanging out with him? Shannon was convinced that Byrne had no choice. If Brady was keeping him on a short leash, then it made sense that he was staying at Byrne's farm. Shannon waited until after dinner in the hope that Brady would get back to him. He didn't receive any call so he left for Kingarrow Farm. When he found the farm he left his car in the lane and some distance away from the entrance. The light was beginning to fade as he approached the farm which was a single storey building. There were lots of bushes and trees surrounding the building. The lights were on in a number of windows. He looked into the first window he came to. He could see Byrne sitting at a table, looking fairly glum, with a mug of something in front of him. Keane was tied to a chair and from the bruising on his face he had had a beating. Brady and another man, Shannon didn't know, were standing near the fireplace deep in conversation. Brady had threatened to kill Keane if the police were informed so he couldn't take that risk. Somehow he had to save Keane. He owed him that much, perhaps more. He had asked Brady to do an exchange but that was risky too. If he went into the farm house Brady could kill them both. On balance, he decided, that to try the exchange may be the lesser of two evils. He tried the front door. It wasn't locked so he walked straight into the hall and through into the living room.

'Well, well,' said Brady, 'we have a visitor. We've been expecting you.'

'You knew I would find you eventually.'

'I was depending on it. I knew the idea of an exchange would bring you here.'

'Okay, let's get on with it. Release Sean and I will take his place.'

'I'm forgetting my manners. I haven't introduced you to my friend, Alan. Alan has something for you.' Alan produced a hand gun and pointed it at Shannon.

'What's the idea, Brady? I thought we were going to arrange an exchange?'

'I didn't agree to an exchange. What's to stop Keane contacting the police when he is free?'

'I'm sure that Sean will agree to keep quiet in exchange for his life.'

'You must think I'm stupid. I'm not going to leave any loose ends.'

'You won't get away with it. My people know where I am and they will have informed the Garda.'

'I'll be long gone before any of your friends get here. In fact we are leaving now. Alan, tie his hands behind his back. Get his car keys, his mobile phone and his weapons. He must have parked the car down the lane. Bring it to the front of the house.' Within a few minutes he was back with Shannon's car.

Byrne had been watching Shannon and Brady with a look of consternation on his face. Brady turned to him, 'Peter, get Keane up

243

out of that chair and check to make sure that his hands are securely tied behind his back.' Byrne got Keane up onto his feet. Keane staggered and Byrne had to steady him. He was obviously still suffering from the beating they had given him.

'Declan, what are you going do?' asked Byrne, obviously very nervous.

'I'm going to get these two out of my hair forever.'

'Shannon's people know I am living here. I'm sure that they know that Sean Keane is here too.'

'Not necessarily, Peter, or they would be here now.' Byrne still looked very worried.

'Alan, you and Peter get these two outside.'

Shannon and Keane were taken outside to the parked cars. Shannon was bundled into the boot of his car and Keane was lifted into the boot of Brady's car.

'Peter, remember you haven't seen us. Keep your mouth shut and you won't see us again. Okay?'

'Okay, Declan.'

'Let's go back inside and check that we haven't left anything belonging to Alan or me.'

Brady followed Byrne back into the farmhouse. As soon as they were in the kitchen Brady shot Byrne in the back of his head.

'That's another loose end taken care of, Alan,' grinned Brady when he returned to the parked cars, 'you drive my car and I'll drive Shannon's car.'

The cars headed west and it was some twenty minutes before they turned off the main road and made their way down a narrow lane. The cars stopped in a clearing near the mouth of The River Finn. Both Brady and his companion got out of their cars.

'What's the plan Declan?'

'When I was a kid my uncle used to bring me fishing in this area. If we walk through the gap in those bushes we should find a small jetty. We are going to rope these two to the jetty's support legs and when the tide comes in – kaput! We are going to hang around and listen to them struggle or if we're lucky we may hear them scream.'

They lifted Shannon out of the boot and dragged him down the embankment and roped him to a wooden strut. They did the same to Keane then returned to Brady's car. Brady had brought a flask of coffee and they sat drinking it waiting for the tide to come in.

39

Back at The Priory in Manchester, Stella was telling Clarke that she had become very concerned for Shannon. He was in Donegal without any back up. Clarke said that there was nothing they could do until Shannon contacted them. He felt frustrated that he was unable to get out there to help him. Stella said that as far as she was aware, there had been no further communication since his phone call to Peter Blake. She decided to raise the matter with Peter.

'Peter, has Tom contacted you again?'

'I'm afraid not.' It was then that Colonel McDonald came into the room.

'Jim,' said Blake, 'we are discussing Tom and we are concerned that we haven't heard from him.'

'Contacting him may be dangerous. If he is watching Brady, a phone ring may disclose his position, although I would have thought that he would have switched his phone off. Can we take the risk?'

'When I last spoke with him,' said Blake, 'I should have arranged some sort of safe means of contacting him. He did seem to be in a hurry and switched off immediately after I had given him the information he asked for.'

'Perhaps it's time to speak to our friends in the Garda,' said McDonald.

McDonald went to his desk and tapped a number on his phone.

'This is Colonel McDonald. May I speak to Chief Superintendent Brendan Jennings?' McDonald put his phone on loudspeaker and after a few minutes Jennings came on the phone.

'Hello, Jim. How are you?'

'I'm fine. Brendan, I want to ask you a favour, a big favour.'

'It sounds interesting. Ask away.'

'As you know Declan Brady is at large somewhere in Northern Ireland or the Republic.'

'We are keeping a look out for him but there has been no sign of him yet.'

'One of my men had a tip-off that Brady was in Donegal. More specifically he thinks he is holding up in Kingarrow Farm which is somewhere between Cloghan and Kingarrow.'

'I don't know that particular farm but I'm sure the local police will know where it is. Do you want me to send some officers to check?'

'I should make sure they are armed.'

'No problem. I'll arrange it straight away.'

'Brendan, we're not sure that Brady is there. Our man has not contacted us for some time so we have to assume that he is being prevented from using his phone. His plan was to find where Brady was holding up and then inform the Garda so that they could arrest him. Warn your men that if Brady is at the farm, there may be some armed resistance.'

'Okay, Jim. I'll keep you informed.' Jennings rang off.
McDonald addressed his team, 'there's nothing we can do now until Jennings gets back to us.'

'Why don't I fly out to Holywood army base?' suggested Stella, 'Captain Cosgrove could provide men and transport to get to Donegal.'

'You would have difficulty finding Kingarrow Farm,' said McDonald, 'and Cosgrove wouldn't allow you to take army personnel into the Republic. The Garda will be able to get there more quickly than Cosgrove and his men.'

'I'm sorry. I wasn't thinking. I...I...' Stella realised that she was allowing her emotions to get in the way of common sense. She went to her desk and sat down.

'I understand, Stella,' said McDonald, 'we are all concerned about Tom. It's not like him to keep us in the dark which makes me think that he's in trouble. Let's wait and see what Jennings finds out.'

About an hour later Jennings called back.

'Hello, Jim.'

'Have you got any news, Brendan?'

'When the Garda arrived at the farm they found the place empty except for a dead body. He had been shot in the back of the head. Documents found on the body identified him as Peter Byrne. It would seem that the local Garda had some intelligence on this man. He was from Northern Ireland and the British police had a file on him but gave an assurance that he was no threat to the community.

'It was the evidence of this man that helped to convict Brady and his gang,' said McDonald, 'he took the reward but refused protection and refused to change his name. He wanted to be left in peace to farm in Ireland. I'm sorry, Brendan, but I couldn't tell you any of this because it was a police arrangement. Now he's dead it doesn't matter.'

'I understand, Jim. I'm sorry I can't give you any more information. The only vehicle on the premises belonged to Byrne so we haven't any evidence that your man was there. Three of the beds had been slept in but we will have to wait and see if forensics can come up with something. We will continue searching the immediate area and I'll let you know if we find anything.'

'Thanks, Brendan. I really appreciate your efforts and I owe you one.'

'Any time, Jim.' Jennings ended the call.

'Doesn't look good,' said McDonald as he looked solemnly at the others.

'Of course, there is a chance that he wasn't at the farm,' said Stella, 'or he could have got away.'

'I gave him the address of the farm,' prompted Blake, 'so he must have gone to the farm. The question is did he arrive at the farm before or after Byrne was shot?'

'Yes, that is the question,' agreed Clarke, 'and the next question is what do we do now?'

'I'm not sure that we can do anything,' said McDonald, 'we don't know where he is.'

'I think the only hope is that he has his phone,' said Blake, 'and he is able to contact us.'

'I think we have to assume that he hasn't got his phone,' said Clarke, 'otherwise he would have contacted us. Jim, I know we have another project going here but Brady is really unfinished business.'

'What are you trying to say, Tony?' asked McDonald.

'I want you to give permission for Stella and me to fly out to Holywood army base. We could borrow a car off Cosgrove and drive up to Donegal........'

'Then what will you do?' interrupted McDonald.

'Please, Colonel,' pleaded Stella, 'let's give it a try.'

'I think it's a good idea,' said Blake, 'these two know how Tom works. They may spot something that the Garda wouldn't recognise.'

'Okay, okay, it's not necessary for all of you to gang up on me,' smiled McDonald, 'we can put the present project on the back burner for a time but when you get back I shall expect double effort from all of you.'

'A deal,' they all said in unison.

Stella and Clarke left immediately for Greenacre airfield. Colonel McDonald rang Chief Superintendent Jennings and informed him that Stella and Clarke would be in his area looking for Shannon.

40

Shannon and Keane struggled hoping to loosen the ropes but they had been very securely tied. The ropes were fairly thick and even if the posts had had sharp corners it would have been impossible to cut through them. The water had now reached their knees and they had begun to shiver with the cold. They could hear music so they assumed Brady had the car radio on. Occasionally they could hear them laughing probably at their expense.

'I'm sorry, Sean, for getting you into this awful situation.'

'You didn't get me into this awful situation. Remember, I insisted on coming with you as back up. If I remember rightly you didn't know that I had followed you.'

'Okay, but I should have known that Brady wouldn't have agreed to an exchange. In spite of all my experience and training I made a major mistake and that's going to cost both our lives.'

'I agree that we are going to die but don't blame yourself. I thought that I could hoodwink Brady but I was wrong and that's why I ended up tied to a chair and beaten up. That put you in a situation where you felt you had to try to rescue me.'

'Hindsight is definitely a wonderful thing. Here we are tied to two posts, water up to our knees and we are arguing about who is to blame.'

'Brady is to blame, Tom.'

Both men fell silent. Shannon was thinking about his grandmother. If he had listened to her then he wouldn't be tied to this post now and his grandmother would be alive. He could see no way out of this predicament. Colonel McDonald and his team wouldn't know where he is. They wouldn't know that Keane was with him. All they would be certain of was that he had gone to Kingarrow Farm. He wondered if Byrne would do the decent thing and inform the police. Then he remembered the gunshot he had heard when he was locked in the boot of the car.

'Sean, did you hear a gunshot back at the farm when we were locked in the boots of the cars?'

'Yes, I'd forgotten about that. I think it would be Brady making sure Byrne wouldn't grass on him again.'

'I'm sure you're right so there's no chance of Byrne helping us out.'

'I don't think there is any chance of anybody helping us out.'

'Where there's life there's hope, Sean.'

'I don't think the guy who thought that up ever experienced being tied to a post with water up to his knees.'

Shannon was now feeling desperate but didn't want to pass on his fears to Keane but Keane was no fool and he was well aware that their position was hopeless. Shannon didn't want to die but would have died more easily if he had been able to put Brady away. It now seemed as if they were going to join the fishes. And there was Stella, his lovely Stella. He now believed that he wouldn't see her beautiful, green eyes again and wouldn't be able to hold her and tell her how much he loved her. He was certain that Keane would be thinking about his wife and family. It must be like torture for him to know that he wouldn't see them again. He wouldn't have the pleasure of seeing his children grow up. He was suddenly aware that the water was now above his waist and would soon be up to his chest. He was convinced that they would be dead before dawn, probably a lot sooner than that.

41

Captain Cosgrove provided a civilian car for Clarke and Stella and they set off for Donegal. They eventually arrived at Kingarrow Farm. A guard was on duty but he had been informed that they would be arriving. They went into the farmhouse. An area in the kitchen had been taped off so they kept clear of that. They looked around the kitchen hoping to find some clue that Shannon had been here. If Shannon had had the slightest opportunity to leave a clue they were sure that he would have done so. They searched the room meticulously for nearly an hour but were unable to find anything. They checked upstairs and as the Garda had reported three beds had been slept in. It was unlikely that Shannon would have slept in any of them.

'I think that this has been a waste of time, Tony.'

'Well, we have satisfied ourselves that Tom didn't leave a clue. If we hadn't checked and later found out that he had left a clue we wouldn't have been able to forgive ourselves.'

'He probably didn't have the time or the opportunity,' said Stella, 'we don't know any more than when we first arrived here.'

'I know but we tried. Let's talk to the Guard stationed at the front.' They approached the Guard and told him that they hadn't found anything. They then asked him if they had any information which would indicate which way Brady may have gone. He said that they had followed the tyre tracks of two cars for a short time along the lane. When they entered the main road they lost them. He said they were sure that the cars were headed west but couldn't be more accurate than that. Stella and Clarke returned to their car.

'Tony, whether the news is good or bad I would like to be in this area when Tom is found. I couldn't possibly go back to Manchester before finding out what happened to him.'

'All right, let's go to Cloghan I believe that The Ramblers Inn has a good reputation.'

At The Ramblers Inn they managed to book two rooms. The receptionist apologised because the rooms weren't ready. The previous occupants had been allowed to stay for a few extra hours so the maid was still cleaning the rooms. She told them that they were too late for dinner in the restaurant but they would be able to get bar food if they wished. They left their luggage with the receptionist and went into the bar.

'What would you like to drink Stella?'

'I'll have a gin and tonic.'

'I'll have a Jameson's in honour of my good friend.' This brought tears to Stella's eyes.

'I'm sorry, Stella, I wasn't thinking.'

'Don't be sorry, I've been looking for an excuse to cry.'

The barman approached, 'Can I help you, sir?' Clarke asked for the two drinks.

'That's interesting, sir,' said the barman, 'you are the second Englishman to ask for a Jameson's in the last few days. The English usually ask for Scotch.'

'Did you know this Englishman?'

'Not exactly, he was a guest here for a couple of days. He often had a bar snack and we often had a long chat. I liked him very much and I had a feeling that he enjoyed talking to me. I was surprised when he left without saying anything.'

'What did he look like?' asked Stella.

'Er, well, he was fairly tall and he had a beard. I think he had blue eyes but most importantly he was a very nice guy. He was interested in the area and was pleased that business in the area was good.'

'Do you know what he was doing here?' asked Clarke.

'I'm certain that it wasn't for the fishing. My guess is that he was looking for someone.'

'What makes you say that?' asked Clarke.

'He was very interested in three fellas who used to sit together at the end of the bar. I told him that the blond, bearded one of the trio used to come in here alone. When the other two appeared he looked really scared and made a move to leave but they wouldn't let him.'

'Did he say that he knew any of them?' asked Stella.

'No, he didn't but a barman sees a lot of folk and you get to know things from people's mannerisms or words they use. I feel certain that he knew at least one of them. Why are you asking me all these questions? I think you knew this man.'

'We're not sure but we think it could be a friend of ours who has been missing for a few days. Did he speak to any of these men?' asked Clarke.

'He didn't speak to anyone only me. Wait a minute, I tell a lie. It was late one night. Most of the residents had gone to bed. There was this fella who had been in the bar previously. He came back in and after looking at some of the fellas still drinking, he made straight for your friend, that is, the man who may be your friend.'

'What did he say?' asked Clarke.

'I made my way down the bar to see if this fella had come in for a drink. As I got near to them I heard the second fella say something like, "I knew it was you because of the Jameson's," I'm not sure of the correct words.'

'Did they leave together?' asked Stella.

'No they didn't. After a few minutes the second fella left by himself and I haven't seen him since. After a day or two I didn't see your friend in the bar again. Of course, he may have been staying for a few days only and decided to move on. I still think it was strange that he didn't say anything to me. Why don't you try reception and see if they can give you any more information?'

'Thank you very much. We'll do that.'

When the receptionist saw them she said that their rooms were ready and she apologised again.

'I wonder if you could help us?' asked Clarke, 'we are looking for two men who appear to have gone missing. One of them we are certain is missing but we're not sure about the other man.'

'What are their names?'

'One of them may have registered as Shannon or Connery. The other may be registered as Keane.'

The receptionist checked the register.

'Yes, we have a Connery and a Keane and they both registered on the same day.'

'Would you know where they are?' asked Stella hopefully.

'I'm afraid not. All I can tell you is that they booked in for a week. I haven't seen them for a day or two. It's not unusual for some ramblers to go into the hills with sleeping bags and other equipment and stay out for a day or two.'

They asked the receptionist if they could check both rooms to see if there were any clues as to where the two men had gone. She said she couldn't do that without the permission of the guests. They told her that they were here with the permission of Chief Superintendent Jennings. Luckily, she knew him well because he was a fisherman and often stayed at the inn. She agreed to give him a ring to see if he would corroborate their story. When Jennings answered he asked to speak to them. The receptionist handed the receiver to Clarke.

'Hello, sir, my name is Clarke.'

'Tell me, Mr Clarke, who is your boss?'

'Colonel Jim McDonald.'

'What is the name of the anti-terrorist unit he commands?'

'Ironclad.'

'All right, Tony, I just wanted to make sure that it was you. Jim had given me your name but obviously I didn't know your voice. If you hand me back to the receptionist I'll give her the okay.'

The receptionist stayed with them until they had completed searching the rooms. Unfortunately the rooms didn't give up any clues. They returned to the bar.

'I need another drink,' said Stella.

'I'm ready for one too.'

The barman served them the same drinks and then left them alone.

'I have a bad feeling about this,' said Stella.

'It's not good that's for sure,' said Clarke, '

'There's no way that I am going to sleep tonight. I'll stay in the bar until it closes.'

'Okay but let me order some bar food. We haven't eaten much today and if we are going to get drunk let's do it on a full stomach.'

The barman brought them some sandwiches and coffee and they took them to a table. Stella found it difficult to eat in spite of encouragement from Tony.

'If Tom is dead then I won't want to live anymore,' said Stella, tears rolling down her cheeks.

'Please don't give up, Stella. Tom is very resourceful and able to take care of himself,' said Clarke, in an attempt to give Stella some hope, although he wasn't very hopeful himself. They hadn't heard from Shannon for some time and his silence was complicated by the fact that his whereabouts was unknown.

'I know he has taken many risks and survived but I think his luck has run out,' sobbed Stella, 'he has been out of touch with us too long. If he were alive then he would have contacted us. We should have insisted that he had backup.'

Stella's mobile rang and it startled her. She couldn't move and for some time just stared at her bag. Suddenly she grabbed her bag took out her phone and switched on. She stared at the phone and then seemed to freeze.

'Stella, what is it?' exclaimed an anxious Clarke.

42

Shannon and Keane had stopped struggling with the ropes. The water was up to their chests and rising.

'I'm freezing, Tom. I'm going to die from hypothermia not from drowning.'

'I feel the same. I have to admit that a rescue now seems out of the question.'

'It seems we are going to die together, Tom. I won't see my children grow up and we'll never see if our countrymen can live in peace.'

'I'm sure they will find a way. I'm sorry about your family, Sean, and if we are going to die then I can't think of many better men to die with. My regret is that I let you get involved.'

'Thanks, Tom, but please don't blame yourself because.......'

'Shush,' Shannon interrupted him, 'there's something happening up there.'

They could hear running feet, scuffles, shouting and cursing. Then there was a gunshot, more shouting and cursing and then everything became quiet. Now it was the turn of Shannon and Keane to start shouting and they shouted until it hurt. Whatever had happened up there Shannon hoped that the good guys had arrived and won. After a short while two men, dressed in black and wearing black balaclavas, came down the embankment. Shannon looked at them. Oh no, more terrorists? He hoped not. The two men didn't speak but quickly cut the ropes and after a struggle dragged Shannon and Keane up the embankment. There they met two more men in black holding powerful torches. Brady and his crony were on the ground facing down and bound and gagged. That's a relief thought Shannon.

'Who are you,' asked one of the balaclavas.

'I'm Tom Shannon and this is Sean Keane.'

'Why were you tied up down there?' asked the same balaclava who seemed to be the spokesman.

'Brady didn't like us,' replied Shannon.

'Why did Brady not like you?' asked the balaclava.

'We wanted to make a citizen's arrest and hand him over to the Garda along with his pal. He wasn't very happy about that.' said Shannon.

'By the way, who are you,' asked Keane.

'Let's just say we are Friends of the People and particularly friends of the deceased Carson family.'

'Ah, vigilantes,' said Shannon.

'What were you going to do with them?' asked Keane.

'Toss them into the sea.'

'That's execution without trial. That's not justice, that's revenge,' said Shannon.

'Somebody's got to stop these killers and robbers. We found out that Brady was at Kingarrow Farm. When we arrived there he was just leaving and we didn't want a shoot out on the public road. We were also interested in what he was up to,'

'Good for us that you did. Hand them over to us,' said Shannon, 'we'll deal with them.'

'Not likely. They'll get a few years in prison and then they'll be out.'

'My friend has good reason to want to deal with these men,' said Keane, 'Brady was responsible for the death of his grandmother. There are also other charges and believe me he'll probably never get out of prison.'

Balaclava hesitated then called the other balaclavas to one side and they had a short discussion.

'Okay, I guess grandmothers take precedence over friends.'

The balaclavas began to move off when Shannon called after them.

'Please stop this vigilante business. It's not justice, it's revenge and you will regret it.'

'We've been doing okay up to now.'

'Well think about this; others who think differently from you will come looking for you seeking revenge. You, no doubt, will retaliate and a vendetta is born. Let the police take care of these criminals. Someone very dear to me warned me that seeking revenge was wrong. She said that seeking revenge would have a devastating effect on my life. She was right. Because of what I did she lost her life and I have to live with that.' The balaclavas didn't reply but continued to walk away.

'You tried, Tom.'

Shannon searched the back seat of his car. He found what he was looking for, his hand guns and his mobile phone and Sean's phone. He searched Brady's car and found the ransom money. Keane rang his wife and Shannon rang the Garda and told them where they were and asked them to come and collect Brady and co. He then rang The Priory and Peter Blake answered.

'Hello, Peter.'

'Tom, it's great to hear your voice. Everybody has been worried. Where have you been?'

'It's a long story and I will fill you in when I see you. Is Stella there?'

'She's at The Ramblers Inn with Tony. They were hoping to find you at Kingarrow Farm. You'd better call her right away, she's been frantic.'

Shannon rang her right away.

'Hello, Stella.' Stella froze for a few moments, not really believing her ears.

'Tom, where are you?' asked Stella through a vale of tears.'

'I'm at the mouth of The Finn River waiting for the Garda to pick up Brady.'

'Are you all right?'

'Yes, I'm fine just a bit wet. I've been in touch with Peter and he told me that you and Tony are staying at The Ramblers Inn.'

'Yes, do you want us to come for you?'

'No, I have my car here so as soon as the Garda get here I'll make my way there. Sean Keane is with me. We are both booked in at The Ramblers Inn.'

'We knew that Sean was booked in at the inn. What's he doing here?'

'It's a long story. I'll tell you all about it when I see you. Make sure there's lots of hot water, Sean and I will need a hot shower. Say hello to Tony for me. I'll have to go the Garda have arrived. Bye.'

Stella switched her mobile phone off and looked at Clarke. She was shaking but smiling through the tears. 'I guess you heard. It was Tom, he sends his regards.'

'Where is he? Is okay?'

'He's at the mouth of The Finn River waiting for the Garda and he has Brady in tow.' Stella seemed in a state of collapse as all the tension subsided. Clarke put his arms around her and as he held her she sobbed. He knew that the tears this time were tears of relief.

'Oh, Tony, I really thought we had lost Tom.'

'He's been in a few serious scrapes and he has always managed to survive them. It must be the luck of the Irish. I think what you need now is a hot drink; I'll ask Adam if he will oblige. He said he was keeping the bar open for as long as we needed it.'

Adam did oblige and they sat in silence enjoying their coffee and the good news about Tom. Stella was thinking about her roller coaster relationship with Shannon. It was her immediate attraction to him which had surprised her. She then thought that she had fallen in love with him. When she found out about his association with the Provisional IRA she had begun to hate him with a vengeance. She felt that he couldn't be trusted and even when Clarke had assured her that she was wrong, she wasn't convinced. When he risked his life to save her brother she realised that she was terribly wrong about him. Her thoughts were interrupted by the arrival of Shannon and Keane. Shannon called from the door that they were still wet and needed a shower and a change of clothes and they would join them later.

Later in the bar there were hugs and kisses. Adam appeared with freshly made sandwiches and coffee. He expressed his delight at seeing Shannon and said how he had missed their little chats. When he had gone Shannon said that he was a nice guy who was a real asset to the inn.

'First of all,' said Shannon, 'I must introduce you to my friend and saviour, Sean Keane. I know that some of you have heard his name before but I don't think you have met him.'

'I'm very intrigued by the saviour bit,' said Keane.

'Well, I'm now going to explain,' replied Shannon, 'I received the credit for rescuing Ian Bellamy, Stella's brother. The truth is that Ian wouldn't have been rescued if it hadn't been for Sean who, unknown to me, had been shadowing me. Ross had me on my knees and was about to shoot me in the head and I'm sure he would have shot Ian too because he had seen their faces. Fortuitously, Sean got him and his crony first. Sean wanted to remain anonymous so I couldn't say anything although Ian was well aware that we had been saved by a "mystery man" at the eleventh hour.'

'I think you are being very hard on yourself,' said Keane, 'you found the tunnel and then risked your life digging away some of the fallen roof. Working on the two doors to get to Ian could have been fatal. If Ross and his thugs had heard you, your number would have been up. All I did was shoot two rats. What do they say "it was like shooting fish in a barrel" or something like that.'

'I'm grateful to both of you,' said Stella.

'I agree with Sean,' said Clarke, 'you took an enormous risk. It was a job which required back up and Sean provided that very efficiently. We are all grateful to you, Sean, for that.' Keane nodded.

'Now, let's talk about today, 'said Shannon, 'again I can't take the credit for capturing Brady. Brady captured me and Sean. If it hadn't been for the balaclavas, who called themselves Friends of the People, Sean and I would be dead. I can't and won't take credit for Brady's capture. I'm so glad that Sean can go back to his family in one piece because for a long time I thought that we had both had it.'

'It's been a rough experience,' said Clarke, 'and I can imagine your concern for Sean and his family which must have added stress to an already stressful situation. Remember, you found out where Brady was holding up. If you hadn't found his hideout then he wouldn't have been caught on this occasion and, don't forget, you got the money back. That was a real bonus.'

'Tom is being very modest,' said Keane, 'he could have caught Brady dead or alive quite easily if it hadn't have been for me. Brady had me tied up in the farmhouse after giving me a beating. Tom could have come into the farmhouse firing on both barrels but then Brady would have shot me right away. Tom's style was cramped because of me.'

'Okay,' said Shannon, 'that's confession time over. Let's enjoy the rest of the evening.'

'I'll vote for that,' said Clarke, 'let's order some drinks.'
Adam arrived with the drinks and everybody began toasting Shannon and Keane's safe return and everything else they could think of. Shannon's mobile phone rang. He looked at the others and put his finger to his lips and said, 'it's the colonel.'

'Hello, Colonel,' said Shannon as he switched his phone to loudspeaker.

'Hello, Tom. I've have just returned from London and Peter tells me that he had a phone call from Brendan Jennings. Jennings said that you had handed Brady over to the Garda. Well done, Tom.'

'Hold on a minute, Jim. We've been discussing Brady's capture here. I can't claim the credit for capturing him. Four guys wearing balaclavas and dressed in black captured Brady and rescued Sean Keane and me. They called themselves The Friends of the People. I'll give you the full details when I see you.'

'I will look forward to hearing about these guys wearing balaclavas. They sound like vigilantes.'

'They certainly do and they could be very problematic for Northern Ireland.'

'I agree but we will have to hand the problem over to the Northern Ireland authorities. We have some major problem here. Soldiers are being murdered on the streets and we need to find out who's behind it. It could be organised or it could be some individual maniac.

'I guess that you will want us back in Manchester as soon as possible.'

'Not immediately. Paul Adams is helping Peter to do some preliminary investigations so I'm hoping they will have made some useful progress before you get back. I'm conscious that you have probably had a bad time. You risked your life rescuing Ian Bellamy and whatever your feelings are about the capture of Brady, I'm confident that you took some risk in that mission too. Take a couple of days or so off and then return to Manchester when you feel fit.'

'Okay, Jim. I'll see you in a couple of days. We'll call in to see how Ian Bellamy is getting on and then Stella can fly us back to Manchester.' McDonald rang off.

'All right you guys. I had my phone on loudspeaker so you heard what Jim said. Soldiers are being killed on the streets in England. It's hard to believe that they are not safe in their own country.'

'It's very disturbing,' said Stella.

'We need to get back as soon as we can to see if we can root out these killers,' said Clarke.

'Well, it's certainly a job for Ironclad,' said Shannon.

They all continued enjoying themselves as another round of drinks arrived. Shannon smiled and looked around the table. His wonderful Stella looked as beautiful as ever and she radiated happiness. Tony Clarke was telling one of his old funny stories which he embellished with new twists every time he told it. Sean Keane was laughing so hard that tears were rolling down his cheeks. He owed so much to Sean. Stella was laughing too even though she had heard many versions of this old shaggy dog story. It was great to be sitting around a table with such fantastic friends. They had all been through a lot together and survived. He was well aware that he owed them all a great deal and he wouldn't forget.

Printed in Great Britain
by Amazon.co.uk, Ltd.,
Marston Gate.